CAROLE HAYMAN

Born in Kent, she graduated from Leeds University and the Bristol Old Vic Theatre School before working with The Traverse and Royal Court Theatres. A founder member of Joint Stock Theatre Company, she became an associate director for the Royal Court Theatre, where she directed many World Premieres.

Carole also writes for television, film and radio, where she is best known as the co-writer of the Radio 4 hit series *Ladies of Letters*. Her first film as a writer/producer, *f2point8* was recently short-listed for a BAFTA.

She has also published a trilogy of novels, *The Warfleet Chronicles*, as well as short stories and journalism including features for *The Independent, The Guardian, The Express* and a regular column for *The Independent* titled *My Lofty Life*.

She lives in Brighton with the photographer Josh Pulman.

Of her previous work:

'There's nothing she doesn't know about life, love or making mischief.'
Fay Weldon

'This is New Labour's *2084*.
Everyone should read it
so that we can make sure
it doesn't get this bad.'

Clare Short MP

CAROLE HAYMAN

HARD CHOICES

AURORA METRO PRESS

First published in the UK in 2003 by Aurora Metro Publications Ltd.
4 Osier Mews, Chiswick, London W4 2NT. 020 8747 1953
Copyright © 2003 Aurora Metro Publications Ltd.
New edition printed in July 2004.
Hard Choices Copyright © 2003 Carole Hayman.
Cover Design and image: Copyright © Direction123.com

ISBN 0-9546912-1-0 Printed by Cambridge Printing, UK.

About HARD CHOICES

'...the most reviewed unpublished novel in the history of English fiction... *Hard Choices* is as good as Julian Barnes *England, England...*'

Nick Cohen, *The Observer*

'An amazingly prophetic dystopian nightmare with a heroine, Grace Fry, who has more balls than Blair.'

Sue Townsend

'... *Hard Choices* is certainly the kind of satirical fantasy that prolonged exposure to New Labour can inspire. New Labour, New Orwell, indeed.'

Rory Bremner

'Compulsory reading for all dissidents and non-conformists.'

Bob Marshall Andrews MP QC

'The absurd, even threatening atmosphere of British politics ten years hence is brilliantly caught in Carole Hayman's *Hard Choices*. It's an unsettling, funny, perceptive book located smack in the middle of the Doubt Zone.'

Stephen Bayley

'This is the book they wouldn't let you see. Sexy. Scintillating. State of the art. Simply sensational. And that's for starters!'

Helen Clark MP

'This book will send shivers through New Labour. Marvellous stuff – full of insight.'

Brian Sedgemore MP

'A hugely funny, futuristic, radical, ripping yarn – a Minister who speaks her mind, no matter how horrifying the consequences?'

Bea Campbell

PROLOGUE

The piercing October sunlight struck Imre full in the face as he panted out of the copse. He winced and screwed up his eyes, momentarily blinded after the resinous gloom. Across the field, the distinct howls of the pursuing pack indicated the hunt was not far away and after a brief gasp at the stabbing stitch in his side, he set off in a stumbling run towards the bramble hedge beyond which, he hoped, was a road. His back was to the sun now and his vision cleared enough for him to see the frost of his breath on the still, blue air. In the distance he could make out the splendid spires of Lord Ransome's mansion. Sunbeams blessed the gothic grey with a touch of Camelot. In the other direction reared the chimneys of the *Ossophate* factory; a white cloud of smoke puffed innocently above them, as if from a picture-book train. The field he crossed was sprout green from recent rain. A cow, munching, raised her soft head and gave him an unconcerned glance, as though accustomed to seeing a man in fox skin, brush dangling, speeding by in the muddy grass. Raucous barks and the sound of hooves churning the sodden turf urged him on. The bramble hedge, still blackberried and spotted here and there with bright splashes of poppy, offered dense sanctuary. Imre threw himself headlong into the tangle and, oblivious to scratches and snags, crashed through to the other side.

A little further up the narrow lane, a chain-gang was working. With dull regularity their pick-axes rose and fell, scattering chips as they hacked into the surface. A large hole had already opened and the leader stopped to wipe his brow. He and Imre made eye contact. Not so much as a flicker visibly passed between them, but a moment later Imre dived into the hole and the gang, without pause in their automatic labour, covered him with rubble. The pointed snout of his fox-head disappeared, just as the first foaming horse cleared the hedge and clattered onto the tarmac. Through a mosaic of chinks Imre watched the hunt dither, the flecked horses snorting and stamping, the dogs winding in and out, whining. Then with a great bellow of the horn, the Master gestured onwards. His chestnut leapt the gate opposite and in seconds, the whole heaving, hallooing mob had followed.

When all sound of it had gone and the day had settled back into a calm, broken only by a skylark and the occasional weary grunt from a worker, Imre thrust an arm through the rubble and with the help of the leader's sinewy grip, clambered out of the hole. No words were spoken, but the leader dragged off Imre's pelt and offered him a tattered denim jacket and a bit of bread. Imre tried to say thank you – that, at least, he knew in English – but his throat was choked with tears. The leader nodded and thumped his shoulder, then watched as the refugee set off up the road. Where, he wondered was he going? Imre too was wondering. His plan was to get to someone who would believe his story. Grace Fry, the Government Minister who'd recently opened the Re-location Centre, might. She'd seemed friendly – had taken his hand in a firm grip, but he had no idea how to find her. The air had warmed a little now and the sky turned deep cornflower. The sun filtered through the russet hedgerows and cast charming, lace-like patterns on the empty road ahead. Even in his despair, Imre could not help noticing that October was particularly beautiful that year. A blackbird chucked. A church clock struck the hour. One might almost think all was right with the world...

CHAPTER ONE

The white skin of the Drome glowed, the seaside sparkle lending a silky gloss to the PVC, as Grace Fry hurried towards it. As usual, she was late, there never seemed enough hours in the day for her small Women's Unit to attack the work she deemed essential. She saw it as attack, for that was her nature. Today however, the first day of Conference 0010, she was late not because of her own over-packed schedule, but because *Ransome Rail* had encountered a cow on the line.

Other ministers had been travelling on the same high-speed, tilting train; all had groaned as it tilted to a standstill leaving them on a tipsy incline. To be delayed for Conference, of all things, and when the Government was heading into election year – the consequences hardly bore thinking about! These thoughts were kept private. It was not done to criticise Lord Ransome. The Drome, towards which they travelled, had been bought by his consortium after the Great Crash of 0000 and re-leased to the Government for a nominal sum. It was one of Ransome's most famous loss leaders. The railways were another. The Government had many reasons to be grateful to him.

Grace was more anxious than most. One of the first events of Conference was the ceremony at which she was to receive the 'Woman of the Decade' Award from the prestigious European Female Federation. Though she courted the media and loved publicity – her detractors said too much – she was naturally a little nervous. It would be a theatrical occasion. Her own performance must be immaculate.

To save time she slithered sideways, particularly awkward in her customary high-heeled shoes, to change in the Elite class 'Fresh 'n' Up!' facility. At the end of the carriage, a Happiness Warden had already begun an uplifting exercise class for the more eager travellers. Idleness was frowned on. Those taking part had stripped down to modest one-piece under-garments, having travelled in expectation, and were jerking earnestly to chants of 'Meat is death!', 'Greens are good!', 'Eat your nuts!' and so on. Grace nodded to Naomi Lord, Secretary of State for Family, in passing. Naomi was leaping with set jaw and dogged determination. Grace knew it would be noted that she hadn't joined in.

As she tottered along the corridor hanging onto the Teflon ceiling straps, thoughtfully provided for these all too frequent unscheduled halts, Grace glimpsed, through the convex windows, fields rolling away to the distant sea. A labourer was ploughing with a horse-drawn plough, churning up great curls of rich chocolate-coloured soil. Seeing his broad, smocked back and gaitered legs, braced against the powerful, tramping horses, Grace thought fleetingly of a peasant Ben Hur. Behind the plough came head-shawled women, scattering seed and trundling huge drums of *Ossophate* fertiliser to spread along the furrows. Apart from the vivid *Osso* logos – she could just make out the slanting slogan, 'Puts body on your table' – it was a biblical image.

Less so were the hoardings, which reared from the track sedges, announcing:
'MORE CEREAL. LESS PROTEIN' and 'VEGGIES R U'.
Grace sighed. She could barely remember steak. She ran her tongue over her lips – she was an unreconstructed carnivore and would sometimes bite them just to taste blood. Not the sort of thing to admit in public.

She bolted herself into the silver loo capsule complete with *Toobs* vanity unit, *Osso* night-soil re-cycler and spouting fountain of Ransome's water and ducked away from the porthole window labelled 'Warden-Watch', clicking her teeth in exasperation. Really, it was unnecessarily invasive, in Elite class – she hated to be scrutinised about her toilette. She ran a comb through her blonde urchin cut, grateful as always she didn't have the bother of a wig, and applied careful make-up, finishing with a dash of bright coral lipstick. Lipstick was power. It was important to look young and vibrant.

Now, an hour later, she clacked down the front in a stunning white sharkskin suit, mirroring, not entirely serendipitously, the shiny Drome. Though Grace was used to the sight – the Drome had been the seat of Government ever since the collapse of the Houses of Parliament, due to faulty underground infrastructure – it still filled her with awe. Drome had an almost animal aura and breathed white light over everything.

She put up a hand to smooth hair tendrils slightly ruffled by the mild sea breeze, simultaneously making a mental check she had everything necessary for the rest of the busy day. Since the loss of her Parliamentary Private Secretary, Martha, after a long, slow illness, at the beginning of the summer vacation, Grace had had to sort out her own affairs, plan her own itinerary and carry her own handbag. Short-staffed as her unit already was, the pressure had been intense. She was unhappily aware of the pile of unanswered – even unread – correspondence. Martha would have dealt with it in her usual, subtly efficient manner, targeting what was important, side-lining what could be ignored or delayed. She had been the perfect ministerial ally.

Grace missed Martha in other ways too. As a listener, advisor, confident and gossip. A minister's life was a lonely one, even with the prizes. How pleased Martha would have been about this award and how she would have enjoyed the celebration. Grace's coral mouth tightened and a short, sharp line appeared between her eyebrows. Naomi had promised a replacement PPS soon, but Grace knew there was no replacement for a long-time friend.

Her hand fell to the simple gold locket she wore round her neck. She fingered it absent-mindedly, as though it had talismanic properties and the mere fondle could reassure. The touchstone obviously worked, for a moment later her brow cleared and her step regained its bounce. Grace was never down for long. Besides, she was aware that shortly, her image would be relayed to many screens. It would not do to look troubled when approaching a moment of triumph.

Outside the twelve-foot steel fence, which cordoned the Drome circumference and separated Grace from the pebbly, wave-lapped beach, groups of National Security Wardens were stationed at regular intervals. Their presence had been worrying when they'd first been created to quell the panic riots in the National Emergency. The appalling terrorist attacks of 0000 had created worldwide hysteria and many countries had resorted to a similar watchfulness. Now, like so much else, the sight of the wardens in their grey Teflon boilersuits had become unremarkable. Only a few years ago these streets would have been littered with beggars, drug addicts, refugees. Now, there was no sign of disturbance in the neat town, which was gaily decorated with national bunting in St George's red and white, and strings of coloured lights for the Conference. Even the security cameras, which hung on every Heritage lamp-post trailed jolly ribbons. The Ministry of Mode had, as always, done an excellent job. Ransome's red and silver logo appeared on many of the Government posters – his company had sponsored Conference this year – along with the Drome symbol which always reminded Grace, to her guilty amusement, of an old-fashioned Dutch cap. Martha had been the only one with whom she could share such irreverent thoughts.

The pricking of her wrist-bleep urged Grace to a trot. As well as giving messages and time by the nanosecond, it emitted small electrical shocks, which increased in sharpness, the later its wearer became. Adam Solomon had first seen one when years ago, as Secretary of State for Business, he'd made a visit to a Japanese theme park. He'd been charmed by an ingenious toy, then called a *Tamagotchi* and commissioned this customised version, to be distributed throughout the Party. No one knew quite how highly charged they were. High-ranking ministers, who wore more powerful bleeps, could often be seen careering across Millennium Green, but the unpleasant tingle they caused at warning level was enough to spur most to action.

A few seconds later, the whirr of a security camera marked her arrival, a little out of breath, at the giant reclining figure of the entrance. Encouraged by the huge banner which draped the creature's breasts, proclaiming, 'Creating Stability. Go with Gideon.' and pursued by the swivelling lens, Grace hurried through the androgyne's mouth and down its transparent throat towards the foyer of the huge saucer-shaped building.

Inside the Draconian security area, dotted with dead-eyed Special Forces, their machine guns cocked and ready, delegates were being stripped and blood-sampled. Grace, as a minister, had only to endure a bag search – the Security Warden clicked her teeth over the bright lipsticks – and a personal patdown and voiceprint. Beyond the conveyor belts and body scanners, the busy foyer was hung with giant posters of the Prime Minister, the boyishly handsome Gideon Price. Grace made the obligatory duck of the head as she passed one.

Close by the benign, smiling face she encountered the posse of grey-booted Drome Unit lads who hung about the Government Persuader, Adam Solomon. In their smart designer uniforms, they lounged insolently, staring at passers-by with vague menace as they waited for Adam, who was talking to a police officer.

"I saw a vagrant on the front. Hello, Grace. Send a warden to pick him up, would you?"
The policeman shifted anxiously and dropped his hand to his electric baton.

"Certainly Mr Solomon sir, straight away. I don't know how that's happened... "

Adam waved away further discussion. He shot his wrists out of his grey suede suit, adjusted the cuffs on his immaculate pink shirt, displaying gold Drome symbol cufflinks, checked his bleep and turned to Grace with a smile.

"Grace, dear, how are you? Super holiday? "

"Didn't have one," sighed Grace. "Too much to catch up on, with Martha... you know... You–? "

"Brazil," murmured Adam. "Fantabulous. Of course, I had my vidi-fone with me."

He put an arm round Grace's shoulders; a gesture, she was aware, as much to propel her towards the Great Navel as to display affection.

"Mustn't keep your audience waiting. Can't tell you how happy Gideon is – we all are – about this award. Play your cards right Grace and I'm sure something big's in the offing."

Grace shivered a little. Adam's friendly tone was known to be more unnerving than when he was taking people to task over some misdemeanour. It was particularly worrying when he smiled. The hint was exciting though. Something big? Could it be, at last, her own Ministry? Gideon had been implying for months, years really, that eventually he would create her longed-for Ministry for Women.

The posse, leading in a semi-military stomp, cleared a respectful passage as they passed through the crowds milling in front of the floor-to-ceiling cyclorama, which circled the foyer. A looped video of the town as it had once been, played on the screen; a constant reminder, with its rioters, looters and drug-crazed vandals, of the mayhem from which the country had been rescued. The Old Testament warnings of the Drug Czar, Isiah King, boomed over the scenes: "This country had become the habitation of devils, foul spirits and the unclean..."

Grace barely noticed. The message had long been subliminally absorbed. All she, like the People, could recall of the National Emergency – apart from small details like finding her hoarded noodles eaten by mice and wrestling with a neighbour over a nest of pigeon's eggs – was a violent and economically terrifying moment of history. Albion had been rocked to its very foundations but like the rest of the world, had been at war with mysterious, unseen forces ever since and had settled into a dull, embattled resignation.

The central rally hall, the Great Navel, was an astonishing creation. It had once housed an exhibition and retained that extroverted charisma. No one could be unmoved by the sheer towering splendour of the domed ceiling. All felt dwarfed by its massive proportions. It was like being in a spaceship from an old sci fi movie. The vast space was full of people, large security passes dangling from their necks, seated at round, flower-decked tables. Grace recognised constituency friends and representatives, several of whom waved as they saw her enter. They would be impressed to see her squired by the powerful Adam. No one liked him, but many had reason to fear him.

Adam steered her towards the grand platform in the centre, which was draped and lit in Conference purple and set up with a semi-circle of microphones and cameras from Jethro Stone's *Stone TV,* and it's only rival, GBC, the Government funded corporation. The outer periphery was crowded with photographers and print journalists. Jethro Stone's papers, *The Daily Millennium* and *The Sunday Prophet* were well represented of course, but Grace was pleased to see that *The Independent Satellite*, the only national newspaper not owned by Stone, had also sent a contingent. Among them was an old sparring partner, its political editor Zach Green. They had crossed swords on more than one occasion. *The Indie Satellite* was notorious for anti-Government disinformation – 'whinging', Seth Thomas called it – but Zach apparently bore no malice and gave Grace a supportive smile. He was a good-looking lad and his smile was winning. She smiled back, grateful to him.

A 'Go with Gideon' cheerleader-like routine by the logo bedecked 'BarleySugar Bunnies', was just finishing, as Adam placed Grace at a table near the stage. Naomi Lord, Grace's immediate boss (for her Women's Unit perched not altogether comfortably within the Ministry of Family) was already seated there. She was wearing pale yellow with a frill round the neck. She looked, thought Grace, like a lemon meringue pie. Naomi cast a suspicious glance over Grace's brilliant suit and tastefully ragged hair; she said nothing however, as she leaned over to give her a congratulatory peck. Grace pecked graciously back, her smile disguising the fact that she did not particularly like Naomi.

She couldn't help thinking that this award, though hers alone, reflected quite nicely on the Ministry of Family.

Other ministers and civil servants from Family, mostly male, circled the table, as well her own Women's Unit staff, entirely female, and a young woman Grace did not recognise.

"This is Josie... Josephine Andrews," whispered Naomi. "I told you I'd find you a replacement PPS. I'll introduce you properly afterwards."

Grace shot a quick glance at the girl, seeing plump but not unattractive features, with fleshy lips and dark hair in the regulation virginal haircut. Josie was gazing at her with a mixture of awe and admiration.

"I'm so honoured," she murmured breathily. "I've read all your speeches."

You're probably the only one who has, Grace thought but did not comment.

Outside the Drome, a Government branded stretch-limo drew up by the androgyne's big toe and, after a discreet pause, Gideon Price emerged, smoothing his rather bouffant hair. In his Cuban heels and purple suit, reborn Beatle-style with a tinge of long-dead Chairman Mao, he cut a dashing figure. There was the sense about him that he knew it. Behind him came his wife Hettie, swathed head to toe in unbecoming lavender. She was not a natural 'pastel' and the brown flick-up wig, which sat a little askew on her large head, did nothing to help her image. Last out of the limo was Seth Thomas, Gideon's surly spokesman. In keeping with his reputation he wore black and, unlike Gideon and Hettie, was not smiling.

All three were immediately surrounded by Security Wardens and police and hurried towards the building. Gideon raised his arms and grinned and waved to a small crowd, which had gathered the other side of the cordon. Nudged by him, Hettie gazed myopically in the same direction and waved rather wildly.

The trio entered the mouth and the crowd dispersed as a Ranso-tram stopped on the front and disgorged its neat and tidy passengers. They bustled about their business – loitering was an offence – but one, a tall white-haired man, distinguished looking despite his shabby clothes, was left standing. Unmoved by the attention of a couple of Security Wardens, he stared through the steel mesh towards the Drome and the disappearing figures.

Inside the Great Navel, the buzz of excitement had reached fever pitch. A spontaneous cheer broke out as Gideon and Hettie entered. They stood basking in the warmth of their welcome, then moved slowly through the tables towards the stage, Gideon stopping many times to shake hands, pat shoulders, wave, blessing the throng. Several times he drew Hettie close and once bent to give her a tender kiss. Watching intently, as she always did when Gideon appeared, Grace thought she detected a slight resistance on Hettie's part. She didn't look quite herself and her wig was in need of a dressing. But a moment later she was flashing her husband her usual adoring smile. Grace must have been mistaken.

There was a fanfare of synthesizers, composed specially, the programme announced, by Lord Peregrine Creede, the Musician Laureate, and Hilde the head of the EFF mounted the stage and took up her position beneath the banner announcing, 'Woman of the Decade' (sponsored by *Bonka*). In ringing, if somewhat glottal English – it was Germany's turn to chair the Federation that year – she announced a tribute to Grace.

"Prime Minister, ladies und gendlemen, before de European Female Federation prezent Grace Fry wid dis avard, ve vill a short film show of de oh zo many achiefements vhich haf her made, Voman of de Decade!"

To massive applause and even a few whistles, the lights were lowered and on the raised screen at the back of the stage, a sequence of seminal moments in Grace's history unfolded. With soaring choruses of electronic plainsong and a breathy voice-over from a popular *Stone TV* docu-soap actress, it was very impressive.

Grace glanced towards a neighbouring table where her university friend Miriam Matthews sat, as footage played of them both on a student demonstration. On screen, the tee-shirted young Miriam held one end of a 'Reclaim the Night' banner while Grace mugged to the wobbly hand-held camera. A smiling Hettie Price held up the other end of the banner. She had been a good friend, as well as an active campaigner in those days. Now, she sat clasping the hand of Gideon Price. Middle-aged Miriam, in formal baby blue and the tight chignon favoured by executive women, sat with other *Electra-Telecom* representatives, smiling and shaking her head at the screen. In the audience there was indulgent laughter.

The film moved on to Grace's achievements for women in the now defunct TU movement. Another old friend, Margie Griffiths appeared on the screen. Before Adam Solomon, as Minister for Business, had outlawed trade unions, she'd been a women's liaison officer helping Grace, then a backbencher, draft bills on flexible working, equal pay, crèches and other woman-friendly issues. Grace craned to find Margie in the audience. Margie was sitting at an outer table, staring glumly at the screen. Beside her, her husband Tony put out a hand, covered hers and squeezed it.

Grace's work as a Minister in Dan Jefferson's Government was eulogised: family courts, rape laws, revolutionising care for the elderly – there was a particularly touching scene of her changing an incontinence pad – most of all, her role as the valued, indeed only, woman in Dan's kitchen cabinet. Here, there was a shot of Grace carrying a tray of tea to the stripped pine table, around which sat many men in shirtsleeves and braces. Luke Counsel, then Chancellor of the Exchequer, was amongst them. He took a mug from Grace's tray as Dan Jefferson, the craggy former PM, smiled fondly up at her.

When the voice-over actress dropped into breathy sorrow to describe Dan's tragic early death, Grace choked up and her hand flew to her locket. She quickly recovered, aware that many pairs of eyes were upon her and that her face was undoubtedly on several screens in the room of perpetual night. Though Dan Jefferson was officially revered in the Party, it wasn't done to show overt emotion. Only Gideon reserved the right to be publicly tearful. Now he was looking towards Grace. He locked

eyes with her and nodded sympathetically. Grace felt a rush of
relieved affection; there was an odd attraction between them.

Gideon was on the screen himself in the next shot, dragging
her back from back-bench obscurity after Dan's death, to
appoint her Minister for Women in his newly established
Women's Unit (created, so he insisted, to address the female
issues which had fallen out of fashion in the new world order).
Here he was on a support drive in her own constituency,
Seashoram, surrounded by brawny, brown land-girls and bales of
hay, joining in a 'Happy Harvests' songfest. Yes, she had much
to thank him for. Not least his support in her long battle to
establish a female quota system for Police Officers, Security
Wardens, King's Counsels, Judges and Law Lords, culminating
in her achieving the appointment of the first ever Lady Lord
Chancellor.

On screen were scenes from the investiture in this historic
role of Eliza Barker, who looked remarkably ungrateful, as well
as uncomfortable, in her Elizabethan ruff and farthingale. There
was a rustle in the audience as a close-up showed Eliza poking
at her orange wig and muttering impatiently through her
responses – she was a controversial figure.

Throughout the film there were bursts of clapping, often led,
Grace noticed, by Naomi. She was touched; they did not always
agree on family policy, indeed on anything. Naomi had even
tried, unsuccessfully, to make over Grace's image, considering it
unsuitably vibrant and wanting to turn it regulation pastel. They
were, theoretically, on the same side but Naomi, at thirty-five,
already had a Ministry. And a husband. There was bound to be
rivalry between them.

Ultimately, the film showed Grace's most recent triumph; the
opening of the first National Re-location Centre for refugees and
the homeless, in her own constituency of Seashoram. There were
shots of Grace touring the complex, set in the landscaped
Ossophate industrial park, while the Centre's Managing Mummy,
Christobel Steel, pointed out the excellent work environment
and happy, dome-hatted workers.

Refugees waved and smiled to camera and were seen flower-picking, splashing in jacuzzis and playing football, while the voice-over turned unctuous about Albion's long history of tolerance and sanctuary.

For Grace, the Centre was the climax of passionate efforts on behalf of refugees, many of whom landed illegally at Seashoram. It would, she hoped, serve as a beacon of righteousness to other, less welcoming, countries. It would also house those for whom Grace was equally concerned – dissenters, petty criminals, vagrants, gypsies – all those, in fact, who fell outside the parameters of 'normal' society. No one, in her opinion, should be abandoned when the right care could re-educate and re-establish them as fully functioning citizens.

A freeze-frame on her shaking the hand of a grateful refugee in *Ransome*-logoed National strip ended the film, to thunderous applause from the audience. The Great Navel was an excellent conductor of sound and as Grace rose to accept the award and swayed in her shimmering suit and high heels up the steps to the stage, she felt overwhelmed by her own magnificence.

Gideon came forward to give her the prize, a heavy glass replica of the Drome entrance figure. It would make a great paperweight, she inappropriately thought. Or perhaps murder weapon. Gideon was smiling, his blue eyes full of warmth. He bent to kiss her cheek and his lips lingered slightly.

"Spiffing perfume, Gracie," he whispered. "Sexy!"

Grace looked up, startled, and he gave her an amused half wink. Her head felt light and she had trouble concentrating on his speech, though she understood it to be flattering.

"Nothing could give me greater pleasure than to give our one and only Grace this richly deserved trophy. Done a terrific job as Minister for Women. Think I can say with certainty, no matter how smashing her past, her future will surpass it..."

Grace focussed suddenly. Surely that was more than a hint? It was a promise. The certain promise of a Ministry. She tremblingly took delivery of the statue and turned, heart pounding, to make her speech of thanks.

"Since I've been a Minister, people expect me to watch what I say..."

There was a ripple of nervous laughter in the dark Navel.

"I've never been much good at that..."

Grace's voice gained confidence now, as she got into her stride. This was what had fast-tracked her though her career. Made her exceptional. Her grip, buoyancy, ruthlessness with truth.

"But I speak from the heart when I say a massive thank you to the EFF. I am truly honoured by this award. What's better for women is better for all. I pledge to work ceaselessly for a more equal society..."

She paused for effect:

"... And I look forward to the day when it is so equal, we no longer need a Women's Unit!"

That would show her critics, thought Grace, as the audience howled approval. They sniped at her for ambition, but you couldn't be more selfless than to put yourself out of a job. She raised her arms high above her head in acknowledgement of the cheers and, knowing she looked spectacular, turned in a slow circle, dizzy with fame, glorying in the earlier, dreaded moment of triumph.

On every side were familiar faces, smiling, laughing, shouting praise. She wished more old allies were there to share this with her. Martha, Dan, Luke – they would have meant it. Still, this would do. Not all in the audience were friends, maybe, but at that moment, all were envious.

CHAPTER TWO

Imre was exhausted. He had run all morning after escaping from the hunt, scurrying along hedges and ditches, skirting roads as too dangerous. Finally succumbing to exhaustion on the outskirts of a seaside town, perhaps twenty miles from Seashoram, he'd accepted a lift on a farm cart driven by a ruddy, incurious woman who was going to sell eggs in the market. Sitting on prickly hay bales at the back of the wagon, Imre had stolen one of the speckled brown ovals and frantically sucked out the raw goodness. That, and a few biscuits left out for a snoozing dog, was all he'd had since dawn.

The farmer's wife, a garrulous soul, told him as she flayed the skinny donkey, that she was expecting a high price for her produce as the Drome Conference was on in the town. About time too, she opined; they were desperate for new gates at the farm, the fourway bolt and shock kind – the only way to deter the food-thieving vagrants who still evaded the Security Wardens.

Imre pulled his denim jacket closer when he heard her tone turn nasty. He didn't want her to see the striped shirt, which declared him properly the resident of a Re-location Centre. He strained to follow the woman's chatter. It was difficult as his English was limited and she had a strong country accent. Some of what she said, he already knew. For instance, that the Drome, being portable, moved every three months to a different area of

Albion — Sussex, Wessex, Mercia and so on — to make Government more democratic. She pronounced it 'demicracked'. But he concentrated sharply when she said that for this annual event in Conference Town, all the Peoples' Representatives would be present. Trying desperately to keep the foreign vowel sounds out of his voice, he asked: "Grace Fry... she will be there?"

"Good Gideon yes," said the woman. "She's to receive a great prize for all she's done for the lot of women."
She followed this with a pause and a sigh, perhaps considering her own lot. If she was dissatisfied however, she would not admit it. Not, at least, in front of a stranger.

They were clattering into the streets of the town now and she asked him where he wanted to be dropped off. Rising above the higgledy-piggledy skyline of tiled roofs and pastel paint, Imre saw the great Drome, hovering like a balloon. It reminded him of an ancient tribal tale of a succubus.

"There," he said, pointing.

"Can't get that close," the woman shook her head. "Carts aren't allowed. Security. I'll leave you in the old town."

She dropped him off in a cobbled street, which would have been charming but for the ever-watchful cameras. These Imre had heard about; indeed he was familiar with them from the Relocation Centre. Had he not been designated to take part in the 'fox' hunt — punishment for being a bad parent — he would never have escaped them. Somehow, tired or not, ducking and running, he must make his way to Grace Fry, the only one who could save them.

In a small, old town café, near the seafront and within sight of the Drome, Luke Counsel stirred his cup of *Nut-Noggin*, a greyish groundnut beverage, and stared gloomily out of the window. The little room was steamy and the sharp sun lit the smears on the perma-glass rather cruelly. Only a couple of other citizens sat eating or drinking. The café's euro-board, high on the wall beneath the curfew siren, displayed Conference-inflated prices. Bean stew was twelve euros or the price of a pair of trousers; hay soup was only three, but Luke knew it to be disgusting.

He sighed and drained his cup hoping the bitter nut grains would assuage his hunger. His daughter had made him eat a piece of bread, before he'd left on the *Ranso*-tram that morning. Since she was going on community milking duty, she'd said, she'd get free milk for her and the baby. Luke shook his white hair back – it had an annoying habit of flopping over his eyes – and turned his lined but still striking face towards the large clock on the wall. It had an institutional look to its big white face and black hands, as though from an old-fashioned schoolroom or barracks. The Ministry of Security insisted on every hostelry displaying the time distinctly, so there could be no excuse when it came to curfew.

Noon. Grace, he imagined, would have received her prize by now. He had read about it in the papers – a rather grudging piece in Jethro Stone's *Sunday Prophet*. Jethro had a problem with women of a certain kind, though his wife was rumoured to be one of them. Perhaps that was why. *The Independent Satellite,* on the other hand, had written a very friendly piece. Clearly, Grace had a fan there. Luke longed to speak to her. It was over a year since they'd last communicated. She hadn't answered his last three letters and he despaired of getting a message to her. The Conference security would never let him through without ID. Still he had to try. For the sake of Seashoram.

He rose, pushing back the moulded plastiflex chair to give room to his long legs, and pulling his once elegant overcoat around him – the breeze was chilly – strode towards the door.

Outside, the cobbled old town was pleasantly bright and Luke stood for a moment, face turned up, letting the sunbeams warm his thin cheeks. Behind him, he could hear a scuffling noise and then the clang of a dustbin lid. It was a familiar sound. Someone was going through the café bins, illegally scavenging garbage. Luke could have made a citizen's arrest but he ignored the derelict. He, or she, would be lucky to avoid the surveillance cameras and besides, there but for the grace of – he didn't believe in God, in fact, but he approved of the sentiment.

There was a sudden outbreak of shouting. The proprietor of the *McDennis VegBurgBar*, which shared the alley, had come out.

"Oi, you! Gettaway! I'll call the Warden!"

How many times had Luke heard that threat? It was as common as when mothers in the 20th century had frightened their children with the bogeyman. A second later the derelict came scuttling out of the alley, crashing straight into Luke and knocking him sideways into the wall.

"Zorry... zo zorry..." muttered the small man. His accent was heavily eastern, perhaps United Balkan, or Afghani, and his appearance was dark and gypsyish, his scruffy denim half-hiding some sort of uniform. Accustomed to observation, Luke absorbed all this in the few seconds it took the man to help him to his feet, dust him down and, one eye on the approaching Wardens, set off at a trot in the opposite direction.

Luke stared after him. He looked familiar – had they met before? It seemed unlikely; perhaps it was just the uniform – that of a refugee, evidently, who should be in a holding zone. Shaking his big shaggy head, Luke turned towards the seafront, the Drome and the battle to reach Grace.

Grace was circulating vigorously in 'Conception' (sponsored by *Toobs*) – an area of Drome devoted to women and designed as a giant, red pulsating womb. Men had been known to turn faint and have to be carried out, crying for their mothers. The 'Woman of the Decade' party had got off to a cracking start with the 'BarleySugar Bunnies' in lurex Teflon boilersuits, performing a raunchy girl-power number; in accordance with current correct attitude, the lyrics encouraged girls to be on top.

Grace certainly felt like a top girl as she wove in and out of the crowd, avoiding the trays of *Ransome's* water and radishes, and busily networking. Almost everyone she knew, in both her working and inevitably related social life, was at the reception. She was truly the 'Woman of the Decade' – so many people wanted to meet and greet her, she barely had time for a word with each before another claimed her. She air-kissed Hettie, noting she had straightened her wig.

"Hettie, thank you so much... Peter, hello... Noah, good of you... Christobel, didn't we look glam on screen? Mim, thanks for coming..."

Zach Green, *The Indie Satellite's* political editor, waved and winked, pointing to his notebook and mouthing 'later?'. Grace returned the wave and nodded. He must want an interview, which was excellent news. As she ploughed on handshaking and air-kissing, real friends followed in her wake trying to get a moment's attention.

"You looked great up there," said Tony Griffiths, "very at home."

"I like your hair, duck," added Margie.

"Naomi Lord doesn't," laughed Grace, "Thinks it's 'unsuitable'. At my age I should go grey gracefully, enter a granny zone and sit in front of *Stone TV*. Oh... er... Naomi..." Grace spotted her unsmiling boss, standing inches from her.

"These are my good friends Margie and Tony Griffiths. They live in Seashoram."

Naomi gave the Griffiths a frosty stare; they were not her kind of people. She pulled Grace a little apart to where Josie Andrews was standing with the Chief Whippy, Rachel Church, a tall, gaunt woman in dove grey and a dun-coloured bobwig.

"Come and talk to Josie. I want to be sure she'll suit you." Grace knew there was little chance she'd be allowed her own choice of PPS. She'd actually been wondering about a boy, but she also knew she had to go along with the charade so she smiled and nodded. Rachel, a woman of Grace's generation and, though very different in style, a one time ally, air-kissed Grace and congratulated her.

"And this is your other prize. Josie's one of the brightest from the Ministry of Learning... "

"I'm your greatest fan... " murmured Josie, her plump cheeks quivering.

"Yes," broke in Rachel, "Gideon chose her himself. He said, 'Only the best for our Gracie'." She smiled, a little nervously.

Grace had been known to be unhelpful over staff. The mention of Gideon seemed to have done the trick however, for Grace turned a beam on Josie and held out her handbag.

"May as well start straight away," she said and sailed off to further greetings – so far, on the vast political canvas that was Drome, she'd only tickled the surface. Margie and Tony had caught up with the group and Josie turned to them.

"What happened to Ms Fry's last PPS?" she asked apprehensively.

"She died," said Tony. "Exhaustion."

Grace was in full spin, having bumped into David Timothy, Minister of Mode, a cheerful, plump body, gaily dressed in a flowered shirt and patterned waistcoat. He was one of Grace's best friends inside Drome.

"Luvvie," he cried, falling on her, his Zapata moustache quivering. "Fantabulous, totally fantabulous. As for that suit! Wish I could wear white."

"Naomi hates me," whispered Grace, giggling. "The Gorgon." David giggled too. "You see Gorgons and wicked queens everywhere."

"Particularly wicked queens," murmured Grace.

David looked round in mock alarm and choked on his giggle as he saw Adam Solomon's cold eye upon them.

Margie Griffiths, with Josie in tow, approached again, her grey eyes anxious behind her large red glasses.

"Grace, love, I do need a –"

Before she could finish, Grace caught the eye of Seth Thomas, the Prime Minister's spokesman, who was surveying the group. He beckoned her over. Excusing herself, "Margie, darling, I promise I'll listen in a sec...", Grace crossed to him. Josie, with an earnest expression, scurried after her, as though wishing to be seen fulfilling her bag-carrying function.

Seth was standing in his usual position, slightly behind Gideon's shoulder, and as Grace joined them, the Prime Minister turned to her with open arms.

"Our star!" he exclaimed and bent to embrace her, sniffing appreciatively.

Grace felt herself grow warm and hoped she wasn't blushing. Gideon's attentions, though by no means unwelcome – it was good to be in favour – were confusing. She saw Hettie, at Gideon's side, stiffen slightly and stretch her mouth wider.

"Fans and allies. Spiffing, spiffing!" said Gideon, indicating Lord Ransome who was smiling genially and Isiah King, who wasn't.

"Indeed. Where would Seashoram be without them?" Grace gave a thankful laugh. "We've had such problems with refugees... our coast is so vulnerable, the Citizen's Council's been stretched to breaking point... Now, thanks to you both, and Care of course..." she gestured to Gabriel Strong, the Secretary of State for Care who stood with a fixed smile and shifting, lifeless eyes behind his leader, "We can take care of them..."

All the men nodded gravely. Josie had pushed her way into the circle and Grace felt obliged to mention her.

"Oh, and Gideon – thank you so much for Josie."

Gideon made a dashing bow. "My pleasure." He turned to Josie.

"Heard triffic things about you."

Josie seemed overwhelmed and stared at her feet, shod in neat regulation flatties. Gideon, without waiting for a response, introduced the others. "My organ, Seth Thomas... "

Seth Thomas shook her hand and said a brusque "How d'you do?" Lord Ransome gave her a caressing pat and murmured,

"Charming." Isiah King backed off and grunted.

Gideon drew Grace a little away and said, smiling, "Pop along and see me after lunch, Grace. There's something I'd like a little pow-wow about..."

Grace's heart began to thump. Was this the moment she'd been waiting for? With an effort she remained calm, "Yes... yes of course, Gideon."

The Prime Minister ran his hand gently over her hair. "Ah, Gracie, I'll miss this when you get married."

Grace laughed nervously. She had no intention of getting married. Not least, because it would have meant adopting the wigs *de rigueur* to the state. No – she had been there once, and that was enough, no matter what was recommended by Party Directive.

Gideon gave her a promising nod and bounded back to the group. Seth Thomas, who'd sidled close enough to hear everything, pursed his lips at Grace in an apology for a smile. It was, Grace knew, her cue to move on. She spied Margie pushing through the crowd and, Josie hard on her heels, strode towards her.

"Oh, duck, " said Margie, "I know you're busy, but we've got to get back to Seashoram soon. Tony's got a compulsory fathering class..."

"I'm sorry Margie," said Grace, trying to banish her wild excitement. What did Gideon mean, 'a pow-wow'? It must be good news on a day like today, surely. She was uncomfortably aware that Naomi had got her Ministry, for putting women back in the kitchen. With an effort she concentrated on Margie, for whom she always made time, having shared with her many successful battles. They'd been a good team and good friends. Now Margie and Tony, though only in their forties, were 'retired' with their boys in Seashoram. They were helpful, kind people and often a sanctuary for Grace when she visited her constituency.

"What did you want to tell me?"

"It's just... all this carry on at *Ossophate*." Margie's once pretty face was prematurely aged with worry. "You know, more redundancies now Isiah King's finally accepted this *ET* Fabulous Futures technology... "

"So fabulous a few's looked at the future and topped themselves," added Tony, who had come up behind her.

"Hush Tony!" hissed Margie. "You always look on the black side."

"Death's about as black as it gets." shrugged Tony, his long face set in its habitual melancholy. Margie gave a quick check round and lowered her voice, "It's true, Grace. People are depressed."

Though she no longer had an official trade union capacity, Margie still concerned herself with the welfare of *Ossophate* workers. Both she and Tony had laboured at the pharmaceutical factory for years, before they were made pensionlessly redundant.

"Depressed, yes, it's endemic..." Grace dropped her voice. It wasn't proper to admit to national anomie, one of the worst aspects of endless war, "But... are you saying suicides...?"

Before Margie could answer her alarmed enquiry, Miriam Matthews, Grace's old friend from *Electra-Telecom*, pounced on them. "There you are, at last! I've been looking for you all over to say, well done!"

"Thanks Mim," said Grace, giving her cheek a contact kiss.

"You're totally timely as it happens. I've got some anxious constituents here." She turned to Margie and Tony, seeing them for a moment in their best brown clothes like shabby little animals, clinging together for security.

"Margie and Tony Griffiths," she said, adding warmly, "my oldest, best friends in Seashoram. They're very worried about just what your *ET* 'Fabulous Futures' are going to mean for their future. Perhaps you could tell them?"

As Miriam obligingly began to explain the situation at *Ossophate* – Seashoram's biggest, indeed, almost only provider of work – Grace felt a tug on her sleeve. She turned rather sharply – she hated to be touched in public, especially on her glorious sharkskin, and found herself face to face with her constituency General Committee Chairperson, Noah Petty.

"Oh, Grace, I'm going now... but I wanted to pay my respects." Noah was a short, plain man with an unfortunate ginger wig, worn in the hope of appearing youthful and Price-rite. Grace didn't like him, knowing that respect was the last thing he had for her. She'd been selected for the Seashoram seat over his toupée, with a very substantial majority.

"Thank you, Noah," she said, coldly. "As you know, I always say, what's good for me is good for Seashoram."

"Oh, I agree. Of course." Noah gave an unconvincing grimace as he shook her hand. Grace felt he would have preferred to throttle her. Behind Noah, hovered Christobel Steel, the Managing Mummy of Seashoram's Re-location Centre. They were friends, it seemed. Or allies. Grace had met Christobel when she'd toured the Centre, before and during its opening. She was always polite, yet she gave Grace an uneasy feeling; something about her pebble glasses and the cold, pale eyes behind them. Despite her girlie looks and curly blonde bob – Christobel was unmarried – she was, Grace suspected, steel by name and steel by nature.

Grace watched them go – they were certainly an odd couple, but Miriam quickly claimed her back, saying she'd invited Margie and Tony to lunch, and would Grace like to join them? Eyeing a plate of broccoli spears twirling by, Grace had to agree she was hungry. Hungry for liver, chops, bacon... Oh well, she'd settle for a cappuccino; that, at least, was still obtainable, though in a mild de-caffeinated form.

Josie, who'd shifted awkwardly on the outskirts of the conversation rather like a reject from a playground gang, suddenly jerked forward to whisper loudly in Grace's ear.

"Ms Fry... er ... Grace... Naomi's calling for you."

Naomi Lord was standing with others from the Ministry of Family, artificially grouped in front of a bunch of photographers. Naomi was never one to miss a photo opportunity. Grace hurried across to join them. Now she was about to have a Ministry of her own, Naomi would have to get used to playing second fiddle. Grace manoeuvred herself firmly into the centre and flash, flash, flash went the cameras.

Above the Navel in the room of perpetual night, a bank of television screens monitored proceedings inside and outside the Drome. The surveillance cameras caught a tall white-haired man walking purposefully along the front, past the Heritage fairground on the pier (in use only on annual holidays) and a church from which came the faint strains of jolly music and clapping. On another screen, a small dark man momentarily appeared. He dodged quickly beneath the camera lens and disappeared into an alley. Grace Fry's face appeared on every other screen, two feet high and smiling broadly.

CHAPTER THREE

The photo-shoot over, Grace hurried to the Drome Dames' room to change out of the white suit into something more practical. As she drew a shocking pink trouser suit out of her bag, she saw Josie's eyes turn to saucers.

"Oh, for Gideon's sake, girl," she said testily. "If you're going to work for me you'll have to buck up your ideas. You can't fight for women's rights if you're invisible! Look at Boadicea... Did she wear pastels?"

She stripped to her scanty black underwear and snapped a suspender.

"Women who make history slap on the wode... pass me my lipstick would you... and barge ahead, leaving others in the wake of their stilettos."

She slipped on a pair of high-heeled boots, of a darker shade of pink and checked the effect in the mirror. "And, of course," she gave a brief cackle and pointed one boot, "a stiletto has several uses."

Josie stared at her open-mouthed, as she applied a thick layer of coral to her stretched lips.

"I – oh or a – ow – ar – ee – irehive..." went on Grace, incomprehensibly. Then finishing and smacking her lips together, she repeated, "I know all about Party Directive, Josie. Modesty and virginity," Grace stressed the words comically,

"...the notion women aren't taken seriously if they're sexy. Ha! There's nothing wrong with a bit of glam. Look at me. The men love me for it."

She straightened her locket. "Pastels are for plant-eaters. I'm a carnivore."

She bared her teeth to ensure no lipstick smears, gave herself a liberal spray of perfume – the one Gideon so appreciated – and handed the make-up bag back to Josie, satisfied.

"Right. Lunch. I could eat a horse."

She peeled with laughter as she caught Josie's horrified expression in the mirror.

"Not literally, girl." She gathered her coat and added in a lower voice, "More's the pity."

They sallied forth, Grace a galleon in full sail, Josie her loaded tug. On their way out, they passed through the foyer, thronged as ever with Peoples' Reps and citizens' delegates. The cyclorama was now showing shots of the nice town outside; neat, clean, orderly, intercut with the death and destruction of yesteryear. The latter dwelt heavily on smokers, drug addicts and homosexuals kissing. Clearly, they alone had caused it. Isiah King's thundering voice-over left no listener in any doubt.

"Despite all the Government has done to restore peace and order, there are still some who pursue perversity and sin. Shun those who refuse to conform! They would turn this green and pleasant land into a sulphurous pit with their vile practices... "

Grace grimaced. Vile practice or not, she still missed cigarettes.

"... Never forget. Good Gideon says, "Stability is sexy!""

The word sounded absurd in King's prophetic boom, but most now accepted sexy to mean 'new' or 'modern'.

"Hey, you don't get away that easily!" Grace was grabbed from behind and felt warm breath on her cheek. She spun round to repel the boarder, but it was Zach Green from *The Indie Satellite* and she felt her fierce expression dissolve. Zach was easy on the eye as well as sharp and always stirred the devil in her.

"Talking of 'sexy'," Zach muttered close to her ear, "You look fab. I'd like to see Isiah King's face if he clocks your trouser suit. It would turn the same colour!"

Grace laughed a little awkwardly, aware of Josie's eyes shrinking to black buttons. She pulled away from him.

"Zach, I – "

Zach cut her off. "No excuses Missy, Missy. I want an interview. Something original."

"Double spread? Pages 2, 3, 6, 7 and 10. Pictures?" Grace couldn't help herself.

"All of that and more..."

"Fine, but not now... I'm on my way to–"

Zach, heedless, cut her off, "Now! Come and talk to Paul about it." He took hold of her arm and dragged her through the foyer crowd. Josie skidded behind, desperate to keep up. They thrust through a posse of journalists, amongst whom were Peter Priest, Editor-in-Chief of *The Sunday Prophet* and *The Daily Millennium*, and Jethro Stone, the proprietor of the papers and the head of the global enterprise, Media International. Peter Priest's hand glanced Grace's shoulder as she passed.

"Grace, congratulations on your award. Stiff competition, too. Er... you know Jethro Stone, don't you?"

He turned to the elderly, overweight man at his side. Jethro drew his lips back, revealing the yellowish teeth of one who had once been a nicotine addict.

"Indeed, indeed." Grace nodded emphatically. One didn't offend the mighty Stone. "We've met on several occasions. The last time was at the opening of my Re-location Centre. Mr Stone was so good to us with publicity."

"Yes," agreed Stone, with another self-congratulatory smile. "We gave it six pages."

"We'd like a piece, Grace," pressed Peter, "for *The Sunday Prophet* ... something in-depth... about you personally." Grace hardly had time for a flattered exclamation, before Zach tugged her on. "You're not going to give that lizard an exclusive, are you?" he demanded crossly, when they were barely out of earshot.

"Tricky, pusscat," murmured Grace. "Stone did give the Re-location Centre..."

"Six pages," finished Zach, giving her a warning look.

"Take my advice. Watch out for Priest. You don't want that rag doing 'colourful' stuff on you."

"Ha," muttered Grace. "Only colourful stuff on me is my wardrobe. More's the pity."

"Yeah? Well, just make sure I'm first in the queue. You owe me, don't forget."

He lightened the threat with a cheeky grin, which lit up his brown eyes and handsome features, but Grace was well aware of his meaning.

"I'm not likely to," she said darkly.

They found Zach's boss, Paul Jacobs, propping up a veggie drinks bar. Josie, blundering up panting, eyed the sludge-coloured fluids longingly. The Proprietor and Editor of *The Independent Satellite* was a chunky, energetic man whose small stature was disguised by his large personality. Paul was attractive in a dark, hairy way, as unsuitable to the times as Grace's wayward appearance. He took her hand in a firm clasp and shook it warmly.

"Honoured. Big fan. So's my wife," he chuckled. "Good woman. That stuff you did with the Royal family."

Grace smiled modestly. "Well... officially that was the Ministry of Family..."

"Nah," Paul waved away her diplomacy. "Everyone knows it was you. Naomi wouldn't have the balls."

Josie jumped visibly.

"Suggesting they should be privatised and getting Ransome to foot the bill. Hilarious. As for persuading Charles to spend three months in a Home-Zone with your one-parent families..." He gave a roar of laughter, before downing a glass of murky liquid. "Christ," he spluttered, "What is this crap?"

"*Ransorange,* by the look of it," said Zach. "There's his beetroot juice, if you prefer?"

Paul pulled a disgusted face. "Can't wait to get to a bloody pub," he shouted. People close by turned shocked looks towards them and Josie hopped away, as though to avoid contamination. Grace stared at her stilettos. Paul was known for his outrageous opinions, but she'd have preferred Josie not to have encountered them, today of all days.

"What's with blasted Ransome anyway?" Paul continued, unabashed. "His fingers are everywhere. He's already got his title from Government donations, now he's funding your bloody theme park." He winked at Grace suggestively. "How did you cosy him up for that?"

Grace cleared her throat and gave a swift glance at Josie. The sexual innuendo in Paul's tone was clear.

"I didn't have to," she said coolly. "He approached me. A year ago with the Ministry of Care cuts, Seashoram's Re-location Centre was going nowhere. Now with Lord Ransome and Isiah King on board..."

"King!" exploded Paul. "He's a weirdo."

"New Christian." Zach shook his head ironically.

"Anyone who wants to put electrodes on other men's bollocks is strictly Old Testament!" Paul contradicted. "Drug Czar indeed! Chance'd be a fine thing. Can't even find a bloody aspirin these days..."

"Unless it's *Ossophate*'s brand..." put in Zach.

Paul gave a mirthless hoot. "He's let all this moral minder twaddle go to his head. Thinks he's bloody Yahweh!"

As if to bear out his words, King's voice on the PA split through them. "Tremble! Tremble, all ye who consort with transgressors! Your shame will be uncovered!"

"He's always on about 'uncovering'." Paul's tone was excoriating. "Bloody man's obsessed with stripping!"

Josie trembled as though on the verge of tears and Grace said hurriedly, "I know nothing about Isiah King's motives in helping us, but Lord Ransome lives locally and he's very philanthropic."

"Philanthropic!" snorted Paul. "We've got the files, remember." He tapped his nose and chortled.

Grace couldn't help smiling. Paul was incorrigible. He got away with it because the fearsome information files he had locked in *The Indie Satellite* safe were legendary.

"King and Ransome." Paul shook his head. "Chalk and cheese. Don't be taken in by all this," he waved his hand at the veggie bar, "Ransome's a steak man... "

"And King is water and grass," interjected Zach.

"Grown with his own bloody fertiliser! " Paul topped and the two men laughed loudly.

Grace gave a tight smile. They were well into their double act and the routine could go on for some time, she suspected. It was too much for Josie on her first day. Grace must engineer an escape.

"Guys, I'm late for a lunch date," she said. "No, really..." as Zach began to remonstrate. "I'll catch up with you soon... call me."

Before they could stop her, she turned away, shoving Josie ahead of her. They almost collided with Seth Thomas, Gideon's spokesman. He steadied Josie, who looked mortified, and then bent close to speak softly to Grace, his words made more sibilant by his slight, Scottish accent. "A word of caution Grace... *The Indie Satellite.* We'd prefer you not to talk to them. They're not our sort. Concentrate on local papers, not a national full of scurrilous lies." He threw a look to where Paul and Zach still stood talking and laughing, and drew his black brows together.

"Wankers!"

Grace blinked. Even for Seth, that was vehement. It was a wonder Josie didn't faint. But stangely, she seemed less bothered by Seth's profanity. She was gazing at him with an almost stupid expression of reverence.

Grace nodded without replying and hurried on towards the androgyne's throat. As she and Josie entered it, they encountered more journalists – a flock of Stone's tabloid hacks, poised for celebrity snapping. They held up their cameras and shouted to Grace: "Gracie! Picture! Show us the award!"

Grace stopped mid-stride and gestured to Josie, who fumbled in the big bag and took out the lump of glass, almost staggering under the weight of it. Grace snatched it from her and hoisted it aloft, grinning in every direction. The cameras flashed and flashed.

"Thanks boys," said Grace.

She thrust the award back at Josie and without waiting, tripped on to the Millennium Green, a large area of plastro-turf sprinkled with everlasting daisies, outside the entrance. She continued fast-track instruction, as Josie ran after her.

"Always be nice to photographers, Josie. They can make you look like shit... er... rubbish. Get the media on your side. That's what I've always done." She dropped her voice. "Though Gideon knows, I've been resented for it... Take the appointment of the Lady Lord Chancellor. Adam Solomon wanted that cookbook woman, Celia Thin. I wasn't having that dumb bitch... er... brilliant recipes, a hundred and one ways with a lentil, but can't see the Chancellor having time to cook... I fought him for Eliza Barker through *The Indie Satellite*..."

"*The Indie Satellite?*" interjected Josie in a shocked voice. "But surely they're... I mean..."

"Off-Government message?" queried Grace. "Yes, yes, official shroud-wavers for democracy and all that. But they have their uses."

Josie looked unconvinced. "I didn't like Paul Jacobs," she said primly. "His language!"

Grace laughed dismissively. "Don't pay any attention to Paul. All mouth and trousers. Prides himself on being thoroughly unreconstructed."

They were almost at the edge of the Green and Grace finished the girl's steep learning curve with a grim "Take my word. Play pusscat with the press. Newspapers can make or break you."

They entered the blank territory between the Green and the conglomeration of licensed Drome shops and cafés. Because they moved with the Drome, these were necessarily transitory; they were surrounded by lorries, forklift trucks, and had an unhappy, slipshod appearance, as though in a trailer park, despite being designed to popular taste and heavily logoed in favourite food brands, *S&M* and *Tomnasti*.

The off-aura was asphalted and closer to the security fence
and as they crossed it, they could hear shouting. A ragged posse
of protesters had gathered outside the cordon and some were
gesturing to Grace and waving home-made posters saying, 'Pink
Power'. It was not unlike the scene from Grace's early life they
had just watched in the movie. She craned towards them, trying
to make out what they were shouting. They had certainly
targeted her, as several called her name while others chanted:
"Fuck your quotas!" and made rude gestures. Josie's lips
tightened as she heard, "Shun aversion therapy!" and she gasped
out loud at "How would you feel if your daughter was a
lesbian!"

Grace took a couple of steps towards them but before she
could get close, a National Security van drew up and Wardens
poured out and began to hustle the women roughly inside. Some
broke free and taunted the Wardens with "Fuck Stability! We
want Choice!" Others, undaunted by the buzzing batons, began
a chant of: "Lesb-i-a-n, lesb-i-a-n!"

Knowing there was nothing she could do, Grace turned away
clicking her teeth. "See what I mean, Josie? They go about it all
the wrong way. Look at those clothes – dungarees, Doc Martens
– outdated, even when I was a girl. They look like they've raided
a Home-Zone jumble sale."

Josie looked puzzled. "But... I thought you'd approve. Aren't
they 'feminists'?" She said the word as though it left a nasty taste
in her mouth.

"I don't disapprove," said Grace shortly, irritated by Josie's
ignorance – she obviously hadn't read her speeches very thoroughly. "I don't like aversion therapy. But..."

She finished the sentence in her head, thinking the sentiments ill-
advised to share with Josie. The truth was, if you raised too
many issues you found your own career on hold. Grace had no
intention of letting a few lesbians get in the way of promotion.

"Why are they here, anyway?" Josie asked in an aggrieved
voice. "It's not as though it's a National Demo Day." She had
clearly paid proper attention to the Drome guide to Positive

Protest. Grace shrugged; it wasn't that she didn't have sympathy for the plight of gays. "Can't blame them for trying."

"But..." Josie pressed, "should they be allowed to shout things like..." she lowered her voice to a whisper, " ... lesbian?" Grace clicked her teeth, "As I said before, Josie. We live in a democracy."

Before the argument could develop further, they both became aware of a man keeping pace with them, on the other side of the cordon. He was waving and hissing, trying to attract their attention without alerting the Security Wardens.

"Mees Fry... Mees Fry... Please!"

"That man's calling you..." prompted Josie.

"Oh Gideon, not another raison-head," Grace sighed.

"He knows your name..."

"They do, they do. You get stalkers, flashers... even poisoners."

Josie let out a squeak of alarm. "Shall I call for help? He could be a terrorist!" She fumbled in her bag for her *ET* vidi-fone. The man meanwhile, re-doubled his efforts.

"Pleeease... pleeease... Meees..." He seemed quite desperate.

"Oh, go and see what he wants..." said Grace, moved despite herself. "Don't get too close. I've known them to have shooters."

Josie shot her a terrified look and crabbed towards the fence as though approaching a mad dog. The man thrust an arm through the wire. It was, she saw, tattooed with a number. "I... must speek Mees Fry... I from other contree..."

Grace, unable to resist, had followed Josie. "What is it, Josie?"

Josie said in a low voice. "He's a refugee... looks like a gypsy."

Grace frowned; this was precisely the problem they'd had in Sea-shoram. Homeless refugees roaming the town, thieving and causing disturbance.

"Why aren't you in a holding zone?" she asked, enunciating clearly.

"Bad... I escape..." The man shook his head.

Grace tried a humouring smile. "Now, now, we're doing the best we can. There are an awful lot of you. The Ministry of Care is working on the problem. There'll be splendid Re-location Centres soon. Just like the one in Seashoram..."

"No..." interrupted the man, "I from Seashoram..."

Grace felt her temper rising. Really – some people were never satisfied. "There is a complaints system. A Citizen's Charter. I announced it myself, at the opening."

The man was starting to speak again, but she over-rode him. "I really can't get involved in every case personally – the Ministry of Care– "

"No. You! You!" The man was shouting now. "You meet me. At Centre. You shake my hand. I... Imre Kodaly!"

The name did stir a vague memory, but before Grace could place it, a National Security Warden approached, tapping his baton.

"Is this man bothering you, Ma'am?"

Imre turned feral eyes on the Warden and took off, running.

"Oi, you!" bellowed the Warden, making to follow him.

"Oh, leave him," said Grace, feeling a little guilty. She could have been more understanding. "Just wanted my autograph. He's harmless, really."

The Warden reluctantly backed off. "If you say so, Ma'am." Frustrated – it would have been his first collar of the day – he turned his attention to a courting couple who were unwisely billing on a bench nearby. That sort of thing wasn't allowed in public. He rushed over and gave them both a sharp buzz with his baton. They leapt apart as though they'd been stung and bolted down the promenade, with him giving chase.

The encounter left Grace rather unsettled. What did Imre – was that his name – mean? "Seashoram, bad... "

The Centre was a palace. The incident had not been without its uses, however, in demonstrating to Josie the pressure she was under. "You see what a minister has to put up with?" she said, a little self-righteously as she and Josie headed, at last, into the café. Josie did not reply. Her experience of being PPS to Grace had already rendered her speechless.

CHAPTER FOUR

The café to which Miriam had taken Margie and Tony Griffiths was fashionably retro-style (sponsored by *Babba, Dunky* and *Kiddo*) and decorated with popular toylines from the past. The receptionist was in Bob the Builder costume, the kitchen staff dressed as Noddy, Mr Plod and Big Ears. Grace spotted the group at a *Teletubby* table, as she and Josie hurried into the nursery-like room.

"So. What's the story, morning glory?" said Grace pulling up a glaringly Smartie-coloured plastiflex chair. Though the sweets hadn't been obtainable for years, their popular coatings had been re-franchised to a plastix company. Josie divested herself of the various bags and put her vidi-fone on the table in case of flasher or stalker emergencies. Grace picked up the menu and scanned it glumly. She already knew its contents. They'd walked past a counter piled with pulses, salads and more mud-like vegetable juices – Gideon knew they looked as poisonous as anything a terrorist could concoct.

Miriam indicated a young woman, a stranger to Grace, at the table. "I asked my colleague, Abbie Wright, along as well. I hope you don't mind? I thought it would be useful for Margie and Tony to hear what she has to say?"

"Whatever," shrugged Grace. The word was pervasive slang from the *Stone TV* docu-soap – as eternal as the war – in which 'real' people ' lived 'real' lives in front of the camera. 'Whatever' was one of their favourite expressions and – when she remembered – Grace despised herself for using it. Mim carried on without noticing.

"Abbie works on Fabulous Futures at *Ossophate*; she's my Systems Requirements Operative."

"Come again?" Grace screwed up her face. Techno-speak mystified her, making her long for plain old-speak English. Though she'd once been totally IT literate, she, like most others, had lost the skills after the Great Crash. As soon as the traffic behind the terror attacks had been traced to the internet, it had been outlawed for ordinary users. Now, legally, only Government, big business and the media had IT access and a whole new and exclusive language had developed. Martha, knowing Grace's negative feelings, had always made a point of de-coding the arcane terminology. There were hackers of course – the same self-styled guerrillas who caused train delays and unaccountable accidents – terrorists, according to the Government, but to most people, it was gobbledegook.

Abbie, an attractive girl still wearing her own long, blonde hair, gave an understanding grin. "In plain English... I'm the hands-on person, organising *Electra-Telecom*'s work on the floor. I'm in charge of Fabulous Futures."

Tony gave a snort, but a look from Margie quelled him.

"Abbie was just explaining to Margie that *Ossophate* will have to step up redundancies, now they've accepted the Fabulous Futures Remote Intelligent Monitoring System..." began Miriam, but Margie interrupted angrily, "The company loyalty Isiah King's had – and now he does this! It's so unjust!"

"Things move on, Margie," said Miriam gently. "Isiah can't go global without a system like FFRIMS... and the way *Ossophate*'s agro-chemicals have performed in the market recently... "

"Oh aye," said Tony loudly, "All thanks to us. We worked like slaves when his potency pill took off, then there was all his products when the Government brought in compulsory Home-

Zone contra-conception. Now he's made a killing with his
blasted fertiliser, and he lays people off!"

Margie gave him one of her looks and he subsided. There was a
pause and then Miriam, smiling as though her job depended
upon it, which in a sense it did, said brightly, "There is good
news. Far more de-skilled jobs on the factory floor..."

"For morons," muttered Tony.

"And..." Miriam ignored his aside, "occupational re-
deployment therapy, fully deter-active toddler units... "

"There you are, Margie," Grace broke in. "There'll be work
in those."

"Aye. But that's all compulsory-voluntary." Margie's brow
furrowed with distress. "I'm run off my feet already being a
Home-Zone surrogate granny."

Tony leaned forward and said in a trembling tone, "You don't
know how bad it's got, Grace. You've not been down since you
opened that blasted Re-location Centre!"

"Now Tony," Grace kept her voice calm; she was fond of
Tony but he did over-react. "You know I was disciplined for
spending too much time in the constituency."

She looked round to see if they were overheard, then said quietly
to Miriam, "Adam Solomon warned me I wouldn't get Drome
Unit backing for my female quota system."

Miriam nodded understandingly. PRs were only supposed to
spend certain designated days with their constituents.

"That's all very well," said Tony, his kind eyes filling with
tears. "But if our Steve loses his job, we'll be another family
curfewed."

"Don't be silly." Grace put her hand on his. "It won't come
to that. You're a model family. Look at all those certificates and
praise points you've earned."

Tony shook his head dolefully. "It's a slippery slope once you
start to slide. We know families that... "

He stopped as a waitress, dressed as *Teletubby* Lala, came to
take their order. Grace took a deep breath. Caffeine was what
she needed, but there was little chance of that.

"A double. No, a treble decafesso," she pronounced. Josie shot her a look.

"I'll have a banana and a *Ransome's*," she said pointedly.

"Oh-eh," said the waitress and wobbled off in her *Teletubby* waddle to the Minnie Mouse behind the bar.

The interruption and Josie's request had reminded Grace of Lord Ransome's newest enterprise.

"The condom factory at the Re-location Centre..." she exclaimed. "There's got to be work in that."

"Isn't that just for the residents?" said Margie, doubtfully.

"Aye," grunted Tony. "Work is freedom." He stood up.

"I'm going for a walk." He stomped towards the door. "Don't you get caught smoking!" Margie called after him. She turned sorrowful eyes on Grace. "No offence, duck. He's in a bit of a state."

Grace smiled reassuringly at her. "I've known you too long for that. What's the problem really?"

Margie said in a quiet, shamed voice, "He's in trouble with the Ministry of Family. He took down our Kevin's poster of Gideon Price. There were words and Tony raised his voice..." Margie's own voice shook. "Our Kevin reported him to the Outreach Unit and now Tony's on the bad fathering file."

Everyone at the table was silent with sympathy. Once you were put on a file, it was hard to get off it.

"He's gutted," went on Margie. "Not even redundancy affected him so bad. He's been an angel with those kids and now with Steve the only one working..."

She had no need to say more. A family with no working members swiftly lost privileges and was relegated to curfew status.

Eager to offer a ray of hope, Abbie said, "What department of *Ossophate* does Steve work in?"

"Security," replied Margie and everyone breathed a sigh of relief. Whatever areas *Ossophate* de-personned, it certainly wouldn't be Security.

"And there's another thing that might help," Abbie added cheerfully. "I've discovered *Ossophate*'s got a new product in development. Some anachronistic programme, King's insisting on keeping bespoke..."

The others looked at her.

"PC based," she explained. "Outside *ET*'s brief."

"Will there be jobs in it?" asked Margie; Tony was too old for a job in Security.

Abbie shrugged. "I hope so. Hard for me to say..." She frowned. "It's annoying really. Here am I, trying to create change for them and there's a whole programme I'm not allowed to monitor because he wants to keep it secret..."

She stopped as though suddenly aware she had said too much.

Miriam said fondly, "Our Abbie's quite a sleuth. She's got very close to a young chemist who's working on this programme. What's his name, Abbie?"

"Hush Mim," cautioned Abbie, conscious that Josie was staring. "You know King doesn't allow fraternising between *ET* and his workforce."

There was another silence, while they all considered the draconian aversion therapy measures first instigated by King in his own factory, and now adopted nationally. Though specifically aimed at homosexuals they could, in theory, be used against anybody.

Abbie checked her timer and pushed back her chair.

"I'd better get going. I said I'd meet Sam... er... I mean the chemist, at *Ossophate* this afternoon." She bent forwards and in a whisper added, "I think he's ready to show me what's going on, so I don't want to be late."

"I hope you're not attempting the journey by *Ransome Rail* then," said Grace, attempting to lighten the mood. Everyone laughed uneasily.

"Don't worry," Abbie strode off, waving. "I've got the Kamikazi."

"You be careful on that thing!" called Miriam. To Grace, she said, "It's a motorbike. Abbie made it herself."

Grace was impressed. Abbie was not only beautiful, she was smart. Most citizens in unofficial life – those who had permits to travel at all — had to make do with the crowded and slow *Ranso-trams* and other People carriers.

Tinky Winky minced up with their orders — Lala had obviously gone for her own healthy snack — and as Grace sipped the insipid liquid which passed for coffee, she patted Margie's hand. "I'm sorry about all this trouble, Margie."

"Not your fault, duck," said Margie, woefully. "Global economy. At least in the old days we could have fought it through the unions."

Grace withdrew her hand and said briskly. "Don't go on about the 'old days', Margie." She sometimes went on about them to herself — she was uncomfortable with how many rights the People had lost — but rarely to others. To do so was considered sentimental.

The pricking of her wrist-bleep was almost a relief. She held up her arm and peered at the tiny screen. It told her Gideon wanted her, now, in his office.

"Wish me luck, girls!" she said, rifling through her bag and throwing a hotchpotch of things onto the table. She found the coral lipstick at last and applied it carefully, looking in the little, attached mirror. She pointed the stub at Josie, saying, "Meet me later for that photocall on the pier. In the meantime, you can go shopping. I need lipstick — 'Coral Sunrise' and perfume..." she sprayed herself vigorously, ready for Gideon. "Here, take the bottle. Don't buy any other brand. And for Gideon's sake, get yourself something to wear. Something more carnivorous."

Aware that she had scandalised Josie yet again, Grace bundled the female clutter into her bag, kissed Margie and Miriam and hurried away, chuckling.

In the vehicle park, the other side of the Millennium Green, Abbie kick-started the Kamikazi, a sort of customised pushbike with many excrescences, and zoomed towards the exit. The Warden came out to examine the curious machine, and knowing he was out of range of his own camera, gave the pretty girl an appreciative leer. As he scrutinised her pass and lifted the security gate to let her through, he muttered — too low for the sensitive sound equipment to register – "Wouldn't mind riding pillion to you, cauliflower."

A tall, white-haired man approached the gate on foot and stood aside as Abbie accelerated past him. Luke Counsel followed the Warden back to his booth and asked if he could see the People's Representative, Grace Fry.

"Pass," demanded the Warden.

"I don't have one," replied Luke politely.

"Not possible, then." The Warden turned surly.

Luke knew this was the moment when a few euros should change hands, but unfortunately he didn't have any.

"Can't I, at least, get a message to her?"

The Warden indifferently handed him a *Ranso* logoed pad. Luke thought for a moment, then wrote carefully in his big sloping script. He looked up when he had finished and started, as he saw a blonde woman in brilliant pink, crossing the Green. It had to be Grace; no one else would dare to wear that colour. A moment later, he could make out her blue eyes and coral lips.

"There she is... " he said urgently. "Please!" He tore off the page. "Could you give this to her?"

"Can't leave my post."

"But it's very important," Luke pleaded.

The Warden shrugged blankly. By now, Grace was almost at the androgyne. She was too far away to respond to a shout and Luke watched, his shoulders sagging, as she disappeared into the building.

CHAPTER FIVE

The Drome foyer was as packed as ever. The Cyclorama was now showing pictures of an illegal 'Pink Power' demo, like the one Grace had encountered. This one had taken place in the capital, judging by the shots of the re-built House of Commons Museum, and was rather bigger. Many posters and banners displayed 'Pink Pride' and called for the removal of aversion therapy. Meanwhile, its instigator, Isiah King, incanted hoarily, "Those who spread plague must be contained, re-educated..."
Everyone knew the anodyne phrase meant electro-shock treatment, but the film moved on to show the white wedding of a skin-headed woman and a beribboned young man, complete with church bells and confetti.

In front of the screen, many stalls and booths had been set up. The Drome Consortium, a globalised alliance headed by Lord Ransome, though much of its backing was foreign, had interests in all but a handful of businesses in Albion. The foyer had been transformed into a gigantic market place to advertise and promote its products, all of which were, naturally, 'Government Approved'. Everything from '*Brit-Grip*' Stability equipment to '*Toobstone*' wash-by-hand soap, was on display.

A group of women in peasant dress of sackcloth, clogs and Dutch caps stood at a particularly prominent stall, dispensing monster vegetables to passers-by. A tape of a church congregation singing, 'We plough the fields and scatter' played and above the stall swung an *Osso* fertiliser banner complete with logo of a twelve-foot beanstalk and the by-line, 'Puts body on your table'. Dashing by, Grace tripped over a large marrow which had fallen to the floor, and scattered not seeds, but the contents of her handbag. Zach Green, who was conveniently passing, bent to help her retrieve them.

"We must stop meeting like this," he grinned, as his hand glanced hers on the marrow. "See what happens when you carry your own bags. Sacked the new PPS already?"

"Not yet," laughed Grace, scrabbling under the counter for her lipstick. "I'll give her the day. Bit Price-rite though. Doubt she knows the names of her own body parts. Nearly jumped out of her skin when I said I was a carnivore."

"Your mouth will get you into trouble one day." Zach's friendly smile faded and he gave a swift look round. But under *Ossophate*'s stall, they were unnoticed and reasonably safe if they spoke softly. "Seriously Grace. Be wary what you say. You don't know much about this 'Josie'."

"Insists she's my number one fan," said Grace. "My only worry is whether her brain's up to it. Her frock certainly isn't." Zach threw vidi-fone, audiopad and a few loose euros into Grace's bag, shaking his head at the state of it.

"You need a wife."

"Ha!" responded Grace. "Doormat more like. Slippers and *Nut-Noggin*."

"No sex?" murmured Zach.

"What's that?" Grace snorted. "Can't remember it."

"Pity." Zach's eyes twinkled and Grace felt a slight blush rising.

"What about you?" she turned on him. "Unpartnered hot young blade?"

"Obliging right hand," Zach wiggled his fingers.

"What are you like!" Grace gasped.

"Sensible," returned Zach. "Given that marriage is for life." He dropped the last handful of euros into Grace's bag and stood, saying, "About that interview?"

"Sorry..." Grace shook her head. "I'm on my way to see Gideon."

"Watch out for him." Zach moved his mouth close to Grace's ear. "I hear Hettie isn't giving him the regulation twice weekly."

Grace stifled a giggle. He really was outrageous. It was a nice idea though. Gideon's own Firm Family Values foundering in the bedroom. Maybe that was why he was so... she banished the thought and said, mockingly,

"All this advice. What are you? My fairy godmother?"

Zach raised his eyebrows and lowered his voice, "Don't mention fairies in public."

He escorted her across the foyer to the arm leading to Baby Drome. "What are you going to get from Gideon?"

"A ministry's what I deserve. Mummy's own baby!"

"PM in ten years?"

"Five! I'll be too old to enjoy it."

"Can't imagine you ever being too old," Zach said gallantly. They both knew well though, that for Grace, at forty-something, it was now or never.

"You've got it made with me," he reassured. "I'll love you up large. How do we like a comparison with Elizabeth Fry?"

"We like it," laughed Grace, avoiding his proffered cheek by giving him an air-kiss. Zach would be dangerous at contact quarters, she intuited.

They agreed to meet later at Zach's chosen venue, a pub in the old town called 'The Admiral Nelson'. Outside the Security cordon and less overseen, overheard, he insisted.

Baby Drome housed all Government offices and on her way to Gideon's, Grace popped into her own to drop off her baggage. The Women's Unit quarters were cramped and lightless, though as logoed and branded as all the others. *Radio Digi-tranquillity* played night and day. It drove Grace mad, but her overworked civil servants found it soothing. Now as she checked her hair and make-up in the *Rancon* mirror, it reflected the small room back at her and she knew she would not be at all sad to leave it.

The corridor outside Gideon's office suite was wider and brighter than all the others. There was a sort of reverential hush produced only partly by the soft carpet and knitted bootees everyone was required to wear in Baby. Even Grace was impressed by it. She halted at the ornate door marked Prime Minister and branded with the Government logo – a pink double Drome – looking, Grace thought with a momentary loss of reverence, rather like a pair of blancmanges. She straightened her jacket, smoothed her hair and licked her lips, dry despite their make-up. Before she could knock, the door opened and Christobel Steel came out. Both women jumped slightly. Grace noticed Christobel's blonde curls were mussed and her pearly lipstick looked smudgy.

"Hello again," she said, raising her eyebrows. "I thought you'd gone back to Seashoram?"

"Er... just had to go through a few Positive Image points with Seth Thomas."

Christobel had a background in publicity; in fact at one time, she had actually worked on the Drome Unit's own positive image team. Grace assumed she was talking about the Re-location Centre. They'd had requests for interviews and photo-shoots from countries all over the world wanting to emulate it.

"Everything alright at the Centre?" she asked.

"Absolutely. Top-hole," Christobel said, emphatically.

"It's just that I..." Grace stopped, thinking better of telling Christobel about her encounter with Imre. She trusted to instinct and there was definitely something dubious about the woman.

"You know you're welcome any time." Christobel was smiling. She knew perfectly well that Grace's visits to the constituency were strictly rationed. "Well... I'd better be getting back. They do so miss their House-Mummy."

Grace watched her bottom, unflattered by the silvery *Ranso* uniform, as it swayed down the corridor. There had been gossip, from Zach again, Grace now recalled, that Christobel had had more than one use in the Drome Unit.

She entered the richly appointed suite, based on the original House of Commons mock gothic, complete with escutcheons, busts, panelling, paintings and other Puginesque flourishes and nodded to a group of dark-suited Drome Unit lads, who were seated at incongruously modern work stations. Adam Solomon's uniformed posse was also in evidence, mostly lounging in the leather armchairs. One of them, a handsome young blond, got up to open the door to the inner sanctum.

"Thank you, Christian," murmured Grace, as she passed through to it.

Gideon's office, in complete contrast, was tall, light, airy, and decorated – *Rancon*-style – in the height of simple and restrained modernity. It was clear that the suite, as a whole, was meant to impress as a perfect synthesis of ancient and modern. Gideon, in shirtsleeves and braces was on his exercise bike, peddling furiously. Adam Solomon was draped over a pale grey sofa, reading a report. Seth Thomas could be seen in a cluttered ante-office, speaking on the phone. "C-R- A- P!" he shouted.

The atmosphere was intensely male, clubbable and, to Grace, secret. There was a slight trace of after-shave, perhaps from Gideon's exertions.

He stopped as soon as he saw Grace, leapt off the bike, which continued to spin its wheels without him, and came towards her, his arms out-stretched. A wide smile creased his smooth cheeks and narrowed his blue eyes.

"Grace! Smashing!" He embraced her, pinning her arms and giving each cheek a full contact kiss. "Mmm... What is that perfume? Sexie-wexie!"

Grace shifted her booteed feet. She was, as always, disturbed by his attention. He was famous for pouring love over people, but he made her feel this was personal. When Gideon said sexy, it still had sex in it. He almost vaulted back behind his vast desk, upon which sat a New Gideon bible and a prominent photo of Hettie, their five children and their prize-winning labrador. He rolled down his mauve shirt-sleeves, put his Cuban-booted feet on the desk top and began to peel a huge, *Osso*-logoed orange.

"Had lunch?" he enquired.

"Er..."

"Essential, Gracie. Healthy eating. *Ransome's?*"

"Er..."

Without waiting for her reply, Gideon poured her a sparkling water from his own carafe and went on: "You know how much we appreciate your work in the Women's Unit. Role model. Women love you. Country loves you. We love you. But time to move on, Gracie."

Grace breathed hard. She couldn't disagree with him. Gideon thrust a segment of orange into his mouth, chewed for a moment and then said, bluntly: "Ministry of Mode."

Mode was the last thing on her mind and Grace was struck speechless. Gideon appeared not to notice, going on with "Needs someone topping to give it a spin. Brands are big, Grace, and getting bigger. You'd be fabulous." He threw his hands wide. "Look at you. Style. Flair. Politics is presentation, Grace."

"I– I–" stuttered Grace.

"You're thinking, 'Where's my Ministry for Women?'."

"Well– I – "

"Ah, you're defiantly female and we love you for it, don't we, Adam?"

Adam looked up languidly and said, "What? Oh... yes."

Gideon shook his head humorously at Grace, as though she was a much loved but naughty child and said, "Got to get rid of these out-dated, deadwood, anti-man ideas. Hostile. Non pro-active. New agenda. Instead of conflict; partnership." He grinned encouragingly, and Grace knew she was expected to respond.

"I'm not..."

"Anti-man? Course not. But we'd like to see you partnered, Grace. How long's it been since the divorce?"

"Five years," Grace stammered.

"Long enough. And no children?"

Grace shook her head and Gideon looked grave.

"Talk to Naomi. She got her husband through 'Re-Pair'. Thinks it's spiffing".

"Naomi's– " Grace began.

"Barking!" bellowed Seth Thomas into the phone.

"... a different kind of person," finished Grace.

"Quite," agreed Gideon. He popped another slice of orange into his mouth and surveyed her quizzically.

"That young Zach Green. Seeing him?"

"Not at all." Grace gave an embarrassed laugh. "He's just a – "

"Shit!" screamed Seth.

"– friend." Though it was true, Grace suddenly felt it wasn't.

"Not suitable, Grace. Really. Go to 'Re-Pair'. Love is so important."

Gideon's eyes suddenly filled with tears and he came across and clasped her again, this time pulling her so close she could smell the orange on his breath and his pleasantly soapy skin. Her locket dug into their chests as he said in a tear-choked voice, "You and I remember that well from our days with Dan. We both loved him."

"Bollocks!" bawled Seth and crashed the phone down.

Locked in Gideon's embrace, a headily satisfying place to rest, Grace was vaguely aware of a limo drawing up in the compound and a tall, dark man getting out with bags and cases. She realised with a shock, it was Jonathan Temple, the leader of the 666 Opposition Party. What on earth was he doing at the Government Conference? He turned his fleshily handsome face towards Gideon's window and Grace had a good view of the slight smirk on it. Before she had time to wonder further, Gideon was demanding an answer.

"What d'you say? Brands? Nice office. Pictures. Perfume supplies. Six months, then something super."

"Er... super?" Grace couldn't resist.

Gideon released her. "Adam, explain," he demanded.

Adam uncoiled and wandered round the room, touching the tasteful *Rancon* interior objects slightly obsessively.

"We're thinking of a Ministry of Gender, Grace. A new creation. To nurture gender from cradle to grave. Be responsible for healthy minds in healthy bodies."

Grace gave Adam her total attention. A Ministry of Gender was indeed new. "Would it have responsibility for gay policy?" she queried, thinking of aversion therapy.

"Naturally," Adam was dismissive, even a little petulant, as though it was in bad taste to mention the subject.

"But more, much more. Total influence over how men — and women — develop."

"See Grace," broke in Gideon, bouncing in his chair. "Terrif — make men how you'd like them to be!"

The idea of playing god – or goddess, was not unwelcome, Grace had to admit. Adam had reached the white marble fireplace and stared into the large, *Rancon* pewter mirror above it.

"This country has an ageing population." He ran a hand over his sleek black hair, and turned a little so the light caught the jet undulations. "We need new, young, fertile blood." His tone became quite impassioned and a small spot of red appeared on each long, pale cheek.

"We're going to start a State dowry. Couples who pledge to stay together – the right sort of couples, of course – and produce children..." The right sort of children, Grace added in her head.

" ...will get a helpful handout. The Empty Nesters will pay for it out of Family Fairness taxes."

Grace could think of nothing to say. Many families, especially in Seashoram, would feel they were burdened enough with taxes, she knew. She imagined Margie and Tony's response. Not that they were Empty Nesters. Not yet. Gideon was brimming with delight.

"So, you see Grace, no need for a Ministry for Women!" Grace tried to smile. She distantly heard her vidi-fone ringing, in her handbag.

"Look," advised Gideon, "talk to David Timothy. He's a friend, yes?"

He executed a couple of karate chops then jumped back onto the bike and began to pedal.

"Mummy's the word, Gracie – but I'm announcing a reshuffle at the end of Conference."

He waved gaily. Clearly, the interview was over.

Stunned, Grace muttered a farewell then backed towards the door. She was aware of Adam's black eyes following her all the way in the mirror.

CHAPTER SIX

Grace felt like a sleepwalker as she found herself in the corridor outside Gideon's suite. She couldn't quite remember how she'd got there, except that Christian, Adam's right-hand man, had again opened the door for her. She shook her muddled head, trying to separate the good news from the bad. What did Gideon really mean? He was so overwhelming. Always swept away any doubts or resistance. She must focus.

She stopped for a moment to take out her vidi-fone, which she remembered having heard ringing. The orange message light was flashing and she pressed the digi-button to recover the image. To her surprise, Seth Thomas's face appeared on the screen accompanied by his Scottish growl saying, in almost affectionate tones,

"Hi dear. How'd it go? Call me."

Puzzled, Grace stared at the phone. What did Seth mean, 'how did it go?' He was there, overhearing as always. And why was he calling her 'dear'? In fact, why was he calling her at all? They had no relationship outside official interaction, certainly not one this intimate.

Normally Grace would have investigated further, called Seth straight back and demanded an explanation for this rare friendliness, but in her current state, she dismissed her confusion and digi-ed Zach's well-remembered number. When he did not answer, she left a message on his vidibox.

"Zach? Grace. I'll be a bit late. Off the record, Gideon's offered me 'Mode'. Must talk to David Timothy."

Indeed she must, David was not only an old friend, but one who had supported her through ups and downs since her days in Dan's government. Re-orientated, she tripped through Baby's pastel intestines towards the lofty domain of the Ministry of Mode.

The door to David's office was embellished with a logo of a Restoration-style dandy draped in a red sash proclaiming, as if in an old-fashioned playbill, 'Minister of State for Mode'. Grace smiled at it in passing. The rather portly, brocaded figure was so like David.

Inside, the room was high and splendid with clusters of logos and brand tags, which decorated the walls and ceiling as though for a celebration. Grace's eyes watered at the brilliance. Against the tastefully buff walls, the adverts stood out in jewel-like stains.

David stood in the window embrasure across the room; Grace couldn't help noticing how spacious and light, how unlike the Women's Unit, were the surroundings. David motioned her across with a flowery-shirted arm.

"Oh goodie, you're here. Come and tell me what you think of this."

Grace approached the vast workstation – David was not one who had abandoned computers; in fact, he often professed himself in love with his chatterstack and vast plasma screen. A passion less dangerous than some he had engaged in.

"It's my latest Government marketing plan," he was enthusing. "Open!" he commanded the screen. It did so and, accompanied by the old carol, 'The Twelve days of Christmas,' an advent calendar appeared, each window of it framed by tinsel. "Number one," sang David in a tuneful tenor.

A window opened displaying the sheepdog-like face of Gabriel Strong, Secretary of State for Care. His milky eyes lifted to heaven, he was offering up what appeared to be a steaming

plate of porridge. Window two was Matt Penny, Secretary of
State for Treasure, casting a possessive glower towards his
surrounding tinsel. Next was Naomi, as frost-faced as if she'd
sat on an icicle. Then the Deputy PM, fat-headed Andy Feast,
needing only a sprig of holly in his mouth to resemble the
Christmas turkey. David hummed happily on round the Drome
ministries until he came to Mode, where he ordered Secretary
Pilgrim's dour face out. "Not before time, he's hopeless in
Mode. Rumour is, he's going to Security," and replaced it with a
flattering shot of Grace, "Space now, Gracie! Ooh, looking
good."

Grace had to agree. The bright tinsel reflecting on her blonde
hair gave her an almost angelic halo.

"But, what's it for?" she said.

"Why Christmas, of course. Ministers bearing gifts."

"Gruel?" Grace pointed at Gabriel Strong and raised her
eyebrows.

"Good, isn't it," said David, without irony. "We're going for
Victorian values."

He summoned a picture of a charming, snow-covered village
green, complete with lanterns, carriages, horses, peasants and
other Heritage features. The centrepiece was a sleigh and team
of reindeers. Gideon in full Santa costume, sat with his arms
raised in all-encompassing love, on top of a pile of brightly
wrapped presents.

"I'm thinking of re-branding it 'Santamime'," David
murmured, adding a twinkling star and moving some globs of
snow about.

"How will you make it snow?" asked Grace dryly.

"Oh, that's all fake," said David airily. "Some sort of foam.
Toobs are sponsoring it."

Grace gave an impatient sigh. "I don't think Mode is quite me,
David."

"Could be worse, luvvie. What about Culture? Secretary of
State for ballet dancing?"

Grace shuddered. David tittered and pointed an admonishing
finger. "Face it, Grace. You're not ordinary enough for most

ministries. What's Gideon going to do in a shuffle? Election coming. You're the Peoples' fave PR. He's got to give you something."

"But Mode?" Grace was still unconvinced.

"Look, luvvie. It has its perks. You can wear what you like for one thing." David was a walking example. He wore a wildly flowered silk shirt, with embroidered braces and a paisley waistcoat. "We'll have some fun," he wheedled encouragingly. "We've always had fun together, you and me."

It was true. Back in the days when social gatherings still involved drinking and dancing, they had made a spectacular duo on the floor. David was known for his impersonation of the vintage film star, John Travolta. He and Grace had once entertained Conference with a fully costumed display of 'Saturday Night Fever'.

Seeing her waver, David seized the moment.

"We could get it back. Abba singalongs? 'The Sound of Music' – I've always fancied myself as a nun!"

Despite herself, Grace chuckled. The thought of David's dimples in a wimple was irresistible.

"That's more like it! Now, there's some fabby-dabby ideas coming up from Modus. Look! A medieval artists' colony."

He conjured a gothic, prison-like building onto the screen. A couple of pale faces stared glumly from the high windows.

"And 'Spend' days, where we get hoards of people up from the Home-Zones and give them vouchers to spend in Oxford Street."

The prison was replaced with a view of Oxford Street, its travelator clogged with wild-eyed, disoriented-looking women pushing prams.

"Why?" frowned Grace, thinking of the already over-stretched People Carrier system.

"Retail figures are down. Got to give them a boost. Besides, give the poor things a treat. All they get in those ghastly ghettos is evil EuroSpend."

Grace looked round, but everyone was busy talking to their screens and no one was listening.

"Going to have more ghastly ghettos in Seashoram, soon," she said despondently. "With all the *Ossophate* job losses."

David pounced, jubilantly. "I've got just the ticket. Hang on a mo'...!" Then, "Heritage Theme Town!" he trilled at the chatter-stack and up came a delightful seaside resort, a sweep of sandy beach, painted boats, cutesy cottages and cobbles. "Seashoram's perfect for this new scheme. Lots of jobs, Gracie. Clogs for everybody. Treble the tourist industry."

Grace stared thoughtfully at the screen. Except for the renovation and smart paint, the town depicted could easily be Seashoram, which, since the Great Crash, had suffered more or less permanent recession.

"Well," she said, "I suppose, if I was Secretary, I could push that through."

"Now, you're getting the picture!" David urged her along. "Mode's terribly important, Grace. Remember how good you were at re-branding Camilla."

He called up a picture of Camilla Parker-Bowles, which showed only her eyes as she modelled the once fashionable Afghani burka.

Grace snorted. "Gideon, yes. Years ago. When Charles was still dithering about marrying the wretched woman."

"See what I mean." David was delighted. "It'll give you a lot of power." He knew Grace well enough to use this major selling point.

"I may have even more soon," Grace confided, perhaps unwisely; David was a dreadful gossip.

His eyes grew round. "What's he offered?"

"A new concept. Gender. If I toe the line and get married."

"Well dear, the celibate life's all very well," David's tone indicated he doubted it. "But we all need someone to love."

"Just what Gideon said. Only from him, it was an order." Grace picked up the large framed photograph of David with his wife and family. "You've managed alright."

David's chubby cheeks sagged a little. He looked round and lowered his voice. "It hasn't been easy." Grace nodded, sympathetically.

"There are ways – when were there not – but –" David's voice fell to a sad whisper. "I just hate the pretence of it. You're lucky Grace, believe me. Being straight means never having to say you're sorry." His voice choked up and he took a sip of cranberry juice and cleared his throat before continuing briskly.

"Now, if you're coming on board, give me some advice. Gideon!" he shouted at the computer. "I've had Adam Solomon onto me. Not happy with some aspects of Gideon's image. D'you think this?"

An animated Gideon bounded onto the screen, sporting a Beatle moptop.

"Or this?" Gideon's fringe metamorphosed into a fuzzy afro.

"And then there's the shoes. We've given him Cuban heels... but I think a lift."

Gideon teetered, as if on stilts.

"And gestures. What does this say to you?"

Gideon flung his arms wide and embraced the world, beaming at his audience.

"Or this?"

Gideon lunged in close, giving a leer to camera.

"Too much perhaps. Adam prefers this."

Adam's choice was Gideon mounted on an imperial pedestal, his right arm stretched in a high salute.

"Well?" pressed David, "Which do you think? Shall I add some jack-boots?"

Grace stared at the screen, dumbfounded.

CHAPTER SEVEN

If it weren't for the surveillance cameras and Security Warden presence, the old town would be very pleasant, thought Grace, as she hurried through sunlit streets towards 'The Admiral Nelson'. She winced as a camera caught her off-guard at the entrance. The nanosecond flash, she knew, had just transmitted her image to the room of perpetual night. Oh well, it couldn't be helped; she had the excuse of visiting the pub for an interview. Journalists still had a certain, contained licence.

'The Admiral Nelson' was 'traditional'; a seaside tangle of lifebelts, lobsterpots and fishing nets, the curfew clock circled with shells, even the 'PENALTY FOR SMOKING!' warning draped with seaweed.

It was gloomy inside – the nets cutting out the sunlight. Or perhaps the darkness emanated from the doleful spirit of the drinkers, who with large glasses of *MinCare* absinthe before them, were gawping speechlessly at a huge screen showing the compulsive *Stone TV* docu-soap. There was a smell of chip fat and vegeburger.

Grace stood on the threshold trying to fathom Zach's whereabouts, before plunging further into the rancid fug. She noticed a man at the bar take out a cigarette packet – Gideon knew where he had got it – and light up a cigarette. Those around him backed off, muttering. After he had taken a couple of puffs, two Security Wardens, who were also engrossed in the TV, were alerted by nudges and whispers. They took him by the arms and frog-marched him roughly towards the exit. The crowd watched dully. One or two gave the mandatory hiss. Enjoying his notoriety, the man began to cackle and puffed smoke defiantly in the Wardens' faces. As they passed Grace, he obligingly blew a cloud in her direction. Grace breathed in deeply. Secondary smoke was better than nothing.

She spotted Zach at a corner table and snaked between the groups to reach him.

"Well, well, well," he grinned as she sat. "Mode, eh?"

Grace grimaced and threw a slew of brand-tags, badges and ribbons on the table. Zach hooted with laughter.

"That's just a start," said Grace. "Expect to see me next with logos tattooed all over me."

"Are you very disappointed?" asked Zach with more concern. His face was nice when he dropped the shark act, thought Grace. Gentle. She shrugged. "Of course. Still no Ministry for Women."

"You need a drink," said Zach.

"Don't be daft." Grace looked round in alarm. Only the subclass drank *MinCare* absinthe. "Shouldn't be seen in here at all."

"How about a *Ransome's* then?" said Zach. He poured some from his own bottle into another glass and handed it to Grace. "Cheers."

Grace sipped the water without appetite, then gave a delighted splutter. "Gin and Tonic – you naughty boy," she whispered. "How on earth – ?"

Zach tapped his nose. "There are ways," he said teasingly.

"That's exactly what David Timothy said," mused Grace. Clearly, there was a whole subworld of which she was ignorant. Perhaps, she thought hungrily, one could even get cigarettes.

"David Timothy..." Zach was saying. "Stuff in the safe on him. Other persuasion, isn't he?"

Grace nodded. "Bent as a euro-bond, poor sod."

They both shivered, thinking of cold nights, lavatories on common land and the constant terror of exposure.

"Talking of sex," Zach grinned cheekily, "how about you?"

Grace gave him an old-fashioned look. "We already had this conversation, you reptile. I told you. I'm celibate."

Zach returned the look, raising one eyebrow. "That's the official story, but what's the truth?"

"As if you'd recognise it," said Grace sardonically. "*Indie Satellite?* Flagship of freedom? Punt more like."

"Don't knock it. Saved your bacon more than once," Zach reminded.

"Touché," acknowledged Grace.

Zach had been responsible for an 'in-depth' interview with her at the time of her divorce. The sympathetic piece, told entirely from her side, of course, had detailed her husband's unreasonable behaviour and abuse. There had been hints at a perverse sexuality. More importantly, it laid to rest rumours about her and Dan Jefferson and probably saved her job. Zach was right to point out that she owed him.

"Look," Grace adopted a frank expression. "Drome Policy. No marriage, no sex."

"Wankers," said Zach without rancour.

"Only Seth can get away with language like that – you mean 'bounders' don't you?" said Grace archly.

"No," said Zach with a grin at the Gideonspeak, "I mean wankers. Unless they're on Isiah King's bromide."

"Whatever..." Grace gave a regretful sigh. "I'm a good girl. Haven't had sex since my divorce – that's off the record by the way, I don't need my knickers all over *The Indie Satellite* again – and I won't unless I get married."

Zach whistled, impressed. "You've really never strayed?"

"No one up to it." Grace gave a naughty grin. "I'd tell you, of course, pusscat."

They both chuckled. Something about the atmosphere in the pub allowed them to be mildly subversive. Grace took a sip of G and T and tugged on her locket.

"No time, anyway. This life sucks every last breath out of you. Relax for a second and you're stabbed from behind."

She caught Zach slyly writing a note and grabbed at his copy.

"Great white or what! I don't want people knowing my doubts and fears. This is on record. I'm delighted with Ministry of Mode. I believe in everything the Government does and I'll work my boots — *bootees* off to make it successful."

"So, I'm just your tame mouthpiece?" Zach threw down his pen in a mock tantrum.

"Ah, diddums, pusscat!"

She pinched his cheek, enjoying the smoothness and closeness of flesh, but quickly snatched her hand back as she saw her PPS enter the pub. Josie was wearing a new cardigan in an ugly shade of tangerine and painful-looking sling backs. She looked extremely ill at ease as she hobbled to their table.

"Oh, Grace," Josie spoke in a low voice, as though it was improper to be heard at all in these surroundings. "That photocall..."

Before she could finish, Grace's bleeper emitted a high-pitched wail and zapped her. "Ouch!" she yelped crossly, rubbing her wrist. "Don't tell me. I'm late for it."

"By the way," Josie was smiling nervously. "I think you picked up my vidi-fone by mistake, when we were at the cafe?"

Grace raised her brows. So, it was Josie's fone that had rung. In which case, what was the meaning of Seth Thomas's strange message? Suddenly suspicious, she tweaked Josie's sleeve.

"*Ransorange*. Terrif. Needs a touch of lipstick, though." She rifled through her bag and brought one out. "Go and put this on in the Dames."

Josie's face turned terrified. She trembled towards the women's room as though on the route to Hell. Who knew what you might find in the lavatory of a place like this? She'd heard about dead babies.

As soon as she had disappeared, Grace fished out the vidi-fone and re-played the message.

"Hi dear. How'd it go? Call me."

Seeing her annoyed frown, Zach said, "What is it?"

"That's what I'd like to know," said Grace grimly. "A message from Seth Thomas on young Josie's vidi-fone. Awfully affectionate don't you think, for people who met for the first time this morning?"

"Odd," agreed Zach. "What've you found out about Josie?"

"Very little," shrugged Grace, trying to remember what Josie had told her on their passage through the Drome.

"Comes from Seashoram. A coincidence it seems. Shoved in quick quick at a by-election in the neighbouring constituency – I remember, I was cross at the time; my friend Margie was trying to get selected. Fast-tracked through Learning. Awarded to me. Gideon's choice, apparently."

"Hmm," said Zach thoughtfully. "Reward for something? I warned you to be careful."

These days, it didn't do to take anyone at face value.

Josie was returning, a spearmint gash of lipstick on her fat lips, otherwise none the worse for her experience. Grace handed her the fone saying, "Looks like you've got messages. Haven't had a moment to check."

They both saw a distinct look of relief cross Josie's face as she dropped the fone into her handbag.

A burst of laughter from the TV watchers at some antic on the screen was their cue to move off. The absinthe-befuddled viewers were giving the TV suggestive encouragement. Undercover of the ribaldry, Zach caught Grace's arm and drew her close.

"I'll see what I can find out. Call you later. Mmm, great scent."

"A lot of men like it."

"Have you honestly been celibate all that time?"

Grace smiled. "What's it to you?"

"Awful waste," Zach murmured in her ear. "You're a sexy woman."

The seafront was patchworked with mauve shade and pools of mellow sun and above it the bunting fluttered merrily in the light, afternoon breeze. Out at sea, a vessel or two breached the horizon and seagulls wheeled above the whitecaps, uttering the occasional pained cry. The slight air of foreboding, which had fallen on Grace in the pub, lifted as she and Josie headed along the promenade. There were always plots and counter-plots to unravel; politics was a dirty business.

On their way to the pier, they passed a *Stone TV* logoed camera crew and slowed out of curiosity. To Grace's surprise, the subject of the video-recording was Jonathan Temple, who was being prepared for an interview. One make-up girl was powdering his floridly handsome face, while another sleeked back his thick, dark hair. His brown eyes caught Grace's and he gave a slight smile. She didn't smile back, though they knew each other. She detested Jonathan Temple.

The pier, which had been opened specially, was busy with photographers marshalling the representatives of 'Wimmin Mean Stability' (WIMS) for their photo-opportunity. WIMS was a prestigious national all-woman organisation; so powerful it was practically impossible for a woman to survive in business without its support.

Grace spied Miriam, who was the chairwoman this year, talking to Hettie, whose company, 'Stable Tables', was a member. The two had been good friends, along with Grace, when they were students. In fact, the three of them together had headed up many protests and – it could not be denied – many parties. But since Hettie's marriage to Gideon, a distance had set in. Her dealings with Grace and Miriam were awkward now, as if she was aware she had somehow let them down. Grace joined the couple in time to hear Hettie say, "Isiah King's asked me... er... my company that is... to come in and manage stability during *Ossophate*'s change to Fabulous Futures."

Grace and Miriam exchanged a swift glance. Neither said a word about cronyism, however, as Hettie continued.

"We'll be working closely with *ET*, of course. I've already spoken to your systems operative – Abbie, isn't it? Very helpful."

This was almost the highest praise ever awarded and Miriam bowed her head, conscious of the honour.

"I'll need a list of all the job titles to go, so I can plan counselling sessions... de-skilling, back to reality, visions and values and so on." Hettie frowned. "I understand the staff are under-motivated. A lot of absenteeism. Do you know anything about that, Grace?"

Grace shook her head, though Tony's mention of suicides came back to her. It would not be 'helpful' to bring them up at this moment.

"Strange at a time when job loss has such societal implications," went on Hettie, as though the implications had nothing to do with her husband's policies. Looking at Grace, she added, darkly, "I hope the Sabotage Principle isn't at work."

"Perhaps they don't like aversion therapy," Grace could not resist.

"Nonsense," Hettie gave an uncomfortable laugh. "It's been in place at *Ossophate* for years."

When Grace said nothing, Hettie flourished statistics.

"It has a ninety-five per cent success rate!"

She was hailed by photographers and turned away, abandoning the conversation.

"Pity the poor five per cent," said Grace in a low tone.

"Yes," agreed Miriam. "What happens to them?"

"Isiah King shoots them," said Grace, causing them both to give a silent snort.

They watched Hettie pose and smile for the cameras. Her attitude towards aversion therapy was all the more strange, they were both thinking, given her previous history of campaigning for human rights. Hettie had always been first on the line if she perceived any injustice. They didn't, however, exchange these views.

"She doesn't look well," observed Grace.

Hettie had changed into a pale peach frock, which made her square face look sallow. The flick-ups of her wig now stood out at right angles.

"That wig's a fright. Think she could afford a new one, with their combined salaries."

"Lost sight of herself," opined Miriam. "Spread too thin. Gideon, five kids, full-time job."

"Mmm," said Grace. "And managing Stability's very stressful."

They both smothered another convulsion. But in truth, there was slight envy in their remarks. Though Miriam was married, she and Jim were not blessed with children. Miriam made do instead with prize-winning Labradors. She often encountered Hettie on the competition circuit, where she, too, showed her dogs. Since her divorce, Grace had even less in her home life. No family. No children. Just a small flat and an empty fridge. Her career was everything to her.

The photographers were now moving them onto the big wheel. The bepastelled businesswomen were half pleased, half embarrassed, they pulled their skirts modestly over their knees and giggled coyly like schoolgirls. The photographers urged Grace and Miriam to join in.

"Come on, girls."

"Gracie, Gracie!"

"Up you go!"

"I'd rather have aversion therapy," commented Miriam *sotto voce*. But she allowed herself to be hustled into a swinging basket – she was after all, the chairwoman.

Grace needed no persuading; she loved the fairground atmosphere as much as the attention. As a child she had ridden, skateboarded, skied – activities now considered improper for all but designated sportswomen. She climbed into a bucket seat with Naomi and Rachel, who, stony-faced, seemed less than pleased with her company. The photographers shouted instructions.

"Cram in ladies!"

"Off we go!"

The wheel ground off with little shrieks from the occupants.

"Lovely, lovely, give us a wave!"

The wheel gathered speed. Grace laughed out loud, loving it. The breeze ruffled her hair and brought pink to her cheeks.

"Smile. Don't look down!" shouted the snappers.

"A shot of Miss Fry at the top. With Mrs Lord and Mrs. Church."

The wheel stopped at the top, the bucket chairs swinging wildly. Rachel smiled grimly. Naomi had gone white and was clutching the sides of the bucket.

"Can you stand up for us, Grace?"

"That's our girl!"

"Wave, wave!"

"Careful."

"Arms out."

On her feet, Grace executed twirls and pirouettes as though she was again on the dance floor. The greater the danger, the more she enjoyed it. She quite forgot there was anyone sharing the seat with her.

"Yoo-hoo! Gracie!" yelled the pack.

Tossed from side to side, Naomi and Rachel had a hard time keeping their dignity. Grace laughed exultantly and, hands waving above her head, shouted to the sky.

"I can see the headline now. 'Grace Fry on top of the world!'"

Her shouts alerted Luke Counsel as he wandered along the front and Imre Kodaly as he crouched for shelter from the breeze, behind a beach-hut. The tiny fluorescent figure shone like a beacon against the darkening, lapis sky.

In the bucket, Naomi and Rachel looked up, their faces a picture of disapproval and rage.

"Grace Fry, on top of the world!" Grace bellowed, oblivious to them all. "Top of the world! Top of the world!"

Again and again, Grace challenged the heavens.

CHAPTER EIGHT

The press conference eventually broke up. The journalists had, in truth, been more interested in Grace's future than the future of Naomi's Firm Family Values – to Naomi's fury they repeatedly demanded a statement from Grace on whether she expected to get her own ministry. Released at last, Grace, Miriam and Josie headed back along the promenade, towards the security cordon. The afternoon sun had waned to a rich gold, streaked with orchid and a slight evening chill had fallen. Grace was thinking of warmer clothes and unpacking her bags, left strewn about the hotel room that morning. She and Miriam had agreed to have dinner later, after the church service, which marked the official opening of Conference.

She was just wondering which costume would cover both events, when Miriam's vidi-fone rang. Miriam lifted the matchbox-sized fone on her wrist – as an *ET* executive, she naturally had their most recent state of the art accessory – and said, "Here."

Abbie's face appeared on the tiny screen. She spoke excitedly. "Mim, I'm at *Ossophate*. Sam's promised to take me to his lab tonight. He's going to show me the bespoke programme."

"That's terrif," said Miriam,

"If there's anything important, I'll bring it to Conference – won't take long on the Kamikazi."

"OK," nodded Miriam, "But do be care –."

Abbie's face was wiped from the screen before she could finish the instruction. Miriam shrugged and turned to check that Grace had absorbed the import of the message.

"I guess Security's pretty stiff there. She'll call later when she's got something."

Grace nodded, her constituents uppermost in her mind. She was extremely curious about the job possibilities in this mysterious bespoke programme. She slid her eyes to Josie who had also, of course, heard Abbie's news but the girl was apparently entranced by a dog, bounding about in the spumy shallows. Nonetheless, Grace held her tongue, signalling with a wink to Miriam that they would talk later.

As they walked on, she heard herself hailed in a hissing whisper.

"Mees Fry... Mees Fry..."

She turned sharply – the voice sounded familiar – and was just in time to catch Imre Kodaly's pinched face ducking beneath the promenade. He was on the pebbly beach below and before she could respond, ran off, his body bent low, towards a row of stripey, wooden beach-huts. He had seen what Grace had not. A pair of grim-faced Wardens, bristling with batons, marching down the promenade. Grace shrugged and hurried to catch up with Miriam and Josie. Whatever Imre wanted – and on reflection, she wouldn't mind hearing his grievance with the Centre – it would be impossible to have a frank conversation in the presence of Wardens.

Imre stumbled, panting, to a halt behind the beach-huts and crouched down out of sight of the promenade. So near and yet so far, again. How was he ever to get Grace Fry's attention? He dropped his head between his hunched knees and breathed deeply, trying at once to regain his breath and stave off the pangs of hunger. He heard, as though far distant, the gravelly tow of the busy waves and the crunch of pebbles as a dog threw itself, woofing, into them.

After a moment, he became aware that he was observed. He looked up fearfully and encountered a pair of questioning, grey eyes. The face, particularly the untidy white hair, he recognised and he realised, with a feeling of relief, it was the man he had bumped into earlier.

For some reason, Imre did not find him a threat – perhaps because he was old – perhaps because the expression in his eyes was sympathetic, if a little quizzical. His trust seemed justified when the next moment the man brought half a donut out of his pocket and held it out to Imre.

"Hungry?"

Imre nodded frantically. He edged closer to the seated figure, then grabbed the sugary offering and devoured it. Perhaps, he was thinking, this was a man who could help him. He looked – with his prominent *Independent Satellite* newspaper – educated, literate, at least, and though his clothes were shabby they had once been fine. He had a kind of dignity. Besides, Imre thought, he was getting no closer to his target – he had to trust someone. "I – Imre Kodaly. Refugee from Re-location Centre... Seashoram..." he began, in his halting English.

At the security gate, Grace was stopped by a guard who gave her Luke Counsel's note. She skimmed it hastily then looked around. There was no sign of the writer.

"How long ago did he leave this?"

"Couple of hours," said the guard off-handedly.

"Did he say where he was staying?"

The guard shook his head. Luke's note simply said he was in town and needed to speak to Grace, urgently. He wouldn't say more, knowing that the guard would certainly read it. Grace frowned. What could Luke want that was so urgent? She had no idea how to contact him – he wouldn't have a vidi-fone, they were only for the Elite – she would just have to hope for an encounter in the old town.

The women went their separate ways, Grace and Mim agreeing to meet for the church service later. Josie, Grace dismissed for the rest of the day. She wanted some private time with Miriam.

In her hotel suite, Grace unpacked swiftly, reliving the day's victorious events as she tossed clothes onto the bed, trying and discarding various items before the full-length mirror. The wide-screen TV was on in the background playing news-profile items, but Grace paid no attention until she was arrested by the sound of Jonathan Temple's voice. She snatched up an emerald cashmere dress and struggled into it as she listened. It was the interview she had seen being recorded earlier in the day. Behind Jonathan's head was a cheerful vista of bright sky and beach, but despite that and the heavy make-up covering his pores, Grace did not find him appealing.

The interviewer was asking him the question that had occurred to Grace: 'As leader of the Opposition, what was he doing at the Government's Conference?' Jonathan Temple smilingly explained that *Stone TV* was making a documentary about him, and would be filming as he protested at certain Government policies. Pressed by the interviewer, he agreed that membership of the Euro-Federation would certainly be one of them.

"A corrupt body involved in a catalogue of shame!" he thundered, sounding remarkably like Isiah King. "Euro-economics have been a disaster for this country." Stern-faced, he engaged straight with the camera.

"We're playing second fiddle in an orchestra with no score. Cleaning up after a Euro-potty brothel!"

Clearly, he didn't mind mixing his metaphors. No style at all, thought Grace with a grimace.

"This Government may have absorbed all other opposition, but my Party, once in power, would certainly be looking at opting back out. We bitterly regret the loss of this great nation's sovereignty."

That tallied well with certain of Jethro Stone's opinions. His papers had long mourned the loss of Albion's currency, as the interviewer now pointed out. Jonathan nodded gravely.

"National Pride is perfectly proper. Our surrounding countries use their flags proudly. Here, the use of our patron, St George, has been much undermined by so-called 'liberals'."

He was certainly giving notice to the Drome that he meant business, thought Grace, searching her case for a colour-coded pair of stockings – no government could survive without the support of Stone's enterprises. Temple was now talking about 666 policies, the interviewer questioning him on the proposed 'marriage test'.

"If the right people enter into union in the beginning, there will be no marriage breakdowns. The cost to the State of dysfunctional families is astronomical. Those that fail should be put in jail."

Grace snorted. Even Isiah King didn't go that far.

"So you feel," the interviewer encouraged, "that the Government is wasting money on care and re-education?"

"Outrageous sums!" exploded Jonathan, his cheeks blowing out like hamster pouches. "Aversion therapy? Balderdash!"

They agreed about that at least, thought Grace.

"The death penalty for all sexual deviants would be far more effective."

Grace gasped. She'd never heard him go that far before. She stood, one emerald green stiletto in her hand, as if poised to throw it.

"We believe in a stability this Government has not achieved. Business, Media, Family, King, Church and Government. The Sixth way! 666 Values!"

A seagull circled above his head and seemed about to plop on it. The camera hastily moved away to focus on wave-lapped pebbles. Grace's vidi-fone rang. She expelled air and hopped towards it, putting on her shoe.

"Hi!" Zach's smiling face appeared on the screen.

"How're you doin'?"

"About to put a stiletto through the TV screen. Jonathan Temple's on it."

"Wanker," said Zach genially. It was clearly his favourite term of abuse. "Look. Did a bit of delving. Came up with a couple of things. Can we meet?"

"I'm busy this evening," Grace returned.

"Later then. Say, eleven-thirty? My hotel, 'The Green Dragon'."

"Well..." Grace demurred. She wasn't at all sure it was safe to meet Zach 'later'. Certainly, not at his hotel.

"Oh, come on." Zach gave her a sidelong look, under long lashes. "I won't lay a finger on you. Promise. I know I said you're a sexy piece, but, more importantly, 'The Green Dragon's' outside the security cordon."

He disappeared from the screen before Grace could refuse. As she sat, applying her make-up with even greater care than usual, she found herself smiling.

CHAPTER NINE

The Salutation Service went on for so long, even rigorous New Christians were shifting in their pews. Minister after minister welcomed delegates to Conference and urged them to 'Go with Gideon'. Grace caught sight of Naomi dozing off and being nudged awake by Rachel. In the pew in front, David Timothy was doing *The Indie Satellite* crossword. He leaned back to Grace,

"What's six letters, butter if bigger?" he whispered.

"Bugger," hissed Grace, causing David to thrust his whole fist into his mouth.

Miriam joined in the singing, which she seemed to enjoy, pealing out with a clear soprano. Grace mouthed soundlessly and passed the time by counting the number of logos the Ministry of Mode had managed to squeeze into the 'modernised' Victorian church. The happy-clappy choir was logoed with a *Toobs* tonsil product. There was a bubbling fountain of *Ransome's* 'holy water'. A plaster crucifix with a woeful Jesus had 'sponsored by Dumbo' round his halo. At last, it was over and the congregation filed neatly out behind Gideon, to the choir's rendering of 'Marching in the light of Gideon'.

It was too late, Grace and Miriam decided, to get a restaurant to serve them – even for those who weren't curfewed, hostelries tended to close early – so they would wander the old town in search of fish and chips. It was no hardship for them.

Despite their current elevation, they would both, if asked, still assert they felt most at home in the 'grass roots'. They'd met as students, in a cheap espresso bar frequented by politicos from their redbrick university. Hettie, a little older, was already ensconced as queen bee. Grace and Mim had become friends straight away, drawn by each other's anarchic sense of humour, as much as by shared political ideals and soon became inseparable. Though both had had to suppress the sense of humour and subversion that accompanied it, to rise, they'd managed to remain close through career struggles and marriages; Miriam's to a market analyst and Grace's to a human rights lawyer. When Grace's marriage had failed and she had no family to turn to, Jim and Miriam's comfortable villa had become a second home to her.

The chip shop they found, though certainly 'grass roots,' was not particularly welcoming. According to the large clock above the fog of fat fumes, curfew was fast approaching. It was touch and go how many of the shuffling locals would get served before the sirens went off and they looked askance at the two well-dressed women with prominent security passes, expecting them to jump the queue. They didn't dare say anything of course, beyond a low-level grumble or two, but Grace and Miriam went to the back of the shabby line, aware of the hostility. As the clock ticked loudly to ten fifty-six... ten fifty-seven... the tension in the shop thickened.

"Goin' ter be long?" shouted a man.

"Get a move on," joined in a woman.

"Old yer 'orses." The fishman, red-faced, all but spat into his fizzing fat. "Waitin' for chips. Unless you wan' em raw, carn' go no faster."

Grace and Miriam exchanged uneasy glances. One never knew when a situation like this might get out of hand, which was precisely why the Security Wardens still wielded such power.

A couple grabbed their steaming newspaper parcels and left the shop and the line jerked forward. There was a tapping from outside the grimy window near Grace. She glanced across and to her surprise saw Luke Counsel's face pressed against the perma-glass.

"Luke?" she called and he pushed through the door, a relieved smile on his face.

"No butting in!" and "Get to the back," growled the recalcitrant punters, as he joined her. Luke held up his hand. Cowed, they fell silent; whoever he was, in his old clothes, he had unmistakable authority.

"Luke," said Grace again, kissing his cheek and smiling up at him fondly. This man held so many keys to her past. Before Luke could say anything in return, the curfew sirens emitted a deafening shriek and groans and curses broke out from everybody.

"I've been looking for you all day!" Luke shouted above it.

"Can't hear you!" shouted Grace, covering her ears to make it doubly difficult. The terrible sirens were the worst things about mixing with the people.

"We must talk. You haven't answered my letters."

"Didn't know you'd written," bawled Grace. "Martha, my PPS... ill ... letters not answered – not even opened. Oh, this noise!"

Several Security Wardens had now entered the chip shop and begun checking IDs. They weeded out the cowering folk who didn't have any and, deaf to protest, bundled them towards the door. Luke bent to Grace's ear saying, "I'll have to go. I don't have ID."

"What?" said Grace, appalled. "Why not?

"Withdrawn," said Luke briefly. "Letters I wrote to *The Independent Satellite.*"

"Oh Luke, no." Grace knew all too well what that meant. Luke had never been one to believe discretion was the better part of valour.

In front of them, a scuffle broke out as one man, shouting he was "'Ungry, you bastards," tried to resist arrest. Others took advantage of the situation to make a rush on the door and in seconds, a full-scale brawl was in progress. There were shouts and screams as the Wardens employed their batons with relish, poking and prodding at anyone within reach. Miriam was shoved against the window, and Grace and Luke separated when a woman crashed to the floor between them. In the chaos, Luke made a dash for the door but was collared by reinforcements and frog-marched outside.

"Luke!" shouted Grace, struggling to reach him. "Stop it, I know him, stop it!"

The Wardens, drunk on their power, paid no attention. Luke disappeared, leaving Miriam and Grace trapped in the heaving and howling.

Outside, a large National Security van had drawn up and the curfew enforcers were shoving people into it. Few offered resistance. The restraint methods the Wardens employed were notoriously careless; many had died of asphyxiation. The grunts and moans and the thuds of the batons were drowned out by the screeching sirens. Though electricity for citizens was severely rationed, there was no lack of it for security purposes.

The Warden who had hold of Luke, pushed him towards the van. "In you go." He stopped as he caught a glimpse of Luke's face under the street light. "'Ere, don' I know you?" He demanded suspiciously.

Luke said politely, "I'm Luke Counsel."

The Warden dropped Luke's arm and stepped back, embarrassed. "Mr. Counsel, sir, I'm sorry..."

Luke gave a small smile. "Only doing your job," he observed, gently.

"Don' you remember me, sir?" the Warden entreated.

"I used to be on security at Downing Street, when you was Chancellor?"

Luke surveyed the man and nodded. It was always best to go along with them. The Warden shook his head, sorrowfully.

"Whass 'appened to you, sir?" He leaned in close. "You go on 'ome, I won't say nuthin'."

At that moment, Luke saw Imre being prodded towards the van from where he had left him in hiding, behind the chip shop dustbins. "That man's with me," he said, taking advantage of the Warden's sentimentality. "Could you see your way to..."

"For you sir, anything. You was always that generous." The Warden grinned conspiratorially, but if he was expecting a tip now, thought Luke, he would be disappointed. Apart from a few centimes and his *Ranso-tram* ticket, Luke's pockets were empty.

The Warden seemed carried away with his own emotion however, and elbowed his way through the mob to save Imre. He dragged the terrified refugee from the tailgate of the truck and hustled him back to Luke.

"Go on sir. Quick. Before anyone notices."

Imre clung to Luke and the two of them set off in a stumbling run down the street. The Warden watched them, shaking his head; no doubt pondering on how swift was the fall from grace for those out of Government favour.

Luke and Imre got to the corner as Grace and Miriam fought their way out of the café. Grace's stockings were ripped and Miriam had a swelling on her cheek where she had collided with the window. They were both shocked and frightened.

"Luke!" screamed Grace, almost in tears. "Luke, wait! I'm coming!"

The lights went out all over town, as a sign to the citizens it was slumbertime and in the murk, Grace could no longer make out the distant figures. Miriam put an arm round her and they hurried in the same direction, but when they got to the corner, all they could make out ahead was a silent street and a last *Ranso-tram* rumbling away. Luke and Imre had disappeared completely.

CHAPTER TEN

Grace arrived late at 'The Green Dragon' and, paying no attention to the garish wallpaper, blaring TV or shirt-sleeved Zach, threw herself straight onto the chintzy Teflon counterpane and burst into tears. She was crying as much from shock as from her anxiety about Luke, and Zach, preparing a cold flannel in the en-suite bathroom, was aware of this.

"Here," he said kindly, coming in with the offering. "This'll make you feel better."

"It was awful... awful, to see him like that!" Grace gasped, as Zach slipped an arm beneath her shoulders and hoisted her up. This was not the Grace Fry he knew – sharp as a stiletto, immaculate, always in control. He placed the flannel on her forehead, thinking as he looked at her runny eyes and smudged cheeks, that neither had he ever before seen her without her mask of make-up.

"The Wardens were vile... disgusting!" babbled Grace. Zach was silent. Of course they were. Sometimes he wondered if politicians had any idea at all what went on in the real world.

"Dear Luke," Grace went on. "He looked so thin and poor and... and... old," she finally forced out the word, which, of all adjectives, was currently the most devastating.

"Well," said Zach reasonably, "He is. Gotta be over seventy."

Grace swung her head blindly from side to side as though refusing to believe it. "He was my best friend in Dan's cabinet."

"Apart from Dan," murmured Zach, but Grace appeared not to hear, going tearfully on.

"He was my teacher, daddy, shoulder to cry on."

"Over Dan?" This time Zach spoke more clearly.

Grace pulled sharply away. "God, you're a Hammerhead. What do you want – serialisation rights?"

Zach smiled disarmingly. "Just wondered if he was more than a friend?"

"What are you implying?" snapped Grace, suddenly recovering. "That I shagged him too?" She pulled her jacket straight and scrubbed at her tear-stained cheeks, re-assembling her costume and with it, her *amour propre.*

"I don't know what gives you the right to think you can insult me, just because you've done a couple of half-way decent articles."

Zach put a hand on her arm, "Take it easy, Grace... I only meant–"

"I know what you meant," Grace cut him off. "For your information, Luke would have been one hundred percent the people's choice for PM after Dan died. And mine. He's a lovely, caring, moral human being. If it hadn't been for the Drome machine rolling into action and marketing pretty-boy Gideon..."

She stopped, aware she was getting out of her depth in shark-infested waters. Zach patted her soothingly. "I'm sorry."

He crossed to his briefcase, on a desk next to the burbling TV, now showing a cookery programme; a woman in a countrybun wig was juggling with cucumbers and pumpkins. Zach extracted something from his case and turned to show Grace, producing the articles from behind his back like a conjurer. They were a packet of cigarettes and a bottle of gin.

"Truce?" he suggested, flourishing them.

Grace stopped sniffing and stared with delighted surprise. Then, "Pusscat," she breathed. "Gimme!"

A couple of tots and half a fag later, cordiality was restored. Grace sipped the gin and drew long and hard on the cigarette.

"Magic," she sighed, as the blue smoke swirled about her. Her bliss was rudely interrupted by a loud buzzing from her wrist-bleep, with its built-in smoke detector. Muttering "Shit," Grace dragged it over her wrist and hurled it into the corner, where it bounced about emitting the squeaks of an affronted gerbil. Zach caught her eye and they both laughed like naughty school children. "That's better," he said. "I was worried you'd lost your sense of humour."

Grace stretched on the bed. Though its slippery Teflon coating wasn't exactly inviting – all beds were designed to encourage proper behaviour and early rising – it had been quite a day and she was tired. Zach sat on the side of the bed and gave her a questioning look.

"What d' you want?" he said, "the good news or the bad?"

"Try me on the good," said Grace. "Cuddle me, piranha."

"Josie Andrews has a brother. Chemist. Cambridge first. Went to the outer limits trying his own concoctions."

"Drugs?" said Grace, startled. This didn't fit at all with her image of Josie.

"I'll say. Nineties designer stuff. Dob... flatliners... MDMA... skunk farm in Totnes."

"Very *fin de siècle*," snorted Grace.

"Right. Got busted. Sent down for five years. Round about the time our own dear Drug Czar was appointed."

"So..." Grace wrinkled her brow, trying to follow where Zach's story was heading.

"Comes out. Gets job with major chemical company. Guess which one?

"Not – *Ossophate*?"

"You got it."

"No! An ex-druggie working for the Drug Czar? Priceless."

"Isn't it? Mate on *The Sunday Prophet* tipped me."

"Gideon! Josie's career won't survive if they run stuff like that on her brother."

"They won't. Seth Thomas has put an embargo on it." He paused. "For the moment."

"You mean... "

"Gives them a hold over Josie, doesn't it? Who knows what she's been threatened or promised?"

"So you think she's spying on me?" Grace sat up.

"That's the bad news." He re-filled her glass and they both drank for a moment in silence.

"I don't understand why," mused Grace. "I haven't done anything off-message."

"Maybe they're worried you're going to?"

Zach moved in and took Grace's glass from her hand, "Like say, getting into an 'unsuitable' involvement?" He smiled at her, invitingly. Grace looked at his pretty, boyish face and couldn't help being charmed. Zach's dark eyes sparkled and his curly brown hair looked inviting to the touch.

"I suppose you think you deserve a reward," she said dryly.

"Worth a try," grinned Zach, leaning in.

Grace could feel his breath on her face; it was soft, his face tender. It was a long time since she'd had close contact with another human being. Zach was very tempting...

The hypnotic moment was broken by the beeping of Grace's vidi-fone. She swung swiftly off the bed, ignoring Zach's disappointed sigh and snatched it out of her handbag. Miriam's face appeared on the screen.

"Grace, are you feeling better?" Grace took a gulp of gin. "Much better thanks, Mim. How about you?"

"I've put some ice on my cheek," said Miriam. "The swelling's gone down, but it's a bit bruised." She laughed uncomfortably, "Gideon knows how I'll explain it tomorrow."

"Pancake," advised Grace. It was considered ill-bred to appear in public with bruises. Grace had had plenty of experience of that in the past.

"I've just had a call from Abbie,' Miriam went on. "She sounded very excited. She's found out all about the bespoke programme."

"Yes? What?"

"She wouldn't tell me on the fone. Sam said it was too dangerous."

"Sam?"

"The chemist... so she's on her way here with it."

"What, now?"

"It won't take long on the Kamikazi. I'll call you when she gets to me. By the way... where are you?"

"Er... in Zach's hotel... he's —"

"Mm," Miriam cut her off. "Be careful."

Miriam's face disappeared. Grace replaced the fone then turned to Zach, thoughtfully. "What's Josie's brother's name, d'you know?"

"Sam," said Zach. "Sam Andrews."

CHAPTER ELEVEN

The *Ranso-tram* drew up at the last Seashoram stop, outside the *Ossophate* Industrial Park. Caught in the security arc lights, the smoke from its chimneys spiralled whitely into the dark night air. Luke gave an involuntary shudder. The place always gave him the creeps. He shook Imre, who had fallen asleep leaning on his shoulder.

"Imre, old chap. This is where we get off."

Imre woke with a start and put his chapped hands up, as though to shield his face.

"It's alright," said Luke gently.

They descended and began the long walk to Luke's rambling villa. The route took them alongside the security fence before branching up towards the cliffs, where the road became a chalky footpath. The security guards monitored them as they passed by. Imre was now wearing Luke's coat over his ragged clothes, to give a semblance of respectability and Luke shivered in the cold breeze. Though the days were still warm, the nights gave intimations of winter.

They passed the main security gate, keeping their heads low as cameras swivelled and lights fanned past them. They didn't want to cause an alert. The Re-location Centre was only a mile away, deep in the park and Imre could easily be discovered and forced back there. Both shrank a little as the gates opened and a strange motorcycle contraption came zooming through onto the road. Luke stopped in the shadow of a tree. He had seen the bike before that day; he tried to recall where. The slight figure, blonde hair flowing under the titanium helmet, also seemed familiar.

The bike scattered dust and pebbles and when the explosive crackle of its exhaust, cutting through the otherwise silent, curfewed night had died away, the two resumed their walk. Imre pointed to things in the park and his voice rose above a whisper. Luke hushed him. "Tell me when we get back. It's too dangerous."

Imre subsided and they toiled up the steepening path towards the ghostly white of the cliffs and the black, star-bright sky. They were silent except for a shortening of breath, both locked in their own, disturbing thoughts. Of course, Luke finally nodded to himself – that's where he had seen the bike, and its rider, before – at Conference today, in Drome's vehicle park.

The Teflon cover had fallen to the floor and Grace and Zach lay on the bed kissing. Zach moved his hand softly over Grace's cashmere frock, caressing her through it. The sensual fabric was almost another skin and Grace gave a sigh of pleasure. Zach ran his tongue up her neck and into her ear, taking little nibbles. "Is it good? Is it good?" He pressed her.

"Oh yes, yes..." she breathed.

He slid his hand into the neck of the dress and stroked down towards her breasts. Grace arched to meet him. His touch was assured but unhurried. He knew how to interpret each tiny escape of breath. But as his fingers closed over her hardening nipple, she stiffened and abruptly sat up, pushing his hand away,

"Don't you like it?" Zach fell back on the bed, surveying her.

"Too much." She reached for the cigarette packet and lit one up.

"I wouldn't have brought those if I'd realised they'd be rivals." Zach said. He sighed and raised himself onto an elbow. "Give me a drag?"

Grace put the cigarette to his lips and he held her eyes through the smoke ring. "Were you in love with Dan Jefferson?"

"You know how to get a girl off-guard!" Grace almost laughed at his barefaced cheek. "Once a shark...."

Zach looked hurt. "It was an honest question. I was a big fan of his, when I was a kid."

"You're a kid now," Grace grimaced. "That's another reason you're 'unsuitable'."

Zach reached for her. She didn't stop his hand as it ran over her breast. "I like older women. Maybe I've got a mummy complex." Grace closed her eyes and breathed in, letting his hand travel down to her crotch, parting her legs slightly so he could nestle in it.

"You want to, I know you do," Zach became urgent now. He sat up and took her in his arms, pulling her close. His tongue sank into her mouth and she twined her own around it.

Behind Zach's head, the TV screen was still flickering. Before Grace's eyes fluttered closed, she caught a glimpse of ambulances and sirens – some kind of news bulletin.

Zach pushed her down and moved so he lay on top of her. Grace felt her bones turn to water. It had been so long. So long. She was powerless to resist him. Zach's hand was pulling up her dress, the other was stroking her inner thigh, rising swiftly to the top of her lacy stocking.

"Oh," she gasped, "Oh... oh... "

Her vidi-fone began to ring but for once, she paid no attention. Zach was murmuring and nuzzling into her neck. "Let me... please let me." He had his hand inside her flimsy briefs, stroking and rubbing.

She distantly heard the newscaster's voice announcing the death of a young woman.

"...the woman's identity card describes her as a twenty-eight year-old blonde Caucasian. The bike she was driving was a customised vehicle on which was painted the name, 'Kamikazi'." Grace sat bolt upright, shocked into sudden focus.

"Oh my god," she whispered.

"Anyone wanting further information should ring this number..."

"Oh my god," said Grace again, reaching for her ringing fone.

"What? What!" said Zach.

Grace pointed, speechless, to the television screen. On it was a close-up of Abbie's shattered Kamikazi.

"It's the *ET* girl I was telling you about." Grace managed to croak. "The one involved with Sam Andrews."

Miriam's face appeared on Grace's fone-screen. She looked distraught, "Grace..." she began.

"I know, I know," said Grace. "It's Abbie."

CHAPTER TWELVE

Grace and Josie caught the train to Seashoram by the skin of their teeth. The *Ransome Rail* official at the station had no idea when the next one would be running; several had been cancelled owing to a gas explosion. The official's silver Teflon uniform blew out, balloon-like, as he made it clear to the disgruntled travellers that it was not RR's fault. No one said anything of course, but several noticed he was generating enough hot air for a gas explosion of his own.

Suddenly, a passenger gestured silently towards a moving train and leaving the official in mid-bluster, the crowd on the concourse raced to catch it. Josie, hampered by many bags, had trouble keeping up. Grace had to heave her through the door as the train rolled out of the station. She was already tearful and when Grace deposited her in an empty Elite class carriage, she slumped, blubbering, in the corner.

"Oh, for Gideon's sake, pull yourself together girl," said Grace, pitilessly. She offered Josie a handkerchief, Brussels lace, embroidered with her initials; hankies were another of her personal, stylish touches.

"Why did we have to come?" snivelled Josie. "S'not fair. I'll be disciplined for leaving Conference."

Grace fixed her with a steely eye. "You'll find, Josie, if you toe the line, the line tows you."

Now she was convinced Josie was a spy, there was no need to be nice to her. Josie snuffled into the handkerchief, while Grace unfolded *The Indie Satellite* and flicked to the headline:

'*ET* GIRL DIES IN MYSTERY ACCIDENT.'

She scanned swiftly down the page, but it told her little she didn't know. Zach had been on the fone to his sources about it most of the night. An unidentified vehicle had driven the Kamikazi off the road and disappeared. It had all the appearance of a late-night hit and run. A daredevil faction of the disenfranchised had drunk too much absinthe, broken curfew, stolen an Elite vehicle and gone for a joy-ride. Accidents like this, often fatal, were not uncommon.

Neither Grace nor Zach was convinced by this and by morning, Grace had decided she must go to Seashoram. At the very least, she could visit Luke and find out what he so urgently wanted to tell her.

Josie had been more than reluctant to accompany her, though of course she was not in a position to refuse. "But... you've got an awful lot of functions," she demurred. "There's the 'Praise the Pulses' ceremony, and you're supposed to be presenting a prize at the WIMS' reception."

"Shit," agreed Grace, causing Josie to wince. "For most innovative WIM product – a beef-flavoured female condom, wasn't it?"

Josie blushed and could barely nod for embarrassment. Pity who ever she married, thought Grace. The Ministry of Family's guidebook would need to be well thumbed.

"Oh, that reminds me," she said, "call Naomi and tell her I won't be at the 'Married Love' meeting."

"How will I explain your absence?" said Josie sulkily.

"Make something up," Grace waved dismissively. "That's your job."

She had every intention of keeping Josie by her side. Luke had taught her many years ago: keep your friends close and your enemies closer. She cast an eye at Josie, over the top of the paper. The girl was staring out of the window at the fields flashing by. The train had gathered speed and was now racketing through the otherwise peaceful countryside, on the short journey to Seashoram. Grace felt a momentary pang for Josie. She knew well enough what it was like to be young, thrusting and hungry. She'd been there. Still was really, though now, she hoped, she wouldn't do anything for promotion. Of course, it was more difficult for women. Time after time she had been forced into compromise, in order to pursue equality for her sex. The ends justified the means had become her mantra.

"Feeling better?" she said. Josie nodded glumly. "Well, go and put some lipstick on," advised Grace. "And some perfume. Here, have a splash of mine." She rummaged in her bag and took out Gideon's favourite, giving herself a quick spray before handing it over.

Josie got up lumpenly and left the compartment. As soon as she'd gone, Grace slipped off her wrist-bleep and dropped it into her handbag. She could do without that reminding her every five minutes that she was off-message. Technically, it was a disciplinary offence to remove them, but it was common enough practice even amongst those who sported them officiously, in titanium-plated covers, as though they were precious jewellery. Grace extracted her vidi-fone and called Luke's number. He still had an old landline from his days in office. Luke's mellow voice answered.

"Oh Luke," Grace said, relieved. "You got back OK. I was worried. Look, I'm on my way down. Wait in for me?" Luke agreed, saying he'd prepare lunch.

Grace smiled fondly as she replaced the fone. He was such a dear. He probably had nothing but a few beans and carrots in his larder, but he'd create something.

She glanced out of the window. The countryside basked, its autumn colours glowing, in the blessed sunshine. Grace did not consider herself susceptible to romance – all that had died with Dan – but sometimes on days like today, she was overtaken by a passionate love for the streams and woods of Albion, her country. As she gazed across newly ploughed fields, with their wild flower dotted hedgerows and seagulls swooping above the occasional drum of *Ossophate*, she felt an almost mystical connection.

Chanting from the next carriage brought her down to earth. She got up, straightening her burnt orange linen suit and slid into the corridor. She passed the chanting exercise class obediently following instruction from a Happiness Warden in grass-green Teflon dungarees – "Knees up! Up, I said." and, "Water is Wonderful! Greens are Good!" and followed the corridor round to the ladies, grateful for once for the Warden Watch window. Inside the cubicle, Josie sat on the silver loo, speaking into her vidi-fone. Grace craned to catch a glimpse of the face on it, but Josie's plump shoulders obscured the screen. It was clear though, that she was distressed. Her head wagged vehemently and from time to time, she put up a hand to wipe away tears. Grace pursed her lips. She had a good idea to whom the girl was speaking.

Back in the carriage Grace applied lipstick, checking her face in the mirror. She looked tired, a result of the sleepless night. She frowned – it wasn't good to appear less than fresh and vibrant in public. Josie re-entered on a waft of scent. She had followed Grace's command and her mouth was gummy with lipstick.

"Good start," nodded Grace. "What colour's that?"
Since they were to be together for the time being, she'd decided she might as well encourage intimacy.

"'Petunia Petal,'" replied Josie, without enthusiasm. Not exactly carnivorous, Grace thought, but did not say.

"Suits you. Got a boyfriend, Josie?"
Taken by surprise, the girl stammered, "Er... no... no... that is, I have been to 'Pair' but..." 'Pair' was another branch of the mating agency run by the Ministry of Family.

"You haven't found the right partnering yet?" offered Grace. Josie hung her head.

"Don't be in too much of a hurry," Grace looked out of the window and fiddled with her locket. Two women pulling up cabbages in a field had stopped to ease their aching backs. "In my experience, most women have awful lives."

She returned to Josie's disapproving glance. "Girls don't know what's good for them."

Josie's mouth set in a prim little raspberry. "It sounds as though you don't have Faith in Family," she said. "I thought you'd be a pro-active progressive."

Grace gave a humourless smile. "Don't worry, I am. Particularly for women. But..." she paused and looked Josie straight in the eye. "On some things I'm primeval. Like say, loyalty."

Josie dropped her eyes, while Grace continued to smile dourly.

The train was running into Seashoram station past the usual hoardings, advertising *Ossophate* agro-chemicals and *Ransome's* water, along with the town of Seashoram itself, portrayed as a perfect seaside resort circa 1950. Only Luke, who'd been a child then, would remember it as such. Now its dilapidation caused Grace despair. Though she loved the seat, having inherited it when Luke 'retired', she could have wished for somewhere easier. Naomi, for instance, had Birmiblast, still economically buoyant, as one of the few of Albion's manufacturing areas.

The concourse was crowded with would-be travellers, vainly waiting for the next train to anywhere. They were uniformly well and neatly dressed. Only the Elite could afford permits to travel by train. Nonetheless, Wardens were in evidence and security cameras closely monitored the station. Who knew when these tame folk might suddenly run riot? The expense, the queues, the lateness of the trains. The authorities took no chances.

Outside, Grace flagged down a man-drawn rickshaw and shoved Josie into it. Watching her on the fone had given her an idea.

"I don't need you for a while. I'm meeting some constituents who may be... contagious."

Josie shrank back in her seat.

"Go to the constituency office. You'll find a couple of workers there. Check through the birthdate files and make sure we've sent appropriate cards to everybody. You wouldn't believe how upset citizens get if we miss a birthday."

No wonder, Grace privately thought. It was the only connection most had with their PRs.

"If Noah Petty, our chair's there, give him my regards." That would put the cat among the pigeons, she thought. Give Noah something to worry about.

"I'll meet you back here in a couple of hours."

Before Josie could say anything, Grace shouted, "Forward!" to the boy and the rickshaw set off at a spanking trot. Grace waved to a bicycle one behind and climbing in said, "Follow that rickshaw."

The route to town was busy with bikes, carts and *Ranso-trams*. There were some customised vehicles not unlike the Kamikazi, one or two hung with so many personal belongings they bore more resemblance to tinkers' caravans. There was even the odd pennyfarthing. Grace saw only one car as they passed into the centre of town. It bore the crest of the Commander of the Citizen's Council, an unpleasant man with whom Grace had crossed swords more than once. Like most in his position, he heartily disliked women.

The village green, littered with plastiflex ducks, bore the engraved sign, 'New Millennium Experience'. Seashoram had been the beneficiary of a lottery grant way back then. In the centre of the green was a small pond with a heritage ducking stool – occasionally in use – and round the edges, lottery booths, surveillance cameras, stocks – frequently in use – and a podium labelled 'Speaker's Corner'. A speaker, wearing a faded 'Bravo Britannia' tee-shirt stood on it, declaiming, "Eat more fruit, less protein. Cereals kill sexual desire. Protein inflames the passions!" A small crowd of people had gathered. They watched dispassionately as he flagellated himself with an evil-looking, knotted Discipline.

Grace made sure her rickshaw kept a discreet distance, but as Josie's cornered ahead of them, she urged her driver to keep up.

"Hurry boy. I don't want to lose them."

They trotted through the winding, cobbled streets until the town petered out and they passed into a Soviet-style urbanisation with hi-rise concrete blocks surrounded by tall wire fencing. A large sign announced 'Home-Zones'. These were like townships all to themselves. The inhabitants, a ghetto-ed subclass, forbidden to enter other areas without a special – and hard to obtain – licence. Even in the cheerful sun, the blocks looked depressed. They were largely deserted, the children in school. A dog shat on a patch of scrubby grass. One shabby young woman wearily pushed a pram with a toddler in it.

Beyond the ghetto was an old-fashioned Edwardian terrace. The street furniture now proclaimed, 'You are entering a curfew-free zone'. Some of the neatly hedged houses still had flowery gardens and individual features.

Josie's rickshaw pulled up outside one with rather splendid stained glass panels in its door. Grace motioned hers to stop, where it was shielded by a clipped yew hedge and watched as Josie alighted and went up the gravel path to the front door. Judging by the number of bells, the house was divided into flats. Josie rang one of them and a moment later, a ground floor curtain twitched. After a short pause, there was the sound of bolts clicking and the front door opened a sliver. Peering through the twigs, Grace could just make out the figure of a man. Josie was hustled quickly inside and the door closed with a bang.

Grace got down and, telling her boy to wait, went round to an alley she had noticed at the back of the houses. Keeping low, she scurried along it until, peeking over the fence, she saw that she was level with the house Josie had entered. A padlocked gate at the end of its long, grassy garden gave on to the alley.

No one was about. The only sounds Grace could hear were birds twittering and the distant, classical sound-bites of *Radio Digi-tranquillity*. Silently cursing her tight skirt, Grace climbed over the gate, laddering her stocking on a random nail. She dropped to the other side and immediately ducked and scuttled along the hedge to the back of the house, where she could see French windows. She flattened herself against the wall and sneaked a look in. Josie was sitting on a sofa with her arm round a bearded young man. He was crying and Josie seemed to be soothing him, though Grace couldn't hear what she said.

The young man shook his head and shouted something which, muffled by the glass, sounded like," 'ey 'illed her!"

Grace looked around for some means of entry. She must hear this conversation. There was a small, half-open sash window, at head level nearby. If she stood on the dustbin, she might just make it. With a quick look round to make sure she was not observed – in this curfew-free area there were unlikely to be surveillance cameras, but you never knew – Grace hitched up her skirt and using an upturned flowerpot as a step, clambered onto the dustbin. Her steel-tipped heels made a clattering sound on the metal and she froze for a moment. But no one appeared and, grunting a little, she levered herself through the window and wriggled down the other side, finding herself in a lavatory. The door was open a crack and through it she had a diagonal view of the living-room sofa and could just make out the conversation. Her blood ran cold as she heard the young man say,

"They murdered her, I tell you!"

"Sam!" Josie's voice was sharp. "You can't say things like that!"

Grace gave a tight smile. So, it was Sam. She'd been certain if she left Josie to her own devices she could not resist a visit to her brother. Perhaps she was even under instructions.

"I'm sure Abbie's death was an accident." Josie said firmly. Sam pushed his long dark hair out of his eyes. He looked the archetypal mad scientist, thought Grace.

"I should never have shown her."

"Shown her what?"

Sam shuddered. "No. No! They'll do the same to you... oh Abbie."

He held out a framed photo, Grace caught a glimpse of Abbie's smiling face, before Sam hugged it to him.

"She was the only one who ever cared about me," he wailed. "Except you!"

Grace made a mental note to ask Josie about her family background. Sam jumped up suddenly and rushed to the bay window. He squinted through a chink in the curtains and said in a quavering voice, "Who else knows you're here?"

Grace saw Josie hesitate. Then "No one," she said, a shade too definitely. "I had to come with Grace Fry but..."

"Grace?" Sam interrupted, "Grace Fry? D'you know her?"

"I've just been made her PPS," said Josie shortly. "Everybody knows her."

Grace thought she detected contempt in her tone.

"Abbie was trying to get to her." Sam sounded excited. "To tell her. About the bespoke programme! When she... she..."

Josie did not give him time to continue.

"No one's to know about it." She shook him. "No one, d'you hear? Company disloyalty! If Isiah King finds out– !" She left the threat hanging, as though the consequences were too dire to think about. People had been imprisoned for long periods for company sabotage.

"But someone's got to know! Got to stop it!" insisted Sam, lowering his voice to a frantic whisper.

Josie stood up. "I know you're upset, but you're talking nonsense, Sam. You sound as though you're heading for one of your states."

There was threat in her tone and Sam looked at her fearfully.

"You wouldn't want to have to have more therapy."

Sam shook his head, his eyes registering terror.

"Right. I'm going to make you something to eat. "

Grace shrank back as Josie passed the lavatory door on her way to the kitchen. Josie put on the kettle, then buttered bread and placed a large tomato and some lettuce on a plate. She made tea in a King Charles mug and carried plate and mug back to Sam. He pushed the proffered food away.

"You don't know what's in it."

Josie sighed. "It's a tomato, Sam."

Sam's face took on a cunning look. He smiled slightly.

"Looks like tomato. Tastes like tomato. That's the beauty of it."

Josie tapped her foot.

"I'm not listening to any more of this. Eat or I'll have to call the ManiaMedics."

Sam snatched up the tomato and took a bite, a second later he was on his feet. "Mmm... going to be sick..." he mumbled and ran towards the lavatory.

Without thinking, Grace was on the seat and up and over the windowsill. She crashed down the other side taking the dustbin lid with her. Accompanied by the music of Sam retching – it certainly drowned out *Radio Digi-tranquillity* – she staggered to her feet, covered in vegetable peelings.

CHAPTER THIRTEEN

As her rickshaw bumped over the stony, cliff-top path to Luke Counsel's isolated villa, Grace had time to consider the man she was about to visit. She and Luke 'went back' to Grace's earliest days in politics. It was true, as she had told Zach, that in many ways, Luke was her mentor. He had been a kindly presence in Dan's kitchen cabinet. He was far from soft though, as Grace also had reason to remember. He had rebuked her more than once for her behaviour. He had a challenging and sometimes confrontational nature, particularly if he felt some moral lapse was being countenanced or injustice perpetrated.

Luke's own record on human rights was impeccable. Even in retirement, he had been active on behalf of democracy; protesting by letter on everything from the removal of parliament and the embrace of Drome – he termed it a balloon of hot air – and made many comments about Nazi architecture and Lord Hodge's distant relationship to the infamous Albert Speer – to the dissolution of the second chamber and the methods of control and restraint used by Security Wardens. Though this endeared him to *The Indie Satellite* and other smaller samizdats, it had hardly improved his stock with the Government watchdogs, hence presumably, the withdrawal of his ID card.

After Dan's death, it was plain he would never again achieve high office and rather than remain a powerless backbencher, had given up his seat in Seashoram using the time-honoured excuse that he wanted to 'spend more time with his family'. The town had become part of Grace's fiefdom during a regional re-alignment. The whole area caused her heartache, having never really recovered from the Great Panic. But over the ensuing years, she had worked hard to give its constituents a higher, and more prosperous, profile.

Ossophate had been a gift, as Isiah King's empire, originally built on indigestion powders, expanded and expanded. Now, with the new technology, the opposite – at least in terms of workforce – was again happening. Her concern was obviously for her workers but also, she could not deny, for her own power base. She wouldn't hold on to a ministry for long with a failing constituency. There were as many enemies as friends in the local party; Noah's coterie on the caucus was strong. There was no way Grace would call on him for help; indeed, she strongly suspected he was plotting to undermine her. When things went wrong, or seemingly insoluble puzzles arose, her first port of call was still, and always, Luke.

The rickshaw jerked to a halt in a cloud of chalk dust, the rickshaw boy coughing and sweating. They were at the summit of the white cliff, where Luke's gracious sprawl of a villa over-looked the sea. Behind it was a woody, overgrown garden, which sloped down the cliff-side towards rocks and foam-capped waves. It must have been delightfully full of hidey-holes and dens for Luke's children when they were growing up. Both had long since left home, his son to work for the Euro Federation in Berlin, his daughter to get married. Luke's wife, Margaret, had died some years previously, but though the big old house was far too large for a man alone, he had clung on to it for what Grace imagined to be emotional reasons.

Grace dismissed the rickshaw and walked up the chalky gravelled drive to the porch, which was adorned with an ancient, but still flowering, rambling rose. Not unlike Luke himself, she thought wryly, as she rang the doorbell.

Luke answered the door wearing a worn, pin-striped suit and holding in his arms his young grandson. Grace was amazed at how the toddler had grown; she'd been at his christening, which seemed to her only a few weeks ago. A further indication of how long it was since she'd really talked to Luke, she reflected guiltily. Luke, though, was smiling without censure and ushered her into the wide drawing room saying, "My daughter will be back to pick up young Tobias soon; it's her week on milking duty."

The drawing room was charmingly Edwardian with a tiled, open fireplace in which smouldered some logs, comfortable – if battered – chintz-covered sofas, a baby grand piano, vases of garden flowers and many framed photographs. One wall was lined with oak bookcases, but except for a few children's books – "Proactive Pupils" and "Children into Citizens," – a Celia Thin cookery book or two and a prominent Gideon bible, these were largely empty. Candles and oil-lamps were dotted about to counter electricity rationing. Few private dwellings had their own generators. Through the french windows was a view of a paved patio with a few tended herb pots, and the beginnings of the bushy garden. A small plot had been cleared to grow vegetables and Grace could see the tops of potatoes and winter greens. For once, there was no obvious drum of *Ossophate*.

Luke excused himself to bring in the lunch and Grace watched over Tobias, as he played with a toy Dinosaur Park, which Luke had laid out on the worn Indian carpet. The child had hold of a plastiflex Tyrannosaurus Rex and Grace gently pulled it away from his mouth, as he attempted to chew it. Luke re-entered, bearing a wooden tray, decorated with a rose and loaded with rice and vegetables. They sat at a low table with the food on their laps and Grace marvelled again at Luke's ability to concoct delicious meals out of few and humdrum ingredients. In Dan's day, he had been much valued for it; often throwing together a late night feast as they sat round the kitchen table, arguing and, in Dan's case, drinking.

When Luke brought in the *Nut-Noggin* coffee substitute – even this he somehow made palatable – Grace embarked on her story, starting with the 'bespoke' programme and Abbie's sudden death, through to her suspicions of Josie and what she had learned from spying on her that morning.

"Sam Andrews is Josie's brother, so there's got to be a reason she was assigned to me. And he was in charge of this 'bespoke' thing, so obviously he knows all about it." Grace was putting two and two together for herself, as much as for Luke.

"He seemed terrified. Kept saying, 'Someone's got to stop it.' Stop what, d'you think?"

Luke gave a grunt. "Arrogance, greed, recklessness. Big Business as usual."

Grace threw him an irritated look. "I'm talking practical, not existential, Luke." He had always annoyed her when he turned philosophical.

"Sorry." Luke took the warning humbly. "Actually, it's what I was trying to see you about. There've been rumours, a couple of mysterious deaths."

"Tony Griffiths said suicides," interrupted Grace.

Luke shook his head, doubtfully. "Maybe, but I don't think so. It was those who were complaining who disappeared. I wrote to *The Indie Satellite* about it, but even they don't listen any more..." His voice tailed away and he picked up the toy dinosaur from the floor. "Sometimes I feel like this."

"T-Rex?" Grace raised her eyebrows.

Luke nodded gloomily. "Extinct."

Grace touched his arm encouragingly. "I'm still a carnivore."

Luke turned on her, suddenly angry.

"Are you? Are you sure, Grace? A lot of people here suspect you're so on-Drome you've abandoned your constituents. You used to care... be engaged... now you're totally out of touch!"

Grace withdrew her hand, hurt. Luke's attack brought back those he had made on her in the past, reducing her to novice status. "That's not fair," she said, her voice trembling with emotion. "I'm doing my best for Seashoram. I'm only accepting Mode so I can help... Christ, Luke...!" She stopped and hastily looked round.

Luke's face crinkled into a grin. "It's alright. I'm not bugged any more. Too old and irrelevant. Still it's good to see you fired up, Gracie. Perhaps I was wrong. If so, I apologise."

Grace bowed her head. She was all too aware that Luke had a point. But she'd soon have no career prospects if she totally abandoned Drome constituency directives. And how would that help Seashoram?

The toddler began to grizzle, alarmed at the raised voices, and Luke picked him up and walked the room with him. He stopped in front of a framed photograph of himself with Dan Jefferson, and said, a lament in his voice, "How different things would have been if Dan had lived."

Grace nodded, soberly. "For both of us. The fool. God knows I tried to stop him drinking."

Luke picked up the photo and stared at it intently as though trying to divine something from Dan's expression. "A question mark hangs over his death," he muttered, almost to himself.

"He fell six floors from a balcony," said Grace bluntly. "What's to question?"

"Did he fall? Or was he pushed?" Luke faced her, sombrely.

"He was drunk, for chrissakes. You know as well as I do, he'd been drinking."

Grace's emphatic tone disguised her own unspoken fears. She knew very well what Luke was implying, but she couldn't afford to let such doubts surface. Besides, Luke had always been too fond of conspiracy theories.

Luke shrugged away from her. "You really have bought the tee-shirt," he murmured. He caught up another photo.

"Look at you here." He held out the picture: a much younger, idealistically open-faced Grace, along with Dan and Luke. Behind them stood Gideon, Matt, and Adam, who'd all been junior ministers in Dan's government.

"You had everything at your feet."

Grace looked away, disturbed. "So did you," she countered. Luke gave a sad smile. "True enough. But when Dan died and I failed to..."

"Get elected leader of the party," Grace finished for him.

"You preferred to bottle out. Your choice. I hung on in there."

Luke shook his great shaggy head, more in sorrow than anger.

"I'm your friend, I hope. But I have to ask you... why Grace? How can you stand them?"

"I didn't... don't have a choice," said Grace irritably. "I was young; I had a career, a life in front of me. I wanted everything at my feet again. With proper recognition!"

"Well," Luke sighed. "Now you've got it, I hope you're happy."

Grace frowned. Why did Luke still have the power to make her feel small and insignificant? Why, indeed, did she give it to him?

"At least I haven't done it on my back," she snapped.

"This time." Luke was surveying her under his heavy brows. His glance made no apology for the insinuation. Grace looked away, her fingers fumbling for her locket.

"I'll tell you a story," Luke said, much as he might have to Tobias. "Dan was about to sack Adam Solomon, when he died."

"What?" Grace gasped. It was an impossible idea, Adam was one of the bright young men Dan had championed and promoted.

"Oh yes," Luke affirmed. "There was an insider-trading scandal. Involving our dear Lord Ransome. Dan had just made Adam Secretary of State for Business, remember?"

Grace nodded, remembering also that she had felt cross and betrayed at the time; though far too young and inexperienced, she should have had the appointment.

"Jake Ransome's always made sure he was close to power," continued Luke. "He was the same when we were at school. He'd do favours for the teachers and take the kids for a ride." He chuckled rather bitterly, recalling the days when he and Jake Ransome had been boys at boarding school together. "He even used to auction off the contents of his tuck-box! Anyway, the Solomon scandal rumbled on, implicating several other cronies."

"Just a minute," Grace held up a peremptory hand. "How was it kept so quiet? I didn't know."

"Adam was sent on a fact-finding tour to the United Balkans, while Dan investigated. Dan was good at secrets."
Of that, Grace needed no reminding. She was annoyed though, that he had kept this one from her. Annoyed too, at her own lack of observation.

"Don't blame yourself," Luke smiled, guessing, as he so often could, her thoughts. "After all, people can live with spies for years without knowing."
That, thought Grace, was hardly reassuring.

"When Gideon took over, he sacked a couple of low-level rotten apples, brought in Seth Thomas from *The Daily Millennium* to spin the cover-up and the rest, as they say, is history." He shook his head sadly. "If Dan hadn't died, they'd all have gone." Luke sighed. "Under Gideon, they've risen like dough."

"What are you suggesting?" said Grace slowly, unwilling to follow where Luke appeared to be leading.

"I wouldn't put Dan's death past Dracula here." Luke pointed to Adam in the photo. "There were other reasons they wanted rid of Dan." He stopped as though wary of testing Grace too far. Then, with another gesture at Adam, finished, "His court of serpents will stop at nothing."

"Luke," said Grace dryly, "you see serpents under every bed."
Luke gave a laugh that sounded like a bark. "I have that in common with Isiah King, then. According to him, only a Millennium of celibacy can redeem the Fall of Man!"

"Pity he includes women in that," Grace sighed, thinking of her last encounter with Zach.

"You've never...?"

"Not since Dan."

"Really? That long?" Luke looked amazed.

"I couldn't, I just...couldn't. Not even with my husband." Grace's voice dropped away. The conversation was too intimate for a relationship which was almost father and daughter. "Ha!" she continued, after a moment. "No wonder he divorced me." Her voice was bright but her eyes filled with tears.
The old statesman put a large friendly hand on her shoulder.

"Ah, Grace. I knew you hadn't completely sold your soul. You've gone a long way down their road, though."

"I've managed some good things for women." Grace was defiant.

"Mm." Luke gave her a sceptical look. "Surrogate grannies. Compulsory contra-conception."

"Far too many subclass women were ruining their lives with unwanted pregnancies," began Grace in righteous self-defence.

"Unlike you," Luke silenced her.

Grace fiddled uncomfortably with her locket. There was a pause filled with Tobias's baby burblings. "This is getting us nowhere," said Grace, at last. She was unprepared to take up Luke's accusation. "How can we find out what Sam Andrews is so concerned about? I mean, what is this blasted 'bespoke' programme?"

"I don't know," said Luke. "I've tried to find out and only drawn blanks. I fear the Drome Unit's involved."

"Oh really, Luke." Grace was scornful now. "Paranoia."

"You say that," Luke wagged his big head. "But I've kept documents of some pretty wacky ideas Gideon and Adam came up with, even when Dan was alive. They're very much influenced by Isiah King, you know."

This, Grace did know. The word was, Isiah was to get a Government appointment in Care during the imminent reshuffle. He and Gabriel Strong were two of a kind, though Gabriel always presented himself as the caring, sharing face of human resource management.

Luke went on, mirroring her thoughts. "King and Strong are bonded in suppressive measures. The Great Panic and Dan's death gave them the perfect opportunity for all this 'back to the future' nonsense. Don't forget King's already involved with Care and Ransome on the Re-location Centre."

"What's wrong with that?" Grace bridled. "My Re-location Centre's lovely."

"So *The Sunday Prophet* tells us." Luke gave her a sardonic look.

"You'll be telling me next Jethro Stone's involved in this 'conspiracy'," Grace laughed, as though to ward off a prophecy, but when she glanced at Luke, he was far from amused.

"You may not think it's so funny, in a moment." He took her by the shoulders and looked into her face searchingly. "Can I trust you, Grace?"

"Of course," she said. "You know you can. I don't think you're irrelevant."

"Then there's someone I'd like you to meet." He put Tobias in a playpen with his toys and opened the french windows.

"Come with me," he instructed.

CHAPTER FOURTEEN

Outside, there was a sharp breeze off the sea and Grace pulled her jacket around her. Luke led the way across the terrace and past his neatly staked rows of vegetables. The crazy paving path sloped steeply down through terrain that became more dense and overgrown as they descended. Brambles snagged Grace's stockings and overhead twigs caught in her hair. She wondered if Luke was taking her to a den or cave, but after about five minutes they ducked through giant rhododendrons into a small clearing and, to her astonishment, she saw in front of them a second world war gun emplacement.

The brick building was dug into the cliff. From its other side there must be an uninterrupted view out to sea – Grace could hear the crashing of waves on the rocks below. It looked shuttered and empty and there was a large rusty padlock on the wood and iron-barred door.

"Heavens," she exclaimed. "I didn't know any of these still existed."

"Never been discovered," said Luke, taking a key out of his pocket. "Lucky. We're outside the zone system here. Another reason I've never moved."

He turned the key in the padlock, which Grace now saw had been recently oiled. "I've made it into something of my own private bunker."

Grace's heart started to thump as Luke pushed open the heavy door. She couldn't imagine what he was going to show her. Luke gestured her to follow as he entered and in the musty dark, lit a candle. The flame flickered upwards and discovered, to Grace shelf after shelf of books, tapes, files and documents, many with the old House of Commons portcullis logo on them. She stared, awed. "All these books," she breathed. She hadn't seen so many in one place for years. Here was everything Luke would need to write a political autobiography, if such a thing were still possible.

"I thought somebody should preserve them. And the files." He gave a grim laugh. "If anything happens to me, this is where the bodies are buried."

Grace shuddered. If anyone found this cache, most assuredly Luke's would be.

Luke's candle travelled the walls and illuminated another door in a cobweb-hung corner. It was slightly ajar and Luke pushed at it.

"It's alright, Imre. You can come out."

A pale worried face appeared in the gloom. To Grace's astonishment, it was the man who had been chasing her at Conference.

"But, you're..." she began.

The man nodded.

"This is Imre Kodaly," said Luke. "He's been here since we gave the Wardens the slip." Luke placed the candle on a table and drew up some tattered rattan chairs.

"Sit down, Grace," he said. "Imre's got a story I think you should hear."

"I try to tell you," said Imre, when they were all seated. "Before. At Conference. The Centre... bad, bad! My wife... they give her pills ...say to calm ...she has..." he pointed to his head, "...mental troubles. Then they take her to the hospital wing. I not allowed see her... they tell me she too sick." He paused and struggled for composure, then finished in a low voice. "She die."

There was a silence. Luke had left the big door a little open and through it filtered leafy green light and the sound of birdsong.

"I'm sorry," said Grace at length. She looked at Luke. "But I don't quite see..."

Imre shot out a hand and gripped her arm. "She not ill, before pills. Nothing wrong." He tapped his forehead. "Nothing!"

His fingers were biting into Grace's flesh and she winced with pain.

"OK, OK!" she exclaimed. She wrinkled her brow at Luke. "What about these pills?"

Luke opened his hands wide. "It's *de rigueur* to give people in detention calming medication. The prison system would have collapsed years ago without it. But —"

"Men too. Disappear," Imre interrupted impatiently. "One day there... the next not. And my son."

"Your son's... disappeared?" said Grace. It was hard to unravel the story through Imre's erratic account and thick accent. Now he was nodding his head vigorously.

"They take to 'Protection Unit'." He spat out the words.

"Say for his own good, because I bad parent." His voice choked with distress. "Not true! Not true!"

He broke into angry sobs and Luke patted his shoulder.

"Imre's family's had a tough few years since they were displaced and now this on top of it," he said to Grace.

She nodded, but at the same time was thinking that any abusive husband or father might say the same as Imre. For this reason, she'd been keen on sex segregation and the Child Protection Unit.

"What do you think we should do?" she asked Luke.

"Go there!" Imre answered for him. "Find my sister Eliana. She Team Leader in factory. She know, she know what happen! My wife not dead. I don' believe it!"

Grace exchanged a glance with Luke. Again, it was what any distraught husband might say. Imre clutched at her. He brought his face close and fixed her with piercing black eyes.

"I never see her body. She not dead. Believe me."

A little later, Luke backed his ancient, once ministerial *Rover* out of the garage and opened the door for Grace to climb in.

His daughter, dressed in nineteenth century milkmaid's costume, complete with long white apron and mobcap, stood at the front door holding baby Tobias. She watched as Luke carefully negotiated the curve in the drive, but did not wave. No outing in the rarely used car was ever for a joyful occasion. The gears cranked rustily as Luke reached the cliff path and heaved the old car round to descend the steep gradient. Grace said nothing, knowing he had to concentrate, but as soon as they reached the main road, she asked him for Imre's story. His eyes fixed on the road ahead, Luke told her in measured tones, Imre's troubled family history.

Imre and his family had been cleansed from their village over a decade previously as a result of the interminable war. Janos, their young son, had been carried on their backs over snowy mountain passes. It was miraculous the family had stayed together, when so many had been broken up and lost to each other. But despite being law-abiding and working at whatever came along, they were never welcome in any of the countries through which they passed. Fear of exposure was a constant. In Holland, Imre had a job rearing plants in a nursery. He was good at it, having worked on the land at home, but when he was promoted, he was threatened by a jealous employee. It was time to move on again.

Imre's sister Eliana and her husband were living well in Albion, where they had a vegetable stall in a country market. Albion was the zenith of most refugees' ambitions – Gideon was regarded as almost a god for the stands he had taken during the endless war, visiting desperate people with the saintly Hettie, making thrilling speeches and promising restitution – so Imre and Anna decided to join what was left of their family. They'd entered illegally on a boat carrying tulip bulbs, shortly before the Ministry of Care's refugee round-up. They'd been concerned, at first, at the loss of freedom – wandering was in Imre's gypsy blood and too many walls made him ill – but Anna was exhausted and after all their troubles, the Re-location Centre – luxurious, healthy, offering work and hope for the future – seemed like paradise. Janos loved the play facilities and Imre had been delighted with the football team. Luke had seen them play once or twice at special events in the town stadium. It was from these occasions that he'd recognised Imre.

At this point, the *Rover* made the sharp turn onto the road to *Ossophate* safely and cruised slowly along the perimeter wire towards the entrance of the Re-location Centre. Inside the car, having listened intently, Grace was now applying make-up.

"When we get there, you should stay in the car," she advised, waving the mascara wand. "They'll never let you in without ID. You can wait for me by the main gate." She sprayed a blast of perfume round her neck. She had found it never failed with Security.

Luke braked the car to a standstill and watched with concern as Grace got out and approached the security booth, holding out her ministerial pass. After a moment, she was nodded through and put into a small jeep to be driven the extra distance to the Centre. The security guard went back to the booth and lifted the telephone.

Luke settled back against the headrest and took out his pipe and *The Indie Satellite*. She would be at least half an hour. Besides, it gave him pleasure to flaunt the provocative, off-message newspaper in front of the security cameras.

CHAPTER FIFTEEN

The jeep carrying Grace drew up in front of the Re-location Centre's impressive red and silver entrance. Gardeners in refugee uniforms were pruning and weeding banks of blooming plants; the whirling glass doors were *Ranso*-logoed and the slate-flagged foyer full of magnificent flower arrangements. Christobel Steel, looking rather flustered, came rushing to meet Grace as she entered.

"Well, this is a surprise," she said, adjusting her pebble glasses.

Grace smiled graciously. "Sorry not to have given you more warning. Didn't have it myself. *The Indie Satellite* people are coming down later in the week to do a spread on the Centre."

"*The Indie Satellite*?" Christobel's mouth gaped, giving her the look of a netted fish. "Seth Thomas didn't say anything."

"They approached me directly," said Grace briskly. "I could hardly say no, could I? Would have given the impression we had something to hide. You know what they're like."

She swept past Christobel who was standing dumbly, fiddling with the belt on her uniform. Grace smiled to herself. Clearly Christobel had been having an after lunch siesta.

"Just thought I'd check. Better safe than sorry. It's a DPS. Double page spread, yes? Interviews with residents and lots of photos. Wouldn't want them getting the wrong end of the stick."

"No, no indeed." Christobel caught up with her and hurried alongside, a worried crease on her forehead.

"Gideon knows what they'd print! Displaced people can't always separate fact from fantasy."

"Fortunately," Grace gave her pusscat smile, "I can. Shall we start with the condom factory?"

Christobel winced slightly at the word. The official term was, 'Choice Control Construction'. She led Grace along wide white corridors decorated with paintings and plants, and through connecting doors to the work area.

The condom factory was announced by a giant rubber erection, which hung threateningly above the entrance. Grace wondered if it was modelled on Lord Ransome. His reputation was certainly priapic. She averted her eyes from it, as Christobel tapped in the code and the titanium doors slid back revealing regular rows of workers.

"All our workers are productive and happy," assured Christobel, blowing the large whistle attached by a chain to her belt. All the workers looked up and smiled.

"This is Grace Fry, Government Minister for Women," announced Christobel. "She's come to look at the way we pro-act, so just continue as normal."

The workers, as one, returned to their mechanical tasks. Stretching, pulling, snapping, stabbing. Overhead, whizzed cables dangling quality controlled condoms. Watching their flying hands, Grace became aware that each worker had a number tattooed onto the wrist. Something she hadn't noticed on previous visits.

"They have numbers?" she said, with a frown of displeasure.

"Their names are so difficult," said Christobel airily. "Foreign. Unpronounceable. They don't mind, really."

Grace doubted that, but she held her tongue.

"I'm especially proud that all my Team Leaders are women," continued Christobel. "Like you, I'm a firm believer in Mummy power."

"So I see," responded Grace, eyeing the condoms.

"Oh, yes," Christobel turned coy. "I don't usually tell people, but I was called 'Christobel' after 'Pankhurst'."

"Really," murmured Grace. "I was called 'Grace' after 'Amazing'."

Christobel appeared oblivious to the irony and droned on with her spiel about the best worker care anywhere in the world, becoming quite lyrical on the subject of Lord Ransome's benevolence.

"He's such a generous, caring man," she enthused. "He'd be terribly distressed if he thought our workforce wasn't productive and happy."

They were passing down the rows now and Grace stopped by a worker who was staring blankly head, doing nothing.

"Here's a candidate for his concern then," she said. "This man doesn't seem very productive and happy."

Christobel prodded the man, who pitched forward onto the pile of rubbers which had built up at his workstation. Christobel clicked her teeth and blew her whistle to summon help. Several boiler-suited guards appeared but the rest of the workers took no notice.

Grace took advantage of the hiatus to hurry on down the line, checking the red and silver ID badges at each station until she came to a larger one with the words 'Team Leader' and 'Eliana Kodaly'.

"Eliana," she hissed, bending over as though to examine the work. "Don't look up, but listen. I've been in contact with your brother, Imre.."

Eliana gave an involuntary, startled glance, but she returned immediately to her routine as Grace went on, "He's safe, don't worry. But his wife... Anna?"

Eliana shook her head. "I don' know... maybe dead... maybe still in hospital... secret ward... I have friend, an orderly."

"This medication," Grace whispered.

Eliana gave a slight shrug, "Everyone must take."

"Yes," urged Grace, "... but what is it?"

Before Eliana could answer, her name was called loudly by Christobel, who had sneaked up behind them.

"Ah... I was just asking..." Grace peered at the ID badge, "Eliana, is it? To get me a glass of water. It's very warm in here."

"For the rubber," said Christobel shortly. "Get Ms Fry a *Ransome's*, 2167."

Eliana rose and scurried to a bubbling water fountain. She filled a beaker and held it out to Grace, avoiding eye contact. Christobel, Grace noticed, was watching closely. Obviously, Lord Ransome's concern for his workers did not stretch to giving them freedom of speech. Smiling innocently, Grace reached for the beaker, but before she could take it a loud siren went off and Eliana clumsily dropped it.

"Weald Worship!" called Christobel, clapping her hands. The workers rose and filed obediently towards the door, as around Grace's feet spread a large pool of *Ransome's*.

Once the workers had departed, Christobel offered refreshment. Grace, fearing vegetables would be involved, declined and after a perfunctory check of other areas, empty since everyone had gone to the service, left the building saying she must get back to Conference.

"I think you'll find *The Indie Satellite* a very positive media opportunity, Christobel," she smilingly insisted, as they stood on the immaculate forecourt.

Christobel looked unconvinced. "As long as this visit's set your mind at rest," she said with a sniff.

"Oh yes," Grace was emphatic. "Absolutely."

Her gaze was caught by the distant towers of *Ossophate*, steaming gently. The wispy vapour circled whitely into an otherwise clear, blue sky.

Luke was leaning against the bonnet of the *Rover*, soaking up the sun. His eyes were closed and he clutched his empty pipe between his teeth. Grace was assailed with a poignant memory of its smoke swirling fragrantly round Dan's kitchen.

"Let's drive round to *Ossophate*'s entrance," she suggested, "I may as well check."

"I suppose so." Luke opened his eyes and gave her an uneasy glance. "Well?" he said, when they'd set off. "What did you find out?"

"Not a lot," said Grace. "Except that they're paranoid about anyone talking."

Luke nodded. "No more than I expected."

"I found Eliana. She managed to tell me they're all on this medication. As for Anna... she doesn't know what's happened to her, though she did mention a secret ward in the hospital."

"Secret? Did you ask about it?"

Grace shrugged. "According to Christobel Steel, the only thing I haven't seen is the re-hab unit. Unsuitable for visitors. Violent. She repeated her mantra about drunken asylum seekers, as if they were somehow my fault."

"Colditz," said Luke lugubriously.

"Trust you to jump to the worst possible conclusions."

Luke drove on, a wounded silence emanating from him. After a few moments, Grace conceded, with exasperated affection, "It is a bit odd. There's a sort of... compulsory tranquillity. Hard to put your finger on it."

"Christobel's a cold fish," opined Luke. "I've often wondered about her and Seth Thomas. They were students together."

"Are you suggesting she's the Drome Unit bike?" said Grace, recalling Zach's gossip and the sight of Christobel's oscillating bottom in Baby.

Luke gave a dry laugh. "I'm not sure they'd be into her. Except Seth, before he was married. I meant, I wonder what she's been promised?"

Grace was still pondering on that, visualising Christobel even now on the phone to Seth tittle-tattling about her visit, when they pulled up in front of the main gate to the industrial site. The complex of grey concrete buildings had an almost Gothic air, despite the hi-tech features. Like the Re-location Centre, it had been built by Lord 'Natty' Hodge, though several years earlier. Above the phallic towers – Grace was reminded of the giant condom – the huge *Ossophate* sign sprang into the sky as though daring some deity. It bore out Paul Jacob's contention that Isiah King now considered himself to be one.

As before, Grace approached the security booth alone. A large man in a black Teflon boilersuit and dark glasses came out to speak to her. She held out her pass and in case, like many on security, he couldn't read, said,

"Grace Fry. Women's Minister. Here to check on working conditions."

The guard stared at the pass then asked politely, "Are you expected, ma'am?"

Grace waved the pass. "That's the whole point. It's an impromptu visit."

The guard shook his head. "I'm afraid it's impossible without an appointment."

"This is my constituency," said Grace, feeling her anger rising.

"Only doing my job, ma'am. I'm sorry."

The guard smiled and gestured towards the car, inviting her to leave.

"You are refusing entrance to a Government Minister?" Grace turned on her heel.

"Outrageous! I must and will inform the Prime Minister." She stalked away, uncomfortably certain that behind her he was still smiling.

Back in the car, Grace told Luke to drive round the perimeter fence to where the woods began. High cameras swivelled after them and a low level buzzing filled the car. At each entrance, black jeeps were parked, their engines purring in readiness. The gates nearest to the woods opened as they passed, to let in a large, covered lorry. Grace checked it in the car mirror.

"Turn down there," she said to Luke, indicating an unmade-up path into the woods.

When the factory was out of sight, they stopped and Grace, after many cautions from Luke, climbed out and made her way through the trees. They thinned out as she neared the perimeter fence and she dropped to her knees and crawled forward, keeping behind the bushes. She was aware that on screen her orange suit would create a striking blot of colour.

From a vantage point behind a thick blackberry bush, she could see the lorry parked outside the building with the smoking chimneys. Men in black, *Osso*-logoed boilersuits were unloading and carrying large, apparently weighty, plastic bags inside. Puzzled, she half -rose for a better view, but the slight whirr of a security camera quickly deterred her and bending double, she scurried back to the car.

"Drive on," she gasped. "Quickly."

Luke did as he was bid, plunging through the undergrowth until the narrow path came out onto a poppy-bordered lane the other side of the wood.

"What did you see?" he said, when they had both caught their breath.

"Not sure. Big black bags. Rubbish disposal?"

Luke was white-faced with anxiety. "That place gives me the willies."

"Mmm," agreed Grace, examining her shredded stockings ruefully. It was her second pair of the day. She never travelled without a spare, as she couldn't bear the slatternly look of ladders. Her suit too, was crumpled and moss-stained. She must clean up before returning to Conference.

"Last port of call," she said. "Drop me at Margie and Tony's."

CHAPTER SIXTEEN

'Welcome to a curfew-free zone', announced the street sign, as Luke's car slid into a quiet, tree-lined suburban road. Margie and Tony's pastel-painted bungalow, with its modest net curtains and tidy garden blooming with massive chrysanthemums and dahlias, was distinguished from others in the row only by a large *Osso* security van parked outside.

"Are you coming in?" Grace asked Luke.

He shook his head, taking his *Briar* out of his pocket.

"I'll sit here and keep watch," he said, clamping the cold pipe firmly between his teeth.

Margie answered the door in an apron, being careful to hold floury fingers off the woodwork. She looked harassed, apprehensive even, but her face broke into a relieved smile when she recognised Grace.

"I thought it was the blasted Happiness Warden. Hello, m'duck. Whatever are you doing here?"

She took a quick glance up and down the road, recognised Luke's car and nodded, then ushered Grace in, shutting the door hastily behind her.

"Come through, duck." she bustled ahead, along the hall.

"Sorry to entertain you in the kitchen, but I'm just making the bread and I've got to finish while we've got the electricity."

They passed the door to the living room from which blared the ubiquitous *Stone TV* soap.

"Steve, turn that down, please!" shouted Margie.

Grace glanced into the room. Steve, a lumpen lad, was sprawled in his *Osso* uniform in front of the huge screen. He gave no sign he had heard his mother's request.

Margie clicked her teeth. "I could set the house on fire, he'd never notice. The others are at school. Thank Gideon."

The kitchen was poorly equipped, but neat and spotless. The sink was chipped, the cooker ancient, the table on which Margie was kneading dough, scarred and scuffed, though newly covered in pale pink plastiflex.

There were other little, typically Margie-like touches of colour. The magnolia walls were gaily decorated with hand-embroidered samplers, 'Fruits of the Earth' and 'Bread is the staff of life'; Grace knew them to be Margie's painstaking work. She'd been the same as a TU rep; every job undertaken with acute attention to detail. Now she'd transferred her abilities into home-making for her four men. A certificate of praise for 'Firm Family Values', awarded by the Citizen's Council, had pride of place above the table.

Margie glanced at the big clock on the wall and returned to pummelling the dough as though her life depended on it. Occasionally she stopped, picked up a pen with her sticky fingers and added something to a form she was filling, on the table.

"Would you like a cuppa, love?" she said, suddenly remembering her duties as Hospitable Hostess. Without waiting for an answer, she snatched up the kettle and crossed to the sink to turn on the tap. A grinding noise but no water came out of it.

"Drat and blast!" cried Margie. "That's the third time this week. And never a warning." She hurried into the pantry.

"You'll have to have *Ransome's*, is that alright? I resent using it to boil," she added, almost to herself. "It's so blasted expensive."

"Don't bother Margie. I'm fine. Really."

"Are you sure, duck?" Margie's expression hovered between concern for her bread and duty to her visitor.

Grace made a dismissive gesture. "Is Tony about?"

Margie's face turned doleful.

"He's been hauled up in front of the Neighbourhood Committee. It's this bad fathering business... the Outreach Unit's instructed them to take action." She clenched her fists. "Ooh, I could brain our Kevin!" She smacked her fists onto the table then subsided swiftly, aware she had overstepped propriety.

"If he had one," she finished lamely.

"I'm sorry, Margie."

Grace left a pause for Margie to recover, then said,

"I wanted a word about those deaths. You know, at *Ossophate?*"

Margie pushed the kitchen door closed and lowered her voice.

"Two of Tony's work-mates he kept up with after he left. They told him they'd complained about things there... the de-skilling programme and wage cuts... Next thing we heard they'd committed suicide. Tony was stunned! I mean they just weren't the type."

She shook her head to emphasise their disbelief.

"Tony used to meet one every day to play bowls, the other had just got married. We told Luke Counsel, but..." her voice trailed away. Grace knew she was thinking that there was little, any longer, Luke could do about it.

"He has tried to find out what's going on there," Grace said, "and so have I, but it's difficult. Does Steve know anything?"

"Steve!" Margie yelled. There was no answer. "Deaf as a post," snorted Margie. "He'd sit in front of that dratted telly all day, if he didn't get hungry. I doubt he'd tell you, anyway." Margie set her mouth in a line. "He's like a clam about *Ossophate.* Scared he'll lose his job."

It hardly needed to be said. Margie turned a worried look at Grace, as if wondering about her intentions.

"Well, we all are. If we get curfewed we'll have to move to a Home Zone." Her voice rose. "It would break Tony's heart to leave this house after all the work he's put in. We live off that garden."

She waved towards the kitchen garden. Through the bow-tied print curtains, Grace could see trellis and orderly rows of vegetables. A large pot of *Ossophate* stood outside the small potting shed.

"At least Steve gets the fertiliser free," Margie went on. "Even if it is low wages," she broke off suddenly and wrote 'garden' on her form, in big, simple letters.

"What's that?" asked Grace.

"Units of Satisfaction form," said Margie shortly.

"The Happiness Warden will be round to pick it up any moment." She sighed. "Blasted thing always needs filling in when I'm at my busiest. And I have to print everything because she can barely read. Now... " She checked down the list.

"Do I prefer knitting to embroidery? No. Cooking to cleaning? Yes. How many units shall I give to being a surrogate granny? Well, I love to see the poor little mites cleaned up and read to, the mothers never bother, but on the other hand it takes up such a lot of time. I feel things here are neglected – that's why I'm late with the bread making. Great Gideon, that reminds me..."

She dashed over to the cooker and flung open the door. Cold air billowed out.

"No," wailed Margie, "the heat's gone off! Now there won't be any bread for tea and the children will be angry with me."

She ran back to the form and began feverishly ticking and crossing, muttering,

"Jamming yes, pickling no, mending bother, darning urghh! Oh, it's so difficult."

She rubbed her forehead, leaving a trail of flour.

"I wish there was a pill you could take for all this!"

Steve, tall and ominous in his black boilersuit, sloped in as Grace watched in consternation.

"Isn't tea ready, Ma?" he demanded in an aggrieved tone. "My shift starts soon."

"There's salad in the larder," said Margie, distractedly.

"The fridge was seized by the National Security Wardens," she flung, as an afterthought, to Grace.

"They insisted it had been bought by the proceeds of crime."

"Crime!" exclaimed Grace. It was unthinkable. Tony and Margie were the most honest people she knew.

"Our Darren," said Margie, sorrowfully. "He was caught selling black market hamburgers."
Grace couldn't think of anything comforting to say. Instead she turned to Steve and asked,

"Have you heard anything about a 'bespoke' programme at *Ossophate*?"
Steve stared at her blankly. "Dur..?" he said.

"He won't understand 'bespoke'," said Margie. "It's not the sort of word they use on *Stone TV*."
Her tone was apologetic. "Steve was only educated in practical de-skilling."
She spoke of him as though he wasn't in the room. In many ways, thought Grace, he wasn't.

"A new product," she tried, "Under wraps. A chemist called Sam Andrews has been working on it?"
Steve gave a disinterested shrug and shoved a large tomato in his mouth.

"Right," said Grace, *sotto voce*. "Just doing your job, I suppose."
Steve slouched back to the telly with a plate of monster vegetables. Margie waited until he had gone, to say in a low voice. "That *Stone TV* soap is addictive. If you ask me, it's addled his brain."

The back door opened and a wretched-looking Tony entered.

"Tony, love," cried Margie, catching his arm. "What happened?"

"I've been sentenced to three hours in the stocks," Tony said dully. He slumped into a chair, as though drained of all life. Margie ran to him. "No," she begged, beating his shoulders. "No!"

"Only one short of tagging," Tony moaned. He fell forward onto the floury table, burying his head in his hands.

"Oh, Tony," murmured Grace. She had never felt more helpless.

"They'll put a black cross on our door," Margie whimpered. "The neighbours won't speak to us. The kids'll be shunned."

"We'll end up in your bloody camp," Tony barked, a sudden surge of rage lifting his head. Grace was upset, but she couldn't let that pass.

"It's not a camp, Tony. It's a Re-location Centre."

"Well, we don't want to be bloody 're-located'," Tony returned, belligerently.

Margie was storming up and down the kitchen, wringing her hands. "The shame, the shame," she kept repeating. "How has this happened to us?" She addressed the ceiling. "We've always been good. Done everything by the rules."

She picked up the dough and threw it violently from hand to hand. "It's all the fault of your blasted ministry. Telling us what to do!" She turned on Grace, mimicking, "Faith in Families. Faith in Families. Firm Family values!" She lobbed the dough onto the floor and kicked it around like a football.

"I'm sorry," Grace whispered. "So sorry... I don't know how to help."

"Why don't you just chuck the first tomato?" said Tony bitterly.

Grace backed away from his accusing stare. Her last sight, as she left the kitchen, was Margie jumping up and down on the dough. She almost seemed to be enjoying it.

CHAPTER SEVENTEEN

Seashoram station was thronged with people staring desperately at the departure board. No trains were in evidence. Josie had already been waiting for half an hour before she saw Grace alighting from an old *Rover*. She hung back behind a pillar and watched as Grace bent to kiss the driver goodbye. His face was familiar and after a moment, she placed him as Luke Counsel, a minister long gone before her time in Drome.

Grace came hurrying onto the concourse. She looked flustered. Not her usual smart self. Her suit was splattered with damp patches and she was wearing strange stockings. She peered round, obviously searching for her PPS. Josie stepped out from behind the pillar and waved to her.

"Oh, there you are," said Grace. "How did you get on?"

"Fine. I did as you said and went to the office. The birthday files are all in order. Noah... er... sends his regards."

Josie had prepared this speech earlier, deciding to leave out Noah's snide comments about Grace's unwarranted presence in Seashoram. But when Grace asked her what else she had done, she was stuck for an answer.

"Well – I – " she stammered, "I went for a walk.... to er... to get to know the town." She gave an ingratiating smile. "I did as you said. I bought some make-up."

She produced a handful of loud nail varnishes from her pocket. Those, at least, should please Grace.

Grace gave them a cursory glance. There were more important things on her mind than Josie's carnivorous conversion. The scene at Margie's had left her deeply dismayed. Though it was, in a sense, nothing to do with her, she could not help feeling responsible.

Her appearance was also of concern. She had returned to Luke's, sponged her suit and borrowed some tights from his daughter, but they were far from satisfactory. If she'd been forced to name their colour, she would have said 'swede'. She glanced around, wondering if there was a lingerie shop on the station, but the only retail outlet was a booth selling soya-grain sandwiches and *Nut-Noggin*.

"What about you?" Josie was saying. "Did you see the poorly family?"

"Poorly?" Grace gave a puzzled frown. "Oh, yes, yes. Disturbed, very disturbed, Josie," she nodded gravely. "Do you have family, Josie?"

Josie stared at the platform, to hide, Grace suspected, a blush.

"My parents are dead," she said briefly.

"Mine, too," Grace took on a sentimental, hopefully bonding, tone. "When I was a student. Rotten isn't it?"

Josie shot her a quick, suspicious glance, then continued, reluctantly.

"Actually, I never knew my father. He left when I was a baby."

That explained a lot, thought Grace. To Josie, she said dryly,

"Good job Jonathan Temple's 666 policies didn't operate; your parents would have been prime candidates for incarceration."

Josie gave a sickly grin.

"No siblings?" Grace pressed.

"Er... a brother."

"Lucky you. I was left all alone. Older or younger?"

"Older."

Really, thought Grace, it was like extracting teeth. Though under the circumstances, hardly surprising.

"What does he do?" she pursued.

"He's a... a chemist."

"Skilled, eh? Who does he work for?"

Josie looked round wildly. Her eye was caught by a logo-embellished hoarding. "*Toobs!*" she blurted desperately.

The transparent lie was the final straw for Grace. The day's distresses overwhelmed her and dropping all pretence of sympathy, she shot Josie the look of an enraged tiger.

"Don't lie to me, you little turnip! I know perfectly well your brother works at *Ossophate!*"

She grabbed Josie's arms and shook her. Josie's head rolled about until the whites of her eyes were showing. People on the concourse stopped to stare at this eccentric behaviour but for once, Grace was oblivious to them.

"Who put you up to this?" she yelled.

"To what?" croaked Josie.

"Lying. Spying. Don't think I don't know."

Josie's lips trembled and a frightened sob escaped her.

"I've no idea what you're talking about."

"Really. Really," snarled Grace, baring her teeth. "Next you'll be telling me you'd never met Seth Thomas before yesterday, 'dear'. "

Josie dragged her eyes away from Grace's.

"I – I – never..." she stuttered.

"Never what?" said Grace, nastily. "Aspired to convictions? No, I'll bet. What do you believe in, apart from plant-eating?"

"I – believe – in – the – Government," Josie managed between shakes.

"Of course you do, yoghurt face," spat Grace. "Well, believe me, if you do as you're told, you're told you're dispensable!"

She gave Josie a final joggle, then let go so suddenly, the girl almost fell over.

At that moment, the station PA crackled into life and a female voice announced that the station must be evacuated as

"A remark has been made." This was usually an encoded message, to station staff, that suspect baggage had been found. Lord Ransome insisted there was a guerrilla group, which targeted his trains. No one believed in them, though the occasional arrest was made, and no one took any notice now, until staff in *Ransome* red began shooing people from the concourse. Everyone shuffled, grumbling, outside, as the loudspeakers continued to insist a remark had been made.

"I can think of a remark I'd like to make," said a city-smart businessman loudly.

A Security Warden approached him, tapping his baton and the businessman shrank into the crowd, no doubt regretting his boldness.

"Good," Grace grinned unpleasantly into Josie's face.

"Plenty of time to pay a visit to brother Sam." She indicated a waiting rickshaw. "Shall we?"

Entry to Sam's flat was easier the second time, particularly for Grace, as Josie now had a key. Despite the still bright day, the flat's interior was in darkness. The heavy curtains let in only a crack of light. A melancholy dampness prevailed and Grace, shivering, drew her jacket closer.

While Josie went quickly from room to room calling out in a quavering voice, "Sam. It's all right. It's me, Josie." Grace took a speedy inventory of the living room, of which she had seen only a corner from the lavatory. Bland, soporific music came from a sound system somewhere. Grace whistled through her teeth to Vivaldi's 'Autumn' without thinking, so familiar was she with the tunes of *Radio Digi-tranquillity*.

Josie ran back into the room.

"He's not here!" she said, in a voice close to panic.

"Are you sure?" demanded Grace.

Josie, fighting tears, seemed unable to reply.

"I'll look." Grace pushed the girl aside. She was determined to find Sam before it was too late. If they'd killed Abbie... She swept rigorously through the flat, pulling back curtains, throwing open doors, wardrobes, cupboards. Sam Andrews was not tidy, she noted as she tripped over scattered underwear, plates of mouldy food and abandoned trainers. The flat could definitely use a woman's touch. The kitchen was disgraceful.

On her way back to the living room after a search that yielded only smelly clothes and rotting vegetables, Grace trod on something in the doorway. She bent and retrieved a picture frame. It was the one she had seen Sam Andrews holding that morning. She held it up for Josie to look at. The glass was broken and the photograph had gone.

"I think," said Grace, "Sam left in a hurry."

Josie burst into the tears she could no longer contain, and collapsed onto the settee moaning,

"Sam, oh Sam."

Grace surveyed her for a moment, then drew up a chair and said in a matter-of-fact tone. "You'd better tell me everything."

Josie buried her face in a cushion.

"I don't know, I don't know..." she sobbed.

"What was he developing at *Ossophate*? This 'bespoke' product?"

"He wouldn't tell me," Josie's muffled voice hiccuped.

"And Seth Thomas didn't say?"

"Only that it was important work for Isiah King and if I wanted the job, I'd got to make sure he finished it."

Grace nodded, grimly satisfied. Carrot and stick. She and Zach had guessed correctly.

"And you wanted the job alright, didn't you?"

Her question was rhetorical. Seth Thomas's ruse was easy to spot: Josie promised a fast-track PPS in return for keeping Sam on-message and Grace out of the picture.

"Even if it meant betraying the person you work for."

"I... didn't mean..." Josie looked up, her tear-stained face shameful. "I do admire you, honestly I do. Seth just said you were to be kept away for your own good."

"But not," said Grace darkly, "for the good of the people. It was you who warned Seth that Abbie was on her way to see me, wasn't it?"

Josie nodded reluctantly then said quickly, "But I'm sure her death was an accident."

Grace gave a sardonic snort. "You've been eating too many greens."

Josie began to shake, as though having been the cause of a murder was too much to contemplate.

"What did Seth threaten you with?" Grace drove on. "Exposure in *The Sunday Prophet* as the sister of a convicted drug criminal? DPS with pictures? You could kiss goodbye to a career after that."

Josie raised round eyes to Grace. "How do you know about it?"

"I told you." Grace permitted herself a small smile of triumph. "Get the media on your side."

Josie shuddered. She scrubbed at her swollen face with a shred of tissue, looking the very picture of frightened misery.

"So," Grace took a softer tack, "If he's so upset, where d'you think he'd run to?"

"Now Abbie's gone, he's got no one but me," Josie said helplessly. "It's true what I said about my parents. Sam and I are very close because of that. We've only had each other."

"Abbie must have been quite a shock, then?"

Josie's face turned mean. "She used him. Sam's so unworldly. Vulnerable. It's her fault he's in this state... I don't know what he might do." Her voice began to shake again. "Like one of his old nervous breakdowns. He's out of control."

Your control, Grace thought but didn't say.

"He even seemed scared of the vegetables. Kept on about 'too much tranquillity'."

"No danger we'll have that," Grace replied grittily. "Right Josie, here's the plan. You think hard about where he might be... favourite places, drug haunts, whatever. In the meantime, one word about any of this to Seth Thomas and I will personally give your entire story to *The Indie Satellite*."

Josie breathed in sharply and clutched the cushion.

"I mean it. I warned you I prize loyalty. After what you've done, I would take great pleasure in destroying you."

She paused for the message to sink in, then growled,

"I'm a carnivore, pusscat, and don't you forget it."
Judging by the expression on Josie's face, thought Grace, she wasn't likely to.

CHAPTER EIGHTEEN

"Flee fornication! Deliver those who sin to Satan! Through the destruction of the flesh, the spirit may be saved."

So bellowed Isiah King, to an indifferent crowd as Grace hurried through Drome's foyer. The cyclorama showed shots of a poor sinner in the stocks, being pelted with rotten fruit. Grace was reminded briefly of Tony, but she didn't have time to dwell on his dilemma.

When she and Josie had finally caught a train back, she'd dashed straight from the station to her hotel, where an 'urgent' message from David Timothy was waiting. She'd taken time to re-do her make-up, dump the offensive stockings and change swiftly into a daffodil yellow tailored frockcoat. With her blonde hair and blue eyes, she made a stunning picture. Several snappers had taken advantage of it as she'd swept into Drome.

"Colour, boys!" Grace had instructed, wagging a finger, laughing.

In the foyer, she smiled to the left and right, aware her image would be transmitted to many screens in the room of perpetual night. It wouldn't do to seem at all apologetic. She waved to Miriam, who was standing with a group of *ET* reps, but she didn't appear to notice. Entering Baby, she slipped on a pair of the woolly bootees laid out in rows, trying to pick a colour which was reasonably complimentary. She settled, with a grimace, for pale blue; the pearl and plain knitted slippers looked bizarre stretched over her snappy, royal blue stilettos.

David Timothy's office was, at first appearance, empty. The many workscreens flickered, as though peremptorily abandoned. It took Grace a moment to locate David, whose quiff was barely visible above the high-backed chair in front of his chatterstack. Adam Solomon was standing over him. He was very still, snake-like almost, as if about to strike.

"Ah, Grace," he said suavely, straightening up at her approach. "Good of you to honour us with an appearance. Seashoram splendiforous?"

"I was only away a few hours, Adam," said Grace, defensively. Though she'd been expecting comments, she was ruffled at the speed at which the Drome Unit had pounced. She had Josie to thank for that, she presumed. She'd have words with her later.

"Mm. A long time in politics," Adam murmured. "Do be careful, Grace. We don't want any more accidents."

Without waiting for a response, he glided away.

"Was that a threat?" Grace called after him, annoyed enough to be incautious. Adam turned at the door and lifted a hand.

"Let's say... a warning."

He gave his cold-eyed smile and disappeared. Grace thought she detected a puff of smoke. "News travels fast," she muttered.

"If it's bad," returned David, in a voice full of doom.

Grace focussed her attention on him. He looked half his normal size, crumpled in the chair as though all the air had been squeezed out of him.

"You left a message for me," she said.

David didn't look at her. He plucked at the gold ring on his wedding finger. "Oh – I – I wanted to show you some ideas I'd had for styling 'Horny Hands'..." he said, vaguely. "It doesn't matter now."

He stood and began pulling framed photos out of a drawer. They were all of himself with his family – happy, smiling, in the garden, by the Christmas tree, on the beach. He stacked them feverishly around his workstation until it looked like a kind of shrine. Then he sat in the centre of it and put his head in his hands.

"David," said Grace carefully. "What's the matter?"

"I've done something foolish," said David in a low voice. "A moment of madness." He picked up a large photo of his wife and strained it to his bosom.

"What is it?" said Grace, with growing concern. "Can I help?"

"Help yourself, Grace," said David bleakly. "Safety first."
His voice sank to a fierce whisper. "I know you're not attracted to it. But for god's sake, safety!"
While Grace stared, lost for words, he leapt to his feet and, still clutching the photograph, ran out of the room, leaving the door to slam behind him.

Grace had returned in time for the last scheduled event of the day: the 'Horny-Handed Sons of Toil' reception. This massive charity function, hosted by Jethro Stone's *Media International,* was to begin with a sponsored swim on behalf of one of Jethro's favourite charities, The Foundling Foundation.

Judging by the amount of logos and banners, thought Grace, alighting from one of the country-style flower bedecked wagons laid on for the occasion, David had done a pretty comprehensive job, despite his state of mind. There were enormous posters of happy, smiling children with rosy faces and muddy knees, all clasping huge red apples and beakers of foaming milk. Others were pictured tucking into great wedges of brown bread spread with honey. The girls wore ringlets and pinafores, the boys flat caps, knickerbockers and lace-up boots. They were posed in front of a cosy cottage with a thatched roof dotted with robins, looking for all the world like a currant bun; never had being a foundling looked more desirable.

The event was taking place in the grounds of an impressive country mansion Jethro Stone had hired for the occasion. Banners for *The Sunday Prophet, The Daily Millennium* and *Stone TV* announced it for half a mile along the road from town, leaving no doubt about its sponsorship.

By the time Grace arrived, having dashed back to her hotel to change into a black and white polka dot cocktail frock, elbow length gloves and a tiny hat with spotted veil, those competing were already lining up by the brilliant turquoise swimming pool. They wore modest Edwardian bathers: the women covered neck to knee, the Drome Unit young men bare-chested, but in long striped drawers. Matt Penny, circled neck to knee in busy bee bands, and Gabriel Strong, blinking like a myxamatosis-struck rabbit, looked equally uncomfortable. Grace spotted Naomi and Rachel emerging from a blue and white tent in ugly one-piece costumes, with plastic jelly sandals and Teflon mobcaps. Arms crossed in front of their constrained breasts – though whether from cold or embarrassment wasn't clear – they scurried to greet other female swimmers: Hettie, in strawberry bloomers which cruelly exposed her bulgy thighs, Josie displaying not unattractive puppyfat encased in ruched buttercup-scattered cotton and to Grace's surprise, Miriam, a little more stylish in pistachio satin.

Grace scanned the crowd for Zach Green. She couldn't resist licking her lips as she imagined what he'd look like, stripped. There were many people crowded round the pool – press, paparazzi, the lower echelons of the Party, as well as the Elite. Some genuine workers from the estate had been drafted in to provide competition, even a few of the security men were taking part. They'd abandoned their boilersuits for knitted long johns, though some still wore dark glasses.

As she vainly searched the crowd, Grace became aware that to her right, where a bank of *Stone TV* cameras was assembled, an interview was being conducted. Yet again, Jonathan Temple was being solicited for his views, and yet again, unashamedly, he was giving them. She turned to watch, noticing that Jonathan's striped jersey one-piece was rather flattering, revealing good legs and a taut abdomen, and heard him say he'd agreed to take part in the swim at Jethro Stone's personal request.

"It isn't necessary to approve of Government policies in order to give support to as worthy a cause as the Foundling's Foundation," he assured the interviewer.

"Generosity is essential." He made a generous, inclusive gesture. "The 666," he finished, "firmly believes in charity."

At this point, Gideon emerged from the men's tent wrapped in a mauve towelling robe. To the accompaniment of cheers and whistles, he dropped it to display a finely honed body, with downy dark hair and shapely legs; the hours on the exercise bike had paid off, evidently. The interviewer abandoned Jonathan Temple and rushed, mike poised, to get a comment. Jonathan Temple stood, one hand on his hip, surveying the scene and smiling slightly.

At the poolside, those in the first heat made ready to dive. Grace edged closer and shouted good luck to Miriam, who did not appear to hear her over the shouting. She was standing close to a fully-dressed Adam Solomon, who had his head bent as though to whisper into her ear. Adam moved away, as the contestants stepped onto their plinths. He oozed through the crowd towards Grace, people melting away before him.

"Not swimming, Grace?" He tweaked her veil. "Tut, tut. Not like you to shirk competition."

Grace, regretting her earlier indiscretion, smiled as charmingly as she could manage. "I'm allergic to chlorine."

It was true. But she was also allergic to wearing awful clothes and getting her hair wet in public.

"Me too," murmured Adam. "Rotten bad luck."

He was gazing over her head, his eyes travelling over the strapping young bodies at the poolside.

The starter-gun went off and there was a great splash as the divers hit the water. Grace, shouting and cheering with the rest, felt a touch on her arm and saw Zach Green in clinging knee-length shorts, behind her. Her eyes were irresistibly drawn down his trim body.

"Any excuse to show your rippling muscles, pusscat."

She was pleased to see that, as she'd imagined, he had many. Zach grinned ruefully. "I'm in the next heat. Got to fly *The Indie* flag. Paul Jacobs insisted. Listen..."

He tugged on her arm until she moved a little away from the screaming crowd.

"I didn't want to tell you here, but I felt I must warn you..."
he tailed off, as though he didn't know how to continue.

"What?" prompted Grace.

Zach sighed. "Sometimes I just hate my job."

"There, there, pusscat. Beat your breast when you lose the
race." Grace's tone was teasing, but a frown had appeared
between her finely pencilled brows. "What's the story?"

"*The Sunday Prophet*. My mate on it tells me they're going to
run a piece on you."

"So? Jealous they got to me first, pusscat? "

"Not that kind of piece. You and Dan Jefferson. The
affair..." he stopped at Grace's sharp intake of breath then began
again, almost in a whisper. "DPS, Sunday after Conference.
Peter Priest has got letters, photos... Worst of all... medical
records."

"Oh my god," Grace breathed.

"Yes," Zach gave her a humourless smile. "You didn't tell
me about the abortion."

Grace stared at him, shocked out of self-defence. He relented a
little and touched her shoulder. "Seth Thomas spun it to them,
so somebody knew enough to tell him."

"Fucking sharks!" Grace's voice was a breathless squeak.
"You're all the same!"

Zach backed off slightly and held up his hand. "Hey. Don't
shoot the messenger."

There was a loud burst of brass band music and cheering.
The first heat had finished in a win for Rachel, who had, in the
days when girls still pursued sport, been the All-Albion Upper-
School Champion. Still in the water, she raised dripping arms to
acknowledge the victory cheers.

Over the PA, the Starter ordered the next contestants to
make ready for the gun and Zach, with a reassuring squeeze to
Grace's arm and a muttered, "We'll talk later", raced off to join
the line-up.

Horror-struck though she was, Grace could not help but see he
cut an extremely attractive figure as he leapt onto his plinth. The
silk shorts outlined muscular thighs and his naked shoulders

looked lean and powerful. She noticed Jonathan Temple casting an eye at them, as he lined up between Zach and Gideon.

The pistol shot cracked the air and they were off. The cries, as the men ploughed through the choppy water, reached a wild crescendo. Zach somersaulted smoothly and sliced along shark-like underwater. He was neck and neck with Jonathan and Gideon, both powerful swimmers. Despite everything, Grace was caught in the elation. She waved her parasol and shouted Zach's name. Nearby, Adam Solomon cast a displeased glance in her direction.

Two lengths later, the whistle blew as all three touched the edge in the same second. Gideon and Jonathan stood waist-high in water, grinning and thumping each other on the back. To the shouted demands of the paparazzi they turned, still smiling, and shook hands. Many flashes froze the moment. Zach, they ignored completely.

CHAPTER NINETEEN

The after-swim reception was a bucolic triumph. All the guests changed into nineteenth century, agrarian costume and foregathered amongst straw bales, hay carts, tethered cows and corn dollies. A catering-scale barbeque dispensed chargrilled courgettes and aubergines to the sound of the 'peasant' brass band playing a floral medley. On the greensward in front of the band, teams of 'peasant' girls engaged in formation country dancing. There were demonstrations of hand-milking, butter churning and cheese-pressing by women in community milking dress and many stalls crammed with whey, curd and other dairy products. As a special concession, Ransome's *Cidapple* was being dispensed, largely to the press, from a jolly carnival-style marquee.

The music and chatter was punctuated with the sound of leather on willow and cries of "Howzat". A Heritage cricket match, 'peasants' versus 'gentry', was being played on a well-kept pitch beyond the celebrations. Gideon, now dressed in full horny-handed labourer's kit complete with hat, gaiters and scythe over his shoulder, was standing with a Government group, watching Jonathan Temple bat. Jonathan hit a six to polite applause and leant, casually smiling, on his bat, seemingly relishing the image he made in the graceful Edwardian flannels.

Grace wandered through the crowd, careful to side-step the cowpats, stopping now and then to smile and twirl her parasol at photographers. Many snapped her. Her choice of *Dior* 'new look' retro was seriously at odds with the cheesecloth and sprigged muslin of the other women. Between poses, Grace searched the throng for friends. She was anxious to find Zach and hear more about *The Sunday Prophet*. What records, exactly, did they have? What photos? One or two came blushingly to mind. Dan had kept a very private collection.

David Timothy was nowhere to be seen, which was odd as he had masterminded the decor, but she saw Mim, now in peasant sackcloth, learning to ride a donkey and Josie, as a puff-sleeved milkmaid, taking part in a cream whipping competition.

At last she spied Zach, charming in open-necked cricket whites, standing, notepad poised, close to Gideon's posse. Gideon, surrounded by global businessmen and journalists, was holding up a front-laced leather boot for inspection.

"Hand-crafted years ago in Afghanistan. Look at the workmanship." He turned his foot so they could check the perfect seams. "Spiffing leather industry. No conflict, see, with the workforce. Yep. We learned a lot from the Taliban. But give back." He threw his arms wide, embracing the occasion. "Like this. Smashing. Invite workers. Celebrate Heritage. Top hole. Everyone happy!"

"And sport of course," prompted Seth Thomas, close to his ear as usual.

"'Course. Yep. Fab." Gideon turned back to the game, in time to see Jonathan smash another ball to the boundary.

"*Mens sana in corpore sano,*" murmured Adam Solomon.

The businessmen, an ethnically mixed bunch, all dressed in straw hats and sons-of-toil smocks, nodded vigorously, while the journalists, Peter Priest of *The Sunday Prophet* amongst them, scribbled down Gideon's words of wisdom.

His attention was now, apparently, on the game and one by one they began to drift away. Grace had been standing on the outside of the group, but as she moved closer, intending to catch Peter Priest, it shifted away from her, as though on some unspoken cue. Hettie looked uncomfortable, as well she might in her frightful Heidi costume complete with plaited wig, and avoided looking at her, but Rachel and Naomi gave her hat a spiteful glance, before turning their backs.

"Peter... I'd like a... " began Grace. But Peter Priest, perhaps alerted by her chilly tone, evaded her, going off in the middle of a group of businessmen. Grace was about to follow when Gideon shot out an arm and pulled her to him.

"Grace! Groovy hat."

He lifted the veil and raised his brows suggestively, before bending to nuzzle her cheek. Under the veil, he sniffed at her, murmuring, "That fabby perfume. You are so naughty."

Grace cast about for the appropriate response, but Gideon didn't wait for one, going on, "Super. 'Cos Naomi's got someone she wants you to meet."

He gestured to Naomi who was now talking to a Chinese-looking businessman, in full hunting pink. "Naomi! Over here!"

Naomi approached with a sulky face and thrusting the man towards Grace, said curtly,

"This is Jimmy Wang. He's applied to Re-Pair for a new mate. We thought you might be... suitable."

"My last wife die," said Jimmy.

He grinned broadly, revealing a mouthful of gold dentures. Grace could not prevent a small shudder. Jimmy put a propriet-orial hand on her arm. "I'm sure we get on welly good."

Grace could manage no more than a tight smile, aware of Zach watching from a distance. Gideon had not yet released her and now he drew her aside and lowered his voice to an intimate level.

"Now, Gracie, be helpful. I know you've been seeing Luke Counsel."

Grace shot him a startled look.

"Oh yes. I hear everything." He wagged a playful finger at her. "There was a little girl and she had a little curl right in the middle of her forehead. And when she was good, she was very, very good, and when she was bad..." he paused meaningfully.

"She was horrid?" finished Grace, giving him a wondering glance.

Gideon nodded forcefully. "We love you, Gracie. But even you can go too far. We wouldn't want anything to jeopardise that ministry, now would we?"

Grace shook her head, dumbly. But Gideon had already moved on, greeting and glad-handing another group of corporate acquaintances.

Adam Solomon stopped by her. "I'm hosting a small private soirée, Grace." He nodded to Jimmy Wang. "Perhaps Jimmy would like to escort you?"

Jimmy needed no more encouragement. All in the group watched as he encircled Grace with strong, red-coated arms and lifted her as if she weighed no more than a dead fox. She threw an agonised appeal to Zach as Jimmy shone his entire set of gold teeth at her.

Adam's 'small soirée' turned out to be a glittering banquet in the medieval-style hall of the mansion. Grace could not help but be impressed. It was a long time since she had encountered such magnificence.

The elect sat round a long gothic table with Gideon at one end and Jethro Stone at the other. Scattered in between, were members of the Government with their partners and various businessmen, including Lord Ransome and Isiah King. Beyond the table, a cow carcass revolved on a roasting spit and plates piled high with meat were served by 'wenches' in medieval costume. Champagne accompanied the first course of smoked salmon; with the succulent roasted beef, goblets full to the brim with red wine were placed before each diner. The only person not eating and drinking was Isiah King, who sat fastidiously back from the table, surveying the excess with disapproval.

Grace was placed between Jimmy Wang and Naomi, but though aware of being policed, she tucked into the unusual fare in true carnivorous spirit. She was on her third plate of beef, having requested it 'bloody', when Josie, in a serving wench's tight-laced bodice, bent over to re-fill her goblet. It was the first time Grace had encountered her since their return and she took the opportunity to hiss,

"You told Seth Thomas you'd seen me with Luke Counsel, didn't you?"

Josie's hand wobbled on the wine jug and she nearly spilled it on Grace's polka dot lap.

"I had to say something," she said in a terrified whisper. "He knew we'd been to Seashoram."

"Of course he did, blancmange-face." Grace bared a mouthful of beef. "You told him."

Josie shook her head and looked round fearfully. Grace, a little drunk, had allowed her voice to rise above a whisper.

"I didn't tell him anything else, cross my heart."

"And hope to die," Grace completed loudly.

She picked a cow bone off her plate and pointed it at Josie.

"Watch out, Josie. If you stand in the middle of the road," she jabbed the bone towards Josie's nose, "you get run over."

Adam Solomon was working his way down the table greeting all his guests in person. Josie made her escape as he reached Grace and, surveying her loaded plate, asked, "Enjoying the food, Grace?"

"Meat is a treat," Grace responded awkwardly. He had caught her with the cow bone halfway to her mouth.

"And wine, of course," Adam tapped her over-flowing goblet. "Fun being one of us, isn't it?" He placed one hand on her shoulder and the other on Jimmy's and gave them both an avuncular pat.

"Let's hope we see you both at more of these jolly occasions."

"Oh yes," grinned Jimmy, baring gold tusks now encrusted with shreds of red. "Glace velly nice girl."

Under the table his hand sought her knee and gave it a vice-like squeeze. Grace gasped and stood up sharply, almost upsetting the goblet. It splashed blotches of crimson onto the tablecloth.

"Scuse me a moment. Dames' room," she mumbled.

On her other side, Naomi held out her goblet to a passing wench. "A li'l more pleash!" she demanded slurrily.

Adam flicked her a look from narrowed eyes.

"She wants to go easy on that," murmured Grace. "She's out of practice."

The Dames' room was not easy to locate and in her search for it, Grace pushed open several doors in the Old Master-hung hallway. The first revealed a small private bar where several high status journalists, mostly from the Baby lobby, had gathered. She saw Paul Jacobs drinking and laughing with Peter Priest. Seth Thomas approached with a large cigar and clapped them both jovially on the shoulders.

The next door was to a cloakroom where she surprised Lord Ransome with his hand up Josie's many peasant petticoats. Josie's bodice was unlaced and her ringletted wig ruffled. Her face was turned away, buried in Lord Ransome's shoulder and Grace shut the door hastily, hoping she hadn't been recognised.

A third door led to a smoky, oak-panelled snooker room where several of Adam's posse were lounging, dressed in the uniforms of First World War officers. A couple were at the snooker table; another was on it, turning cartwheels to jeering encouragement. A few, clearly drunk, had stripped to shirt-sleeves and were arm wrestling. One was snorting a line of white powder from an antique gilded mirror. Grace observed all this in a stunned second, before swiftly backing away and closing the door very carefully.

Giving up her search for the Dames, she hurried instead towards the front door, and checking she hadn't been followed, threw open the massive brass-inlaid door and exited as though the furies were behind her.

The fresh night air on top of the unaccustomed wine sent her reeling and after stumbling down the flight of stone steps, she leant on a hay bale to steady herself. In the darkness, 'peasants' were wearily clearing away the debris of the day, the band members packing up instruments; only the cider tent was still lit up and raucous with drinkers. Several press boys, glasses in hand, had spilled out onto the green and as Grace made her way uncertainly towards the carriages, one hailed her. To her relief, Zach's face appeared in the gloom.

"Are you alright?" he said, his smile changing to a look of concern as he observed her agitation. Grace put out a hand and he clasped it, supporting her.

"Allergic to the Elite, I take it?"

"Like being with the devil on the mountaintop," muttered Grace.

Zach laughed wryly. "Some banquet."

Grace leaned on him, suddenly drained.

"Just get me out of here before Jimmy Wang calls for an emergency marriage licence!"

They climbed into an open-topped carriage with patiently waiting horse and clip-clopped into town, under a bright moon and clear, starry sky. The only benefit of the electricity rationing was that orange light pollution no longer scarred the night, as it had in the previous century. Grace fingered her locket and gazed up into the darkness, as if seeking, from one or the other, inspiration.

Zach told her all he knew of *The Sunday Prophet's* plans, which wasn't much except that, obviously, some traitor had spilled the beans on her to the Drome spin machine. Respectful of her distress, he didn't for the moment, press for more details.

She, in return, told him everything that had passed in Seashoram, including Luke's suspicions of the Drome Unit. After what she had seen that night, they no longer seemed so preposterous. A question hovered, but neither said anything for a while and the pause was filled with gently lapping waves and the scrape of pebbles, as they trotted along the seafront.

"So... are you having an affair with Luke Counsel?" Zach asked eventually.

"Jealous, pusscat?" Grace stole a glance. Zach's boyish face looked pleasingly disturbed. With a mock scowl, she added. "Or are we just looking for more copy?"

"No," Zach's voice was low, without its usual bantering tone. "I'm ... worried."

"I've already told you," sighed Grace. "I'm celibate."

"I meant, for your survival."

"Oh, I'll survive." Grace thrust out her jaw. "I'm not ready for extinction yet."

A commotion up ahead slowed the carriage down and halted the conversation. A crowd had gathered at the end of the pier. People were pointing and shouting, flash bulbs were going off. The big wheel was outlined silently against the sky, a dark blob hanging from it.

Grace and Zach craned out of the carriage trying to see.

"What is it?" said Grace.

"Dunno. Looks like something on the wheel."

A National Security van screeched up and Wardens poured out and began to beat back the crowd with buzzing batons. There were screams and shouts as people tumbled over each other to escape. Another van drew up and a police vehicle with siren wailing. Several Wardens started to climb the wheel towards the hanging shape at the top of it. Grace stood up in the rocking carriage to get a better view. She peered at the point on the wheel where she'd been photographed only the day before.

The shape, she could just make out, was the dangling figure of a man. As it twisted in the night breeze, the face was lit by moonbeams.

"Oh no. No!" Grace covered her eyes.

Above a pair of throttling, embroidered braces and the photograph of his wife with the word 'sorry' scrawled across it, hung the frozen face of David Timothy.

CHAPTER TWENTY

Grace was too distraught to be left alone and once they'd escaped the National Security cordon round the pier by flashing their passes, Zach took her to a secret, late-night club frequented by some of his 'reptile' acquaintances.

The club, reputedly run by an underworld mafia of Balkan escapees, was in the old warehouse district of the town, by the side of a dank canal. There was no sign of it on the outside of the looming Victorian brick building; the moon lit only a faded red *Ransome* logo high on the wall. But inside, a network of gloomy passages led down to the basement and a large titanium door, with *Club Gothique* hung over it in blue neon letters.

Zach spoke the password into the entryfone and the door slid back to reveal a dark den guarded by several big, swarthy bouncers. The club, thronged with a vacant looking clientele in shredded black drapes and heavy Goth make-up, looked reassuringly old-fashioned. Or so Grace would have thought if she had been in any state to notice. She was blank-faced with shock, except when overwhelmed by fits of violent shuddering.

Zach steered her to a table near the bar and ordered a couple of the club's special – in fact, only – drinks, from the frock-coated barman, who bore a close resemblance to Dracula. The foaming green cocktails were placed in front of them by a waitress with panda-black eyes, set in a face of sepulchral pallor. Grace downed hers in one swallow and immediately demanded another.

"Easy tiger," murmured Zach, but she paid no attention, catching at the black, cobwebbed sleeve of a passing waitress and demanding,

"Another of those Bat's Blood thingies!"

Trance-inducing music was playing and several Goths got up and began to sway to it in a melancholy, unfocussed manner. They appeared to be in a state of near oblivion.

Grace watched them, sipping her second drink.

"I'm going to get as blotto as that," she said, pointing. Zach grimaced. Perhaps it hadn't been the best idea to bring her here. She was close to collapse already, he suspected. She was muttering to herself, between gulps of the cocktail, and leaning closer, he heard, "David was trying to warn me, I'm sure he was trying to warn me."

"Warn you what?"

"The same would happen to me, if – if –"

"If you didn't stop poking around in Seashoram?"

Grace nodded; her tongue was numb with absinthe and speech had temporarily deserted her.

Zach shook her arm, gently. "Grace, concentrate. If I'm to do a spoiler, I need you tell me what *The Sunday Prophet* have got."

Grace swung her head towards him and stared blearily through tear-swollen eyes.

"The whole story," Zach said firmly, taking out his notepad.

Grace's throat jerked and with an effort, she launched into a slurred monologue. She spoke in a slow, automatic tone, as though the story had been stored away in a locked file, after many of her own silent repetitions.

"I got pregnant... after Dan and I had been together... for about a year. I don't know how it happened... it wasn't meant... we were both married. It was impossible. Dan arranged an... abortion... a private clinic... someone who owed him a favour."

She stopped and wiped her eyes, which had welled with tears

again. Zach took a moment off scribbling to pat her hand encouragingly.

"It was all hushed up, of course, but a few people knew. Luke... Miriam... she came with me to the nursing home."

"No one else?" Zach asked, still writing.

Grace shook her head. "My husband... Dan's wife... may have suspected, but we never said. At least... I didn't."

"Someone told Seth Thomas," Zach said pointedly.

Grace looked at him tearfully. "What are you suggesting? Luke? He's like my father. I'd trust him with my life."

"What about Miriam?"

Grace jolted into anger. "She was – is – my best friend. There's no way she'd betray me."

Zach shrugged, without agreeing. "We've got to think of another way round this. However sympathetic I make your side of the story, it still comes out as adultery and abortion. They were bad enough then. Now they're political death."

"Suicide," Grace said dully. "That's what David meant. They're trying to drive me to suicide, like him. Poor David." She put her head down on the table and wept uncontrollably. Zach put an arm round her, holding her gently until the storm subsided.

"At least he did it in style," he said, in an effort to cheer her. "The big wheel. And the braces were inspired."

Grace choked on a sobbing laugh. "He'd love the press attention... he always was a drama queen." Another burst of crying overtook her.

Eventually, she sat up, straightened her hat and took a slurp of the cocktail. "It's a relief to tell someone the truth about Dan and me," she admitted, with the ghost of a smile. "I've had to keep it to myself for so long."

"Mmm," said Zach, dryly, "But I don't imagine you're ready to share it with the world. Grace Fry female icon, a slut and baby killer... to say nothing of your advancement through nepotism, which let's face it, was the story we killed last time."

Grace stared at him, the full horror dawning, even through a fog of absinthe. "It wasn't like that," she said vehemently.

"It wasn't! I truly loved Dan. He was my family. Everything I admired. I didn't set out to fall in love with him. It just... happened."

"I believe you," reassured Zach. Privately he was wondering what on earth had possessed Dan Jefferson. Surely his motives could not have been so pure. When he'd met her, Grace would have been an impressionable fan. A child almost.

"We've got to find a way to stop *The Sunday Prophet* printing," he said, almost to himself. "There's plenty in the safe on Peter Priest."

"Use it, for christ's sake!" demanded Grace, fiercely.
Zach shook his head, smiling at her naivety. "That depends on what he's got on Paul."

"You're all as bad!" exploded Grace. "Lizards! Toads! Piranhas! You all put yourselves before truth! Justice!"
She was half-standing now, flailing her arms.

"Grace," said Zach, catching one. "You're shouting."
He looked round, but the somnambulant Goths were locked in their own world. No one seemed to have noticed.

Grace guzzled down her drink, much of which had slopped over the table and shouted for a refill. But, when panda-eyes drifted up to their table, Zach waved her away.

"You've had enough," he said to Grace firmly.

"Don't tell me what to do!" Grace turned belligerent. "I'm my own woman." She grabbed at the waitress. "Bring me a double!"
Zach sighed. "Grace... please."

"Don't worry, pusscat," Grace gave a nasty smile. "I'm just practising for when I join the Elite. They're all at it."

"At what?" Zach poised his pen.

"Meat, drink, sex, drugs. You name it."
She swung an arm drunkenly round, spraying Zach with the remaining drops of absinthe.

"You can have anything you want, if you're..." she mimicked Adam Solomon's voice, " ...'one of us'... as our Great Persuader puts it! Beef..." she elaborated. "Cocaine... champagne!"
Zach began to scribble. He knew a good story when he heard it.

"Yesh," Grace was completely drunk now. Her hat had slipped over one eye. "One law for 'us' and another for the People!"

A gaunt Goth in a musty Dickensian top-hat approached with Grace's drink and placed it before her. He smiled, revealing blood-red Dracula fangs and leaned forward, saying intimately, "Can I interest you in something stronger?"

"Wha?" enquired Grace.

The Goth discreetly opened his coat and Grace saw it was lined with small pockets. She pushed back her veil and her bloodshot eyes grew wide as he produced beef cubes, cigarettes, miniature spirit bottles, sticks of salami and tins of caviar.

"But, for special customers..." he felt in a hidden inner pocket and brought out some tiny white pills, which he extended on the palm of his hand.

"Zedo," he whispered seductively.

"Whass tha?" said Grace, touching the pills curiously.

"Only high in town," said the Goth. He drew back his lips, fully displaying his wicked teeth. "Look around you."

The Goths on the floor were now dancing as if possessed. Others were twined feverishly round each other on sofas and banquettes.

"Ten euros," tempted the Goth, "for hours of ecstasy."

"I'll have two," said Grace, hypnotised by the fangs. She waved a hand at Zach. "Pay him."

"Grace..." Zach began to remonstrate, but Grace over-ruled him.

"I wan' teeth like he's got."

She snatched a pill and swallowed it with a great quaff of absinthe. The Goth laughed and held out his hand to Zach.

"You, dude?"

Zach shook his head.

"Call yourself a shark?" taunted Grace. "Live dangerously!"

With a reluctant glower, Zach took the proffered pill and fumbled in his pocket for euros.

"Thass it," cried Grace. "And these!" she filched a packet of cigarettes from the Goth's pocket.

The Goth accepted the notes Zach handed him, then gave them both a knowing wink and wafted away to another table.

Grace scrabbled to open the packet and at once lit a cigarette, making a point of puffing the blue smoke ostentatiously. The gyrating Goths barely registered it, but one of the bouncers twitched his nose and in moments a couple of meat-slabs were headed for their table.

"Outside with that, dame," said bouncer one, folding his arms menacingly. The other stood behind him like a concrete bollard. Grace lit another cigarette and blew a long stream of nicotine into their faces. Bouncer one snatched the fag from her mouth, while bouncer two gripped her arms and lifted her from her seat. Zach leapt to his feet, saying in a reasonable tone,

"Hey guys..."

But the bouncers carried Grace off between them, her hat over her nose, her feet not touching the ground. Grace puffed madly on the remaining cigarette, blowing smoke at the few who were watching. "Watch out!" she shouted theatrically. "Dangerous carnivore. I bite!"

Warming to the part, she demonstrated with loud growling noises. When they neared the club door and she realised she was being evicted, she balled her fists and began to thump the bouncers. "Get your hands off me!" she screamed. "D'you know who I am? I can do what I like. I'm a Government Minister!"

Zach ran behind, weaving between the dancers, apologising to right and left. "Sorry, sorry. Excuse my friend. Ha, ha! Had a shock. No idea what she's saying."

The pill imbibers gave back glazed stares without, apparently, comprehending or caring.

The bouncers dragged Grace through the dark corridors, where her shouts echoed off the walls, and deposited her outside the hidden canal-side entry. They propped her against the wall but she reeled away from it and, to Zach's horror, began a sing-song striptease.

"De dah dah, boom. De dah dah boom!" she sang, punctuating each line by discarding a piece of clothing. Her gloves whirled round her head and landed in the canal where they sank swiftly into the murky slime. Her hat followed, but floated off until it caught at a jaunty angle on a semi-submerged tree trunk. She was down to her underwear before Zach could reach her. The bouncers watched the performance with mounting amazement. One took out his vidi-fone, but Zach hastily pulled a handful of euro notes from his pocket and pressed them into the big man's hands.

"No worries, guys. OK? She's just a fruitcake. I'll take care of it."

They exchanged a glance and shrugged at each other as Grace, singing merrily, twirled up and down the towpath in her flimsy bra and stockings. At last, having divested herself of those, she slid down the warehouse wall and collapsed in a heap of giggles.

With a struggle, Zach got Grace back into her clothes. She kept throwing her arms amorously round his neck and biting his nose. Whenever he disentangled her arms, she tried to drag down his trousers. He propped her, one hand over her hysterical mouth, as far as the main road into town, where he flagged down a passing rickshaw. Once they were inside it, she invited the startled driver to 'snog' her, then passed out across Zach's knees.

The curfew sirens were ringing as they trotted into town and Zach directed the driver through much less-peopled back alleys. He couldn't possibly leave Grace at her hotel in this state; whatever wild whim struck her next would be recorded on the security cameras. He decided to take her to his own hotel, where he could smuggle her up the fire escape.

The iron staircase was troublesome. Grace encircled him like an octopus, urging him to, "Love me, baby... lo-ove me." But half an hour later, to his great relief, she was sprawled on his bed, snoring loudly. Zach stroked her hair off her face. This wasn't quite how he'd envisaged the end of the evening. He stared at the other pill he had bought. It looked innocent as an *Osso* aspirin on his palm. Gideon knew what was in it.

The telescreen was on and the newsprofiler announced the death of Government minister, David Timothy. Zach watched intently, wondering what spin would be put on an incident, which was, in the middle of Conference at least, unfortunate.

"Government sources say Mr Timothy, despite being married, had a troubled private life," parroted the newsreader.

Seth Thomas's face appeared on the screen. He had a look of puzzled concern as he explained, "All we know is that he had some sort of... curious encounter and *The Sunday Prophet* got hold of the story."

Zach gave a snort.

"Adam Solomon visited him earlier in the day to warn him... But..." Seth's face took on a woeful expression, "...sadly he took his own life before we could get to the bottom of the allegations."

Zach reached for his vidi-fone.

"He was an extremely effective minister and will be much missed..." Seth shook his head, a slight break in his voice.

Zach gave a grim chuckle of appreciation at the performance. He'd be spouting crocodile tears next. Seth turned to the camera and delivered his last words directly into it. "If only he'd come to us first with his problems."

"You were right, Grace," murmured Zach, putting an arm round her. "They're sending you a message."

By his side, Grace snuggled in and snuffled gently, at last in sweet oblivion.

In another hotel room, Seth Thomas sat wrapped in a towel watching himself on the screen. He, too, admired his perform-ance and as it came to an end, snapped off the telescreen with a satisfied smirk. He lay back, stretching like an animal against the pillows on the double bed.

A vidi-fone on the bedside table began to ring. Seth cocked an ear, but the shower was still running in the bathroom, accompanied by vigorous splashing sounds. He picked up the vidi-fone and pressed 'receive'. There was no picture but he heard Sam Andrews' frantic voice.

"It's me... I'm in a fonebox... I haven't got many euros," Sam gabbled. "Look, it's much worse than I told you... there was an

Osso security van outside my house... I'm in danger... we all are! I can't go on any more... I've got to talk to someone! Grace Fry... she could help... can you get her to meet me? I'm in our special place... you know. Josie? Are you there? Josie!"

Seth snapped off the fone and pressed the erase button. His face was set like stone, but it changed in a second when Josie, hot and damp, emerged from the bathroom with a towel wrapped round her.

"Was that my fone?"

"Wrong number."

Seth put the fone into 'record-message' mode and tossed it aside. He grinned lasciviously.

"Come here, wench!"

Josie approached the bed, tittering coyly. Seth grabbed at the towel and unwound it, revealing her showerpink, quivering body. He pulled her down on top of him and squeezed handfuls of her plump flesh.

"Didn't you look a prim little girlie in your milk-maid crap." Josie giggled and gasped.

"If only they knew you like I do."

"Lord Ransome tried to." Josie's face turned even rosier.

"Did he indeed? Dirty old man."

"I... I didn't like it..." Josie attempted to sit up to admit this. But Seth pulled her back and rolled on top of her. He bit into her doughy neck and ran his hand up her leg until he found her damp crotch. Josie moaned and thrashed against the pillows.

"Don't worry about him," Seth nuzzled into her ear, "All part of the service. Mmm... you're so sexy." Over her head, he checked his bleeper for the time. "I want to know everything about you."

"You already do," Josie murmured, her eyes tight shut.

"Tell me again. About you and Sam."

Josie's eyes fluttered open in alarm.

"What? I calmed him down, like you said."

"Yes, yes," Seth hushed her with a kiss. "And grisly Gracie?"

"Doesn't know a thing," Josie's voice had the tone of repetition.

"Umhum. Cross your heart?" Seth bit into her breast, above her heart. Josie squealed with delight.

"And hope to die."

"Good girl." Seth rewarded her with a buttock fondle.

"We'll take care of Sam. How about a day out? A special place. You know, when you were kids?"

"Lovely," breathed Josie, pulling his other hand towards her pouting nipple. "Yes, yes."

"So... where would that be?"
Seth pinched the nipple, until it hardened like a cork.

"Oh... ah... our beach-hut," whimpered Josie. "By the light-house in Seashoram."

"That was your hideaway?"

"Always. When things got bad at home."

"We'll go there." He heaved up her hips to meet him. "That's a promise."

"But what about your wife?" Josie gasped, as with a brutish thrust he entered her.

"Don't worry about her. Tell me about the wicked things you and Sam got up to."

"Not... as wicked... as this..." Josie's head rolled from side to side; her legs hunched up and wrapped round Seth's back.

"Oh Gideon, Seth! " she wailed. "I looove you."

Sam Andrews left the fone box, when after three more tries Josie's fone was still giving only the 'record-message' signal. He didn't leave one. He didn't trust messages, you never knew who might listen. He just hoped she had understood what he'd said and would act upon it.

He put his head down – the cliff-top was cold and windy – and led by the wink of the lighthouse, battled through the snagging gorse bushes back to the strip of beach-huts. A candle burned in the window of the one he and Josie had played in as children. He felt totally safe, camped in their secret place. At least it would provide shelter from the night chill. He had no idea where he would go in the morning.

Dawn light crept in the window of Zach's hotel room discovering him curled, fully clothed, round Grace. Both were slumbering peacefully. The lights and the television were still on. The vidi-fone had fallen from Zach's hand when he'd drifted into sleep, still trying to rouse a response from Paul Jacobs.

The same light fell on Sam, dozing, with the occasional shiver, in an old sleeping bag on the wooden-slatted floor of the beach-hut. His laboratory at *Ossophate* was overturned and stripped while he slept. The heavily armed, black-uniformed squad found nothing. To their frustration, Sam had removed all traces of his work. The huge computer winked only one message: 'Systems Error'. His flat, despite a thorough ransack, yielded no more – nothing but dirty clothes and a pile of massive, mouldering vegetables.

Meanwhile in Sam's fitful dreams, he and Josie skipped through waves and had midnight picnics of sardines and biscuits...

The drawn curtains in Josie's room kept the rising sun out a little longer. The first beams filtered through the thin naphlon and played around the bed where her figure lay, very still. The maid, coming in with the seven-thirty order of soya-grain toast and *Nut-Noggin,* screamed and dropped the tray crashing to the floor, when she realised the body on the bed was lifeless.

Josie Andrews lay stiff as a poker in her nakedness. Her eyes were turned upwards and a trickle of froth running from nose to chin had congealed to a whitish powder. On the bedside table by her vidi-fone, were an empty pill jar and half a bottle of *Ransome's.*

CHAPTER TWENTY-ONE

The blinking screens in the room of perpetual night registered a hastily assembled press conference taking place in the foyer of Baby. Adam Solomon was speaking into a bank of microphones, in front of a circling crowd of lobby journalists.

"These sad people obviously had personal problems. The tragic thing is they could have been worked out, if only they'd gone to Confessional."

The journalists shifted restlessly, avoiding each other's eyes. They felt uncomfortable and foolish in the compulsory woollen bootees, handed out at the entrance. They also knew very well, there was more to the story and sniffed hungrily, knowing they would never get it from Adam. He appeared as unruffled and urbane as ever; his bootees were a stylish grey and reached his knees, giving the impression of knitted jackboots.

Other screens showed a police cordon round Josie Andrews's hotel. There was a large security presence and gawping spectators were quickly prodded on. Several screens pictured Grace Fry, forced into an impromptu interview at the cordon. *Stone TV* and GBC cameras were lined up outside it and they caught the harassed-looking minister as she hurried from the hotel. For once Grace was not her sartorial self. Her face was puffy and barely made-up and her clothes were crumpled, as though they had been slept in. She was a more likely target for the truth however, and the sharks immediately accosted her.

"Can you tell us anything about the apparent suicide of your PPS, Miss Fry?"

"Did you have problems with Josie Andrews?"

"Can we have a comment?"

Grace stopped in her tracks and smoothed her frown. The morning had already been a disaster – she must not compound it by seeming, as well as looking, out of control. Aware of the many screens upon which it would appear, she composed her face suitably – perhaps it was just as well it was bereft of lipstick.

"I'm as shocked and horrified as everyone else about the death of this bright, young hopeful..." she began. "Josephine Andrews had the makings of a Government star."

In the little village shop nearest to the beach-huts, Sam Andrews placed a couple of euros for teabags and sugar on the counter. His hand froze as he heard Grace's awful words coming from the telescreen above it. Transfixed, he stared at her image on the wide TV.

"Josie was on the Chief Whippy's promotion list," Grace was saying. "I can think of no reason she would want to take her own life."

"She overdosed on sleeping pills, we understand?" an interviewer put in.

Grace shook her head, firmly. "I don't have that information. It's a matter for the police."

"But there's been a suggestion," the interviewer pressed cheekily, "...that she was under stress. Particularly as a result of an unauthorised visit to your constituency?"

The implication that Grace was to blame was plain, but, giving a sad smile, Grace ignored it.

"Nothing happened there, to my knowledge, to disturb her. We were on normal constituency business."

"But surely," called another, "It's hardly 'normal' to go during Conference?"

Grace fixed the journalist with a stern stare. "My responsibility to people doesn't shut off so conveniently. Unlike you, apparently, I am a public servant!"
She turned on her heel and began to march away, but the sharks, wanting blood, pursued her.

"Isn't it a coincidence two people close to you committed suicide?"

"What do you know about their private lives?"

"People are calling this the 'death' Conference, Miss Fry."
Grace stopped and summoning an expression of tragic dignity pronounced: "It is to my eternal sadness that good friends have died. I shall miss them both terribly." She turned directly to the nearest TV camera. "I shall be attending Miss Andrews' funeral in Seashoram tomorrow. I hope you don't think that visit inappropriate."

The close-up of her face on the screen seemed, to Sam, meant for him alone. He dropped his purchases and fled the shop.

"Oi!" the shopkeeper called. "You've left your things!"
But Sam was already far along the path, which led to the lighthouse.

Released at last from the difficult interview – how quickly the press turned against one, only yesterday she'd been their darling – Grace rushed to her hotel to change.

Since Zach had been woken by a call from Paul Jacobs with the news of Josie's death, she'd been flung into a maelstrom of spin and counter spin. Barely conscious, she'd been briefed by Seth Thomas on the Government line: another unhappy suicide. As if the pain from her hangover, and patchily returning recollection, wasn't enough, her wrist-bleep had pricked her incessantly with updates. Josie unstable. Family problems. History of prescription drugs? Demanding job. Overwork leading to breakdown... This last, with its suggestion that Grace abused her loyal staff, had infuriated her.

After they'd left his hotel via the fire escape, Zach had gone to a chemist friend, another part of his underground world, to get the Club Gothique pill analysed. In the fleeting moments she'd had to consider her real thoughts, Grace was convinced there was a connection.

Her room was quiet. Unusually so. She took off the offending bleeper, stripped out of her creased clothes, puzzled by the lack of underwear, and stood gratefully under the hot shower. Sometimes it was good to have privileges. While she scrubbed herself, trying to sluice away the horrors of the previous night, she thought of Dan. Speaking about him to Zach, though she wasn't entirely sure what she'd said, had brought him vividly to mind. He represented, she believed, the better part of herself and she missed him terribly.

Still, politics was presentation and once out of the shower, she forced herself to concentrate on her costume. She chose a draped crèpe suit in aubergine with matching silk shirt, applied pale foundation and discreet lipstick, no eye shadow and moderate perfume. Today, she must at all costs appear respectful.

Pleased with the result – the mirror reflected back a heroine from Greek tragedy – she used the time until she'd agreed to meet Zach, to put in a call to Miriam. They hadn't communicated since before Grace's trip to Seashoram, and Miriam knew nothing of what had passed there. Miriam's vidifone was in 'record-message' mode, so Grace left a brief, "It's Grace, Mim. Where are you? Call me?"

She needed Miriam badly. She was, she had to admit, profoundly shaken by the deaths, particularly David Timothy's. Events were reeling out of her control and yet, she couldn't help the feeling that she was at the centre of them. If David's warning was accurate, it was essential to discover why. Picking up her bag, briefcase and coat – now, she supposed, she would have to carry them all herself; she would soon have a reputation for killing her PPSs – she had a final check in the mirror and left the room for her rendezvous.

Zach and Grace had chosen the off-aura toy café for a belated breakfast. Grace surveyed the food counter, piled as usual, with wholesome fruits of the earth and resignedly chose a bowl of gritty-looking muesli. The beef from the night before had re-awakened her taste for meat. How she longed for the smell of bacon.

She scanned the room for Zach. He wasn't there, but to her surprise, Miriam was. She was sitting at a *Pokemon* table deep in conversation with, of all people, Hettie. They had graph sheets and plans spread all over the tabletop. Smiling with relief, Grace headed for them.

"One or two skilled and semi-skilled left," Miriam was saying. "But mostly de-skilled with a small core of Elite workers."

They both looked up as Grace reached the table and Miriam at once stopped speaking.

"Gideon, am I glad to see you!" Grace plonked down her muesli. "Hello, Hettie. So, what's the story?"

The women exchanged an awkward glance.

"Er... I was just bringing Hettie up to speed on the *Ossophate* situation," said Miriam, not greeting Grace with her usual smile and kiss.

"Oh good." Grace lifted a spoonful of nuts and oats. "I really need to know about that, because... "

Hettie stood up, sharply and gathered her papers.

"We'll continue this later, Miriam," she said, adding pointedly, "In private." With a frown at Grace, she hurried away, leaving the other two women staring. Grace, the spoon still poised half way to her lips, said, "What on earth was all that about?"

Miriam made a dismissive gesture. "She's finding Conference rather a strain. She was very upset about Abbie's death. They'd been working closely together. And of course David Timothy was an old friend."

"We're all shocked," Grace muttered, spooning the muesli into her mouth and grimacing at the sharp bits. "Now there's Josie as well."

"I advise you to concentrate on damage limitation. Josie's death doesn't look good for you," Miriam said brusquely.

"I am, I am, believe me!" assured Grace. "I'm dying to find out what killed Josie. Especially, as with Abbie, there's obviously a link to *Ossophate*."

"Oh really, Grace." Miriam stood and stuffed papers into her bag. "Abbie's death was an accident. That Kamikazi was lethal. I'd warned her about it a hundred times."

Grace gave her an astounded look. "Mim – how can you say that? Of course she was killed – the bespoke programme!"

"Some harmless, little anachronistic games system, no doubt. If you ask me, Sam Andrews is barmy."

"But, Mim..." Grace's mouth fell open, displaying bits of desiccated fruit and nut." You know that's not –"
Miriam held up a silencing hand.

"That's enough, Grace. As an old friend, I'm warning you – " she took a quick look round. "You've been letting your imagination run away with you."
She slung her bag over her shoulder. "I'm in rather a hurry. See you later."
She almost ran from the table. Grace watched in astonishment, choking on the mouthful of muesli.

A moment later, Zach appeared at the entrance. Miriam passed him with a cursory nod, but glanced back at Grace, obviously noting the connection. Zach brought a cup of *Nut-Noggin* to the table. He checked on the security cameras before sitting, but one was flashing a low battery light and the other had its lens covered with a Mickey Mouse head. Clearly, the staff had one or two subversives amongst them.

"Are you alright?" he said, noting Grace's stricken look. "You're very pale."

"Make-up," Grace said shortly, pushing away the bowl of muesli so violently it slopped milk and currants onto the table.

"So. What's the story, morning glory?"

"That pill's a killer," said Zach.

"Tell me about it, pusscat," said Grace, putting a hand to her head. "My hangover!"

"No, no, no." said Zach. "I mean in certain strengths, it could actually kill. My chemist mate said he'd never encountered anything like it. According to the chromato-graphic process, it's a combi of beta-blocker and performance enhancer with a high Seratonin re-uptake inhibitor."

"Wha–?" Grace grunted, " Speak English."

"Feel-good factor. Could send you AWOL."

"As you described it, it did," Grace said ruefully. "Thank god I don't remember."

"Yeh, well... he said this one is probably made for recreation. The feel-good factor would lead to euphoria, and – " he paused and gave a small cough, "... feelings of sexual abandon."
Grace shot him an alarmed look. Was that the explanation for the missing underwear? But after holding her in suspense for a moment, Zach grinned. "Don't worry, we didn't do anything. You passed out." He leaned in close and whispered. "More's the pity."

"What about other forms of this pill?" Grace brushed the innuendo impatiently aside. Zach's flirting was distasteful this morning.

"In different balances, its potential is limitless. Could be used for work, sport, sleep... "

"Josie?" murmured Grace.
Zach shrugged. "Possibly. Like I said, in the wrong dose it could kill. Anyway he checked his pharmaceutical codex and there's nothing like it registered. It was funny really, he said he wouldn't want to see it fall into the wrong hands."

"You'll forgive me if I don't join in the joke." Grace gave an involuntary shiver. "My instinct tells me it's in the wrong hands already."

"We've got to find Sam Andrews," agreed Zach.

"We?" Grace said sourly. "Still after your story?"
Zach gave her an unsmiling look. "For chrissakes, Grace. Three people are dead already. Whatever this is about, it's dangerous."

"Nice to know you care, pusscat." Grace tried a careless smile, but her voice trembled.

"What's the matter?" Zach put a hand on her arm. "Did something else happen?"

Grace nodded slowly and her eyes filled with tears. In a voice Zach had to bend forward to catch, she said,

"I think I just discovered who betrayed me."

Before she could say more, they saw Jimmy Wang bearing down on them with his glinting smile. He caught Grace's eye and gave a suggestive nod.

"Oh no," Grace said under her breath. "Too late. Here comes your rival."

Jimmy arrived at the table bearing a tray loaded with maize porridge, sourdough toast, curds and whey and cabbage juice. This morning he was dressed as a country squire, with tweed plus fours and a hacking jacket.

"Glace... so solly, bad news," he said. He spread his food over the table and sat to attack it. Clearly, the tragic events had not affected his appetite. Grace picked up a napkin and wiped her eyes, giving a little sniffle.

"Ah, Glace..." then Jimmy put a surprisingly large hand on her shoulder. "No cly. I make you feel better." He gave her shoulder a hearty shake. "You come with me to Isiah King's leception."

Grace flashed a look to Zach who was watching Jimmy shovelling down the food, an expression of disbelief on his face.

" Er... no thank you, Jimmy," she said. "I'm really not feeling up to receptions today. I'm far too upset."

Jimmy's grip on her shoulder tightened.

"No. You come. Adam Solomon tell me to bling you."

"Yes," Grace gave a nervous laugh. "But I'm sure that was before this terrible news. I must hold myself free for further press conferences and interviews. In fact..." she gathered her things. "I'm just off with Mr Green to *The Indie Satellite*." She attempted to stand, but Jimmy's hand, now set like concrete, forced her back into her seat.

"In my countly, women do as told."

"Really?" Grace's brows rose and a small temper spot appeared on each cheek. "Wasn't there a slogan during Fanshen? 'Women are half of China'."

Jimmy's gold smile was replaced by a black scowl.

"Is tlue," he growled. "But wives are obedient."

He lifted his hand as though about to strike Grace. She flinched and Zach pushed his chair away and half-stood.

"Alright, Jimmy," said Grace hastily. The last thing she needed now was a public brawl. She gave Zach a quelling glance. "But it's in costume. I'll have to change." She looked at her bleep. "I'll meet you at the Drome... er... later."

Jimmy shook his head. "I come with you to hotel. Wait." He stuffed his mouth with the last piece of toast.

Zach and Grace exchanged an agonised look. Zach bent to tie up his shoe and Grace, to pick up her handbag. Under cover of Jimmy's loud crunching noises – obviously his teeth weren't merely decorative – Grace muttered,

"I'm being policed. You'll have to go."

"To Seashoram?" clarified Zach.

Grace nodded. "For god's sake, get to Sam Andrews before anyone else does."

A stretch-limo with darkened windows drew up outside the beach-side village shop. Seth Thomas got out and peered around through dark glasses. His sights fixed on the cliff path at the top of which, just visible, were a couple of beach-hut roofs and above them, the tall white lighthouse.

"This is it," he barked into the car.

Christian, the Drome boy dozing inside, uncoiled tetchily and got out, exclaiming at the cold wind. Seth shot him a look of contempt. He was furious he'd been saddled with one of Adam's useless posse. There was no love lost between him and the Persuader. They set off up the chalky cliff path; Seth in a sportsman's stride, Christian, in his decorative boots, toiling more slowly behind him.

A line of huts with faded paint stood bravely fronting the wind at the top. Several were shuttered, with padlocked doors.

Seth motioned Christian to use his boots to kick them in. This was activity Christian enjoyed and he dropped his girlish whining about the cold and threw himself into it. The knee-length boots, though not good for climbing, were excellent for smashing down doors. Seth stalked ahead down the line, entering each hut as the splintering wood gave way to reveal dim, mildewed interiors. All the huts were empty. The last one was not shuttered or locked. The door swung open easily at the first kick. It, too, was empty. But over the back of a beach chair hung an *Osso*-logoed tee-shirt and on the table in front of it sat a large tomato.

"Bollocks!" screamed Seth to the wind and the seagulls.

CHAPTER TWENTY-TWO

The office *The Independent Satellite* occupied in the Drome was small and cramped. It was however, the best the newspaper could command. Though larger than a samizdat, its circulation was tiny compared to that of the papers in the mighty Stone empire.

The media offices overlooked the Great Navel, as was appropriate for the reporting of great Conference speeches. Journalists were not supposed to stray into other areas of the building, unless authorised for a special press briefing or staged photocall and Adam Solomon, in particular, became incandescent if he encountered them elsewhere. Lobby briefings were normally held in the subdued Baby, where the hush was deemed to give the hacks a sense of governmental importance. Today, however, Adam was holding 'impromptu' press meetings all over the place and Zach passed him doing an interview for *Stone TV* in the vast foyer. The cyclorama showed clips from the Drome 'Confessional' unit complete with straightjackets and weeping PRs, over which Isiah King exhorted all Peoples' Representatives with 'personal problems' to visit the Drome therapist.

The corridor outside *The Indie's* office was crammed with people, mostly handsome young men, one or two of indeterminate gender. Inside, more pretty youths lounged on a plastiflex banquette which, apart from the computer hack-stacks, was the only available seating. Paul Jacobs sat on a swivel stool in front of his hi-tech workstation. He was snarling into the phone, as Zach strode up to him. "Never mind all that Solomon spin. Get me something I can print, goddammit!"

Zach signalled he needed Paul's attention urgently and as Paul slammed down the phone, gestured round and asked, "What's with all the rough trade?"

Paul waved his hands, disparagingly. "Lining up to character assassinate David Timothy. Poor sod. Want you to do the interviews. We'll run a spoiler before *The Sunday Prophet* do it."

"*Moi?*" Zach looked pained. "Interview a bunch of queens in tights? Hardly my style."

"No one else." Paul looked round the busy room. His small staff was, as ever, fully stretched. "Amazing how many have come forward, considering the penalties."

"Nothing to do with the payment you offered, I'm sure," said Zach ironically.

"Just get on with it," snapped Paul. "I want this in tonight's edition."

Zach smiled winningly. "Can't, Paul. Got to go to Seashoram. Forget the fishnets. I'm on to a story with real legs."

"The stories are at Conference, lad," said Paul turning back to his hackstack. "Two suicides, one queer. How much bigger can it be?"

"That's my point," pressed Zach. "They're linked, I'm sure. What's even better – to Grace Fry."

Paul shook his head, cynically. "Wasting your time, lad. Word is she's the next to be hung out to dry. Lobby lads are running a book on how long she'll last!"

Zach nodded eagerly. "Exactly. And this story's why. Grace has discovered weird goings-on in Seashoram. I've got to go and chase it."

"You shagging her, or what?" Paul gave him a half-admiring glance under drawn eyebrows.

Zach made a modest gesture, but did not deny the charge. "The point is, she's uncovered something. Something big. To do with *Ossophate* and the Re-location Centre."

"That bloody place. Thought she loved it?"

"Not any more."

"What's going on there then?" Paul's curiosity was provoked.

"That's what I'm trying to find out," said Zach with heavy irony. He gave a sly grin. "Betcha there'll be a link back to *The Sunday Prophet.*"

He well knew which of Paul's buttons to press. Paul and Peter Priest were old rivals. "Let me go. You won't regret it, honestly." Paul looked tempted. He surveyed the banquette of preening boys and sighed. "Alright – I'll get Fifi to do this lot. But you'd better come in with the goods, boy." He pointed a finger. "Or you're dead."

Zach flung his arms wide. "So shoot me. But Paul, I'm going to need a teeny bit of editorial assistance."

The long limo cruised down Seashoram high street. The street was busy with official market vendors and neatly attired shoppers; though Seashoram was poor, its people kept up appearances. At the village green, a large crowd had assembled. The limo slowed at Seth's command and he stuck out his head to watch. Normally such large gatherings were illegal, but he saw that a vigorous Citizen's Cursing was in progress. A melancholy-looking man was locked in the stocks and the crowd was pelting him with rotten vegetables. To one side stood a weeping woman, presumably his wife, and in front, three youths who were leading the crowd in shouting and jeering. The three youths were by far the most vociferous.

"Gideonless git!" yelled the youngest. "Bad dad!" screamed the middle one and the eldest, "We disown you as a father!"

They punctuated the abuse with viciously accurate lobs of tomatoes and eggs. Their unhappy father was completely splattered. Seth gave a satisfied smile. The Government's policy of instructing families to report on each other's off-message comments was obviously working well in Seashoram.

Through her tears, Margie noticed the limo. Though un-logoed, it could only be a Government vehicle and when all eyes were on Tony, she made a rude sign at its departing bumpers.

The limo passed on through the market's many fruit and vegetable stalls and down cobbled streets with surveillance cameras and long, orderly lottery queues. Seth pointed out to Christian, how clever it had been of him to suggest the Government use lottery funds to pay for the People's surveillance. He leaned back, grinning wolfishly. Really, it was like taking candy from a baby.

The limo slowed now and then for Christian to alight and make shop-to-shop identity checks. The last in the row was a Heritage-style barber's shop, with gay awning and a striped pole. Christian, bored with his role now, went in and made a cursory check. Two or three men were getting their hair cut in the regulation short back and sides. One, his face covered in foam, was being shaved. Christian checked them against the photo of the dark, bearded young man he held in his hand. No one in the shop resembled Sam Andrews.

"Fuck this for a game of soldiers! " said Seth, when Christian climbed back in. He indicated a pub sign to the limo driver. "Stop there."

This time, when Christian got out, Seth got out with him. The sign swinging over their head announced that it was 'The only pub in town' and in larger letters, 'The King's Head.' Seth pushed at the engraved glass door.

"Surprised Isiah King hasn't had its name banned," he snarled, "given his abhorrence to drink." And in answer to Christian's questioning glance, "You can check who's in the bar. I'm bloody thirsty."

In another part of town, Zach's rickshaw drew up at the gates of the Re-location Centre. Telling the driver to wait, Zach approached the security booth and leant in to speak to the guard.

"Hi there," he gave a big grin. "Zach Green, *Independent Satellite*. I've got an appointment with Miss Steel."

The guard, without speaking, checked with his winking monitor. There, in large letters was the appointment marked for 1 pm. Next to it, was a visual aid of the smiling face of Christobel, for those who had trouble with reading. He handed Zach a security pass, then pressed a button to lift the electronic bar and nodded him through.

Zach walked up to the entrance. It was the first time he had seen it and he was impressed with the ultra-modern design features and general signs of Ransome cash expenditure. Whatever was going on inside, the outside lent it a very attractive coating. *Radio Digi-tranquillity* played in the reception area, which was full of specially cultivated flowers in shades of red and silver. Workers in similarly coloured uniform bustled about; a line of residents trooped through on their way to the restaurant. With a disarming smile, Zach approached the desk. He repeated his mantra to the smartly suited young woman behind it and flashed his ID and the security pass. The receptionist glanced at her screen and then at the overhead clock, which showed twelve forty-five, and with an apologetic smile said, "Your appointment's not for a quarter of an hour. I'm afraid Miss Steel's still on her rounds."

"That's OK," said Zach. "She said to wait in her office."

"Well, I don't know..." began the girl, but Zach turned his devastating brown eyes and seductive smile full on her, and in a second she melted.

"I suppose it's alright." She gave an answering smile. "If Miss Steel said so."

"Oh, she did. She did," breathed Zach, then with a tender squeeze of the girl's wrist, "See you later."
Before she could respond, he was off through the door marked 'House-Mummy'.

The interior of 'The King's Head' was far less jolly than its namesake, whose head was hung over the bar, still smiling despite being separated from its body. Christian made a perfunctory tour of the *MinCare* absinthe drinkers; some tearful, some smiling stupidly, all with their eyes pinned on the large telescreen. They shrugged at Sam Andrew's photo, unresponsive and uncaring. No one in the gloomy room was at all like him. Sighing – this was a tedious occupation – Christian returned to the bar where Seth was now staring into a large absinthe.

"And one for my friend," demanded Seth of the barman.

"Gideon. I don't know... " said Christian doubtfully. "I've never tasted this *MinCare* stuff. I've heard it sends you loco." Seth slapped the large absinthe in front of him.

"Get that down you, you friggin' pansy."

Zach lost no time. He went through Christobel's office like a locust, but with the care of a seasoned journalist, left everything just as he'd found it. He rifled shelves, drawers, filing cabinets, scanned the many framed photographs: Christobel smiling winsomely with Lord Ransome, with Isiah King, with Noah Petty, with Seth Thomas and the Drome unit. He took several snaps with his own minute camera, turning his attention at last to her desk, on which stood a large computer with a screensaver of weaving vegetables. He listened for a moment and checked his watch, then quickly began to search the computer.

To his surprise and delight, the residents' file came up without the need for a password. Christobel must feel very secure in this ivory tower. He typed in the name 'Kodaly' and gave a small whistle as, again without question, their family details appeared on the screen. Zach read: 'Imre Kodaly-missing. File active. Janos Kodaly – housed in Youth Protection unit. Anna Kodaly – undergoing tests in Special Operations unit.'

He quickly deleted all this information and smiling slightly, replaced it with a spin of his own. Then he searched for '*Ossophate*.' It came up instantly and he scrolled down the pages of information, looking for any connection. He just had time to take in "Contract for Re-location Centre waste disposal. Signed April 0010", when a slight sound outside the door alerted him and he swiftly returned the screen to savermode. He stood in front of it, in case the bouncing broccoli didn't appear quickly enough and beamed broadly as the door opened and Christobel Steel entered, looking extremely frosty.

"Ah, Miss Steel..." Zach went forward, hand out-stretched. "Good to meet you. I've heard so much about you and this wonderful Centre."

Christobel looked taken aback.

"Yes," Zach went on, getting close enough to smell her scent, a rather pungent rosewater. "And I must say, the reports don't do you justice." His voice was a caressing murmur now. "I was told how marvellous you are at your job but not that you're also... so beautiful."

Christobel stared at him astonished, through her pebble glasses.

Seth and Christian were on their fourth round of absinthe. Seth was gazing, red-eyed, into the middle distance. Christian was having trouble focussing at all; his knees were buckling beneath him and remaining upright required full concentration.

"I've... had... enough... of this... pissin'... game plan."

Seth's words came slow and heavy. "I'm... gonna take the job G.B.C's offered me."

Christian tried to nod in agreement, but his neck seemed paralysed. If he took his eyes off the smiling King's head, he knew he would fall over.

"Jethro Stone's offered me a column... *Sunday Prophet*..." he managed to slur. His words sounded far away and from someone else's mouth. Seth appeared incensed with this news.

"Fuck off!" He made a rude gesture towards Christian. "A column? You're just a bloody Solomon poodle."

"Wunnerful man," returned Christian. "Prou' to... serve him."

Though Christian couldn't turn his head, he could see Seth's face reflected in the mirror behind the bar. The lips pulled back in a grinning snarl, as Seth demanded, "You shaggin' him, too?"

"You cad!" Christian lunged towards the face in the mirror, but succeeded only in overturning a glass of absinthe. The viscous, green fluid spread stickily over the bar, coating it like sewage. Neither of them noticed.

"Take tha' back!" Christian insisted. "Adam Sol'mon's n'officer 'na genleman."

He tried to pin Seth, but Seth now seemed to have three heads and Christian was unsure which was the real one.

"Unlike you!" he finally blustered, to all three of them.

Seth swung slowly towards him until, even in the mirror, Christian could see that his nose was only an inch away. With a Herculean effort, Christian forced his eyes round to meet Seth's red-rimmed stare.

"Wha d'jou mean by tha?" Seth challenged.

There was no going back and Christian matched him in belligerence. "You an tha' Josie..."

"Shut your gob!" shouted Seth, but Christian was beyond intimidation.

"Behaved like... bounder. Screwed her... an' topped her!" he shouted in return.

Seth's hands came up and grabbed Christian by his epaulettes. "I said... shut it!" He accompanied the words with a furious head-butt. Christian had the impression he'd been hit with a brick. His eyes crossed, his head rolled and he slumped to the floor.

Seth stood over him, his hands clenched. He looked round the pub, but no one seemed to have noticed the fracas; they were too far gone themselves with *Stone TV* or absinthe addiction. Seth prodded Christian's unconscious form with his foot.

"Wanker!" he muttered, contemptuously.

A few moments later Seth staggered out of the pub, propping a chalk-faced Christian. As the cold air hit him, Christian bent double and puked. Green bile shot down his uniform and splashed onto his boots.

"Disgustin' faggot," growled Seth, but the anger had gone out of the situation. Somehow, they stumbled into the limo, and Seth ordered the driver to "Get the fuck out of here."

The limo pulled away and retraced the route to the main road out of town. On the high street, it cruised past the barber's shop again, but neither Seth nor Christian noticed a slight, blond, clean-shaven man exit. He noticed the limo though, and as it accelerated down the street, Sam Andrews turned to watch it.

CHAPTER TWENTY-THREE

The last major event of Conference, apart from Gideon's excitedly awaited closing speech, was the 'Noah's Fludde' reception. Bank-rolled expansively by Isiah King, it was already in full 'fludde' by the time Grace and Jimmy Wang arrived. The floor of the Great Navel had become a millpond ocean surrounded by palm trees and crystal sand, and in the centre of it, beneath many *Osso* banners and logos, floated a huge, green Noah's Ark into which 'animals' two by two were pouring.

The line of guests waiting to be greeted, many of them celebrities from the Arts and Sports worlds beloved of Gideon, was each attired in the fur or feathers of an appointed beast. There'd been a lot of jostling for the favourites – word in the lobby was that euros had changed hands. To entertain them during their progress, children dressed as puppies and kittens gambolled about to vaguely spiritual, tubular bell music. Above their fluffy heads, nubile youths in the guise of monkeys and parrots performed acrobatic feats on the prow of the Ark and over it all, the familiar ear-ringing voice of Isiah King treated them to soundbites from Genesis.

As Grace, in fox fur and Jimmy, returning to his hunting theme as a beagle, joined the queue, Isiah reached a mini-crescendo. He stood at the Ark gateway, majestic in flowing white, grey locks streaming, bubbles of froth clinging to his lips.

"And god saw that the wickedness of man was great upon the earth and the thoughts of his heart were evil continually. And the lord said..." Isiah shook his staff at them. " 'I will destroy man from the face of the earth, for I repent that I made him.' "

The guests, cowed by this threat and trying to appear at ease in their absurdly encumbering costumes, shuffled uncomplainingly forward to the point where they would shake hands with the welcoming Drome Unit. Gideon, as usual, had a special word for everyone. He was splendidly accoutred as a peacock, the turquoise tail eyes enhanced the colour of his own, making them sapphire-like, deep and sparkling. He held out both hands to Grace and squeezed her paws gently.

"Rotten Gracie. So rotten. Poor little Josie. Why didn't you tell us she was so disturbed?"

"I... er..." Grace stammered. This was a new turn of events and one for which she was unprepared. Was all the blame for Josie's death to be laid at her door?

"Don't worry." Gideon leaned forward until his mouth was close to her furry pointed ear. "We're going to take care of you. You couldn't have guessed she came from a dysfunctional family."

So that was it. The game plan was to discredit Sam Andrews also. Both brother and sister were nutters.

Gideon ruffled her fur, enthusiastically. "Foxy lady! Mmm, that ripping perfume. What are those wonderful lines from the Song of Solomon? 'Waters cannot quench, neither can 'fluddes' drown it...' "

He laughed softly, enjoying his own joke. Grace made an effort to join in, but the sound stuck in her throat. The fox fur costume, chosen weeks ago as a witty joke, felt suffocating.

Gideon was already greeting Jimmy with beagle-baiting bonhomie, so Grace passed on to Hettie who looked dull and miserable in her brown peahen costume.

"Oh... hello, Grace." Hettie stuck out a feathered hand.

"Hope you're alright... it's all rather ...distressing." Hettie's own voice sounded distressed and her beak wobbled.

Despite her dislike of what Hettie had become, Grace felt sorry for her. It couldn't be all roses married to Gideon, and whoever had designed that costume needed shooting. The cold fingers of Adam Solomon brushed hers, as though he could hardly bear to touch her fur.

"Tally Ho, Grace. Curious costume. Feeling hunted?"

"Certainly by the press," returned Grace, sharply. She was sure now, Adam had briefed against her.

"Mmm. To lose one friend is unfortunate, to lose two looks like carelessness. One has to wonder who'll be next."

He smiled, the fangs on his anaconda head yawning fearsomely.

"Ah, Jimmy. Having a topping time?"

"Oh yes," Jimmy grinned. His gold teeth looked even more incongruous protruding from the snout of an eager beagle.

"Grace not giving you too much trouble?" continued Adam. The anaconda's jaw appeared to sneer. "She needs a firm hand."

Jimmy gave a honking laugh and waved his arm in the direction of the performing children. "Childlun good."

"Yes," Adam murmured. "Mr Stone thinks he's in heaven already."

They all looked at Jethro Stone, who was surrounded by chubby 'puppies' and even dandling one on his knee.

"But Noah found grace in the eyes of the lord," incanted Isiah.

"Mr Stone same as me," asserted Jimmy, casting a hard look on Grace. "Want many."

Adam laughed with a soft, sibilant sound. The idea of Grace as a mother evidently amused him.

"Childlun make famiry," said Jimmy, to drive home the point.

"I quite agree." Adam's voice took on a sorrowful timbre. "Sadly, I shall never have any."

Jimmy gave Grace a push, to move on. Behind them was Eliza Barker and she was stepping on his tail.

Eliza, looking as disgruntled as ever, was in full Lady Lord Chancellor Elizabethan gear, but as a concession to the dress code, had a standing collar in the shape of a wing-spread eagle.

With her piercing eyes and sharp nose, she looked very like the ferocious bird, without further help from the costume. Trailing in her wake was her long-term partner, a small dumpy woman dressed as a bear.

"Dear Eliza," Adam air-kissed at the collar. "If I may say so, a spiffing combination of ancient and modern!"

Eliza, huffing, ran a finger round the inside of the collar.

"Blasted uncomfortable," she said grumpily.

Isiah's rising voice cut through their conversation. "And the lord said – two of every kind shalt thou bring into the Ark – male and female."

Adam surveyed Eliza's companion. "Not taking the lord too literally, Eliza?"

"Leah's been with me for thirty years," barked Eliza, true to her name. "I'm not dumping her now, just because of your daft gender policies."

"Bold," murmured Adam.

"Some of us still have the courage of our convictions," Eliza snapped.

"Surely, you mean... predilections." Adam's hooded eyes were black with malice. "Be careful, Eliza. Look what happened to David Timothy."

Eliza puffed a blast of cigar-smelling breath into Adam's face and stalked on, without further comment. Leah lumbered obediently after her. From her place further down the queue, Grace heard the encounter and silently applauded Eliza. It was exactly for this feisty refusal to conform, that Grace had fought to get her the Lord Chancellorship. Not that Eliza had ever shown she was grateful.

Inside the Ark, the animals were milling about, gushing over each other's ingenious costumes and snacking on the vegetable offerings – Grace saw a lion turn up its muzzle despairingly at mushroom vol-au-vents. They drew bowls of Ransome's water from bubbling troughs and raised them to each other in greeting. There was eager anticipation of the entertainment – a musical on an epic biblical theme – commissioned by Isiah. Some were even taking part in a tap dancing finale, choreographed by Adam

Solomon, and had been issued with Drome tap shoes in readiness. The fun would begin as soon as all the guests had been herded on board.

Grace moved swiftly through the zoo, hoping to shake off Jimmy, but he followed her scent, making unpleasant snuffling noises as assiduously as a real beagle. She missed Zach, but hopefully he was by now in Seashoram. When the lights dimmed on the raised central rostra in readiness for the pageant, she found herself hemmed in by Jimmy and Peter Priest on one side and Rachel and Naomi on the other.

Peter Priest seemed remarkably suited to his weasel costume; he eyed Grace beadily and twitched his whiskers at her. Rachel was in whippet skin with a hangdog look and Naomi had come as a predatory-looking grey squirrel. Grace had an inward pang for poor David, who'd been responsible for allotting the costumes. He would have been crowing with pleasure that Mode had done such an accurate job. He, himself, had been coming as a rooster.

Miriam, dressed as a frog, stood a little further away with Hettie, but she refused to make eye contact. The only source of support was Eliza who fidgeted close behind Grace, snorting with random displeasure.

Crashing music composed by Lord Peregrine (Piggy) Creede, the Musician Laureate, began. Lord Creede, celebrated for his musicals, which had swept aside all other forms of theatre, conducted the bold oratorio himself. He was dressed as the pig of his nickname, and as the magnificence of his own score over took him, waved his trotters and shook his fat, rosy jowls with passion.

Isiah King processed regally across the stage and took up his place in the spotlight. His amplified voice reverberated round the Ark, ringing its plywood rafters.

"The fludde was forty days upon the earth. and all flesh died that moved upon it. Only Noah remained alive and those that were in the Ark with him."

The kittens and puppies skipped on stage and commenced a beguiling dance drama, showing, in mime, the joy of those on board with Noah. The audience laughed and clapped. Jethro Stone could be seen, sitting close to the stage, gaping at the agile monkeys.

"The stench of shit must have been intolerable," remarked Eliza, loudly. Those close to her shifted uncomfortably.

"Noah's sons and his wives and the wives of his sons..." intoned Isiah.

"Bet it was the wives who shovelled it," interjected Eliza, warming to her theme. Glances of disapproval and hushes came from the bystanders. Eliza was unrepentant.

"When they weren't cooking and cleaning and servicing the menfolk."

"And god remembered Noah and the rain from heaven was restrained."

Lord Creede's crashing chords gave way to gentler, more pastoral music. Noah's daughters-in-law, dressed as nymphs and shepherdesses, performed rites for the return of fine weather.

"And the lord said 'Eat the green herb, but flesh and blood shall ye not eat.' "

On the green-bathed stage, the nymphs made garlands of grass and the lions lay down with the lambs. A circulating waitress offered a plate of cucumber crudités to Eliza, who brushed it rudely aside with a swearword. Other animals had now begun to move away from her.

There was a slight lull as the garlanded actresses tripped offstage to change costume and Peter Priest took the opportunity of nudging Grace.

"Sorry to hear your bad news," he said, in a low voice.

"Really? I understand you're preparing some more for me?" Grace smiled, but her teeth were gritted. Peter hung his head in mock repentance. "Nothing personal." He indicated Jethro Stone, now stroking one of the kittens. "Orders from above. I've always liked you."

"Oh, well that's alright then."

Grace didn't attempt to keep the sarcasm out of her voice. Jimmy was chortling at the female monkeys, who were keeping the audience entertained with feats on the trapeze, so she made her escape and moved quickly towards Miriam. She was determined to get to the bottom of her behaviour.

Miriam didn't see her approach. She was riveted by her companion. Hettie's peahen head was jerking about, her wings flapped and she was emitting strange squeaks.

"Subcontracted – to remote intelligent monitoring system..." The fractured speech sounded almost robotic. "Must ensure human resource development actualisation." Her peahen pipe rose to a hectoring command. "Right objectives! Right de-skills! Dedicated stand-alone!" ...then as suddenly descended into babble.

"Visions and values... hands on, hands off... Stability, stability, stability..."

Animals all around were staring. Hettie suddenly welled with tears and dashed through the crowd to the exit.

"Good Gideon!" exclaimed Grace, under her breath. "The woman's unhinged."

Miriam jumped and her bulging frog eyes swivelled to Grace.

"Oh, Grace," she said, "I didn't see you."

She seemed less than pleased to see her now, and Grace decided to confront her friend.

"Mim. What's going on? You've been avoiding me, and –"

Miriam pushed past her.

"I haven't got time for this now, Grace."

Grace shot out a hand and grabbed her arm. "It's me. Grace. What's the story, morning glory?"

Miriam shook her hand away. "I – I... Excuse me. I've got to go." She gave Grace an agonised look. "I... er... I must look after Hettie."

She ran, disappearing into a welter of fur, scales and feathers before Grace could catch her.

Rachel and Naomi had been watching. Naomi now sidled up and said. "Are you alright, Grace? You look very shocked. Adam's concerned about you."

Grace hastily recomposed her face. "Concerned?"

"About your state of mind. All the tragedies so close to you."

Grace stared at her. Naomi put her squirrel head on one side and smiled in a way intended to be winsome.

"He recommends a visit to the Drome Therapist."

Fury surged through Grace. She recalled that her husband had always hated squirrels, claiming they were really tree-rats. Rachel now joined them and seconded Naomi.

"Could be helpful, Grace. Sort out your priorities."

"I know what they are, thank you, Rachel," said Grace tightly.

"Besides... why would I need the Drome therapist?" She threw a contemptuous glance back to Jimmy. "You've already got me in a straight jacket."

Rachel gave a hurt smile. "You see, Grace. That's not very helpful. We only have your best interests at heart."

She shook her head, warningly. "I wouldn't want to have to put further negative things in my report."

"What report?" Grace demanded sharply.

"The one I've been asked to prepare for your Constituency Caucus."

"Constituency cau – how dare – by whom?"

"I'm not at liberty to say." Rachel snapped shut her snout.

"Bloody Noah Petty!" Grace could not help the expletive.

Rachel clicked her whippet teeth. "That's no way to talk about your constituency chair. No wonder they're considering de-selecting."

She dropped this bombshell in a matter-of- fact way, as though it was common knowledge. She and Naomi stood back to watch the effect of it on Grace. Grace tottered as if she had been struck. She put out a hand to save herself, but encountered only air. A long way away she heard Isiah King's voice.

"And the fear of you and the dread of you shall be upon all that move upon the earth. I establish my covenant with you and all your seed hereafter."

If Grace could have seen Isiah, she would have witnessed steam pouring from his nostrils and foam from his mouth. Despite his famed hatred of sex, he appeared to be having an orgasm. But Grace was blind to everything but her own potential downfall. The screens in the room of perpetual night registered her stricken, open-mouthed face. She looked, in her rough fox skin, like a defenceless, frightened animal – the very antithesis of the glamorous creature who, on the same stage only two days before, had embraced victory. Rachel and Naomi exchanged a knowing smile and melted away, their mission accomplished.

Grace spent the next hour huddled in the Ark's lavatory. The stall was very smelly, some guests having taken animal behaviour rather too literally, but Grace, her head hung over the pan, was oblivious to it. She shuddered and shook between bouts of retching, occasionally raising her head to gaze fixedly at the cistern, as if seeing her future written on it. 'Devoting herself to charity', would be the only option, since she had no family with whom to 'spend more time'. She gulped for air, but the awful stink brought on another spasm of retching.

Eventually she heaved herself up to a standing position and leaning against the flimsy wall, mopped her face with scraps of toilet tissue. With sudden alarm, she checked round for cameras. The final humiliation would be to appear on the screens as yesterday's washed up, vomit-streaked woman. But the stall was mercifully free of surveillance. The Ark had been erected so quickly, there had probably been no time to install it.

She went to the washroom mirror and surveyed the damage. The last two days had certainly taken their toll on her complexion. Her face looked like a runny paint palette. With her usual prescience, she'd had a pocket made in her fur trousers and from this she extracted, powder, lipstick and perfume. She might be yesterday's woman, but she'd go down flying her colours.

After a professional patch-up job – even the stubby fur had been combed 'til it was sleek and shiny – Grace emerged to see Gideon climbing on stage to congratulate the sweating line-up of Drome Unit tappers at the end of the spectacle. After chubbing and hugging each one of them, Gideon stood in the flattering follow-spot and slowly, magnificently fanned out his lustrous tail. There were cries of admiration and girlish delight from the audience. Tail covets fully stretched, Gideon preened, twisting this way and that, to a burst of rapturous applause. Only Eliza Barker, standing close to the spot from which Grace watched, had her arms stubbornly folded.

"Gosh!" Gideon grinned engagingly. "Being Prime Minister's jolly good fun. You get to wear all the best costumes."

There was another burst of clapping, accompanied by laughter and cheering. Gideon held up his turquoise-feathered arms to still the elation.

"Many thanks to Isiah, for staging this spiffing spectacular. Noah's Tale. Moving and true. And what better setting than the story of the chosen male and female of the species, to announce the creation of a New Ministry."

Gideon paused and looked slowly round the vast hall, on which an expectant hush had fallen.

"It is with the highest hopes, I announce today: The Ministry of Gender!"

There were whispers of surprise and interest.

"Pledge to the Future!" Gideon went on. It was one of his favourite phrases. "Nature and Nurture. Male and female in rightful place. Management of Breeding. Selection of Best."

His face shone with belief and his right arm rose slowly. It looked, thought Grace, as if he was trying out David's ideas on body language.

"Blue print for perfect family. Benefit all Civilisation!" Gideon flourished the feathered arm, which now pointed at the ceiling.

The animals murmured, exchanging nervous glances, unsure of the required reaction. Eliza Barker gave an ostentatious snort of disgust. Before the pause became too marked, Adam Solomon started to clap. In seconds the floor erupted in howls of approval and wild applause. Several animals raised their arms in an answering salute. Eliza shook her orange wig in disbelief.

"This is what all that fiddling with soya beans led to," she said sourly to Grace. "Genetically modified human beings. The dickhead'll be cloning himself next."

Grace hushed her quickly. Even Eliza couldn't get away with that kind of language. Fortunately, the animals were carried away with their own ecstasy and no one was listening. All eyes were on the stage as a white dove, bearing in its mouth an olive twig, landed on Gideon's out-stretched hand. There were gasps of astonishment at the perfect timing. Gideon was smiling an Olympian smile.

"Perfect Family in Promised Land," he foretold.

A crescendo of clapping followed this, during which Gideon searched the audience until his eyes alighted on Grace. "Need someone special. Take us over the top."

He gave her, she was sure, the ghost of a wink.

"Woman. Super. More than qualified."

The animals, especially Rachel and Naomi, craned to see where his glance was directed. Eliza was in no doubt.

"You don't go along with this crap, do you?" she demanded.

Grace smiled awkwardly. "Well, I..." she faltered, acutely conscious of being the target of narrowed, animal eyes.

"I approve of everything the Government does," she finished, with brave conviction.

Eliza looked as though she couldn't believe her ears. But on stage, Gideon was nodding and smiling. With a final tremble of his tail, he acknowledged the adulation, then expressing the hope that everyone had a 'splendiferous' time, glided from the stage as a joyful choir started.

The buzz of excitement and speculation in the audience soon rivalled the music and Grace found herself at the centre of it. She caught a look like a witch's curse from Naomi; she and Rachel were huddled together, their faces swollen with outrage. Grace, herself, had no idea what to make of Gideon's behaviour coming so soon after their threat. Was she being punished, or rewarded?

"Minister for Women! Bah!" exploded Eliza, by her side.

"Bring back the pinny, why don't you! How about foot-binding and female circumcision?"

"Now Eliza..." Grace began in a humouring tone. "Don't be absurd."

"Nothing like as absurd as a Ministry of Gender!" Eliza said, acidly. "Imagine what that'll do for women!"

Grace sighed. Eliza wasn't easy to appease; sometimes she regretted her quixotic choice for Chancellor.

"These 'feminist' arguments have been the same for fifty years," she reasoned. "Where did they get anybody?"

"A bloody long way!" Eliza spat the words into her face. "You wouldn't have stood a chance of being a PR without what my generation achieved before you."

"Yeh yeh." Grace was almost rude.

"Why am I wasting my breath? There's no subversion left. None of you lot would say boo to a goose, never mind piss off to a Price."

Grace had heard all this from Eliza before, but not usually outside her chambers. She didn't like to think of the consequences, if anyone reported the things Eliza said about Gideon...

"Really, Eliza," she said chidingly. "Anyone would think he was Big Brother."

"More like Big Sister," Eliza gave a scornful snigger. "Bloody Tiller girl in that costume."

Grace guiltily suppressed a smile. Eliza was incorrigible.

"Where's it all headed, Grace?" Eliza's tone turned serious. "What about the old in this 'super' ministry? Never a mention of them. Are we supposed to volunteer for euthanasia?"

"Hush, Eliza." Grace looked round. Eliza's gruff voice was like a barrel organ.

Eliza cackled. "That's right. Be scared. Be very, very, scared." She took a small cheroot from behind her ear and lit it. "But what are you going to do about it?"

She blew out cigar smoke and prodded Grace in the chest. "It's five to twelve for you, Gracie dear. You're already past forty."

She had hit on – as she well knew – Grace's greatest paranoia.

The surrounding animals had drifted away, leaving them a wide berth. Grace dropped her voice and with it, her attitude.

"I don't know," she said wearily. "I'm sorry."

Eliza fixed her with an eagle eye. "I've told you before. Never apologise. Never explain. I've done my stint, now it's over to you. Just get bloody on with it!"

The party ended in disarray, when unidentified smoke set off the sprinkler system. Gideon, still waving his plumes, was rafted across the pond; it gave him the appearance of walking on water. The guests scattered, clutching wings and tails as water poured down, adding authenticity to the fludde theme. Some deemed it a sign from heaven.

Grace knew very well Eliza's cheroot was to blame. In one of her wilder gestures, she had set fire to her wig. Leah, well used to her lover 's eccentric habits, had doused her in Ransome's water.

Jimmy escorted Grace back to her hotel, one large paw on her all the way, and waited outside her door while she struggled out of the clammy foxsuit. She was longing to contact Zach, desperate to know how he was doing in Seashoram. She took the vidi-fone into the bathroom and shut the door. But when she called Zach's number, his fone rang and rang, not even switching to message mode. She could hear Jimmy banging on the bedroom door. His voice penetrated through the two walls.

"Glace, I am rate! Hully up. Glace! Hully!"

With a sigh, she rang off. Whatever Zach was doing in Seashoram, it didn't include telling her about it. She replaced the fone in her handbag, feeling she had lost her last touchstone with reality.

CHAPTER TWENTY-FOUR

The tour of the Re-location Centre was, Christobel assured Zach, comprehensive. Loading his tenth roll of film, Zach had to admit it certainly felt like it. It had taken five rolls to penetrate Christobel's frost. Only many flattering snaps of her in various locations had finally melted it. She draped herself over desks in the learning centre, dandled babies in the nursery, tested bedsprings in the dormitories, tasted nut-roast in the canteen, blew into condoms in the factory, put a ball in the net on the playing field and all but gave blood in the hospital. By the time they arrived at the watergarden in the middle of the 'tropical' leisure facility, she was cooing as loudly as the birds flying round it.

"Will this do?" Christobel snatched off her glasses and leant seductively against a plastiflex palm tree, toying with a dangling frond. Above her, giant butterflies flittered; in front of her was a foaming 'hot spring' jacuzzi. *Radio Digi'* bathed all in tranquillity. Zach was reminded of a *Stone TV* shampoo advert.

"Lovely," he beamed. "Very original."
He shot another roll of film, as Christobel bridled and simpered.

The atmosphere under the PVC dome was stiflingly hot and damp and after a quarter of an hour of intense photography – Christobel couldn't be faulted on inventive poses – Zach loosened his collar.

"Phew," he said, with a cheeky smile. "Hot."

Christobel nodded. "For the plants." She had already undone the top three buttons of her shiny, silver suit. Teflon had the effect, in heat, of baking foil.

Zach indicated a gushing 'spring' nearby. "Is that water drinkable?"

"I should hope so," Christobel treated him to a coy glance. She was slightly cross-eyed without her glasses. "It's *Ransome's*."

"Perfect," said Zach. He crossed to the fountain, which had a shelf of beakers by it. Zach filled two with the sparkling water and handed one to Christobel, who had followed him.

"Hail Pulses!" he cheered.

"Hail Pulses!" she returned, raising her beaker and clinking his intimately.

A bird swooped so low it almost grazed their heads.

"Good Gideon! Was that a parrot?" Zach pointed into the dense foliage, where a red and silver wing was just visible. Christobel obligingly followed his finger, screwing up her eyes in an effort to see without her glasses. As soon as she looked away, Zach extracted the tiny, Club Gothique pill from a film canister, and popped it into her beaker. It dissolved immediately, a surge of bubbles rising and popping on the surface.

"Wicked," breathed Zach, hypnotised by it. Christobel turned back to him, wagging her finger. "Not quite the word to use," she admonished, smilingly.

"Slip of the tongue," apologised Zach. "I'm so impressed. That bird's wings are even in Ranso colours!"

"Of course." Christobel's smile was patronising. "Lord Ransome's a stickler for detail."

"I bet he is," murmured Zach. He thought quickly.

"How about a picture of you drinking his wonderful water?" Christobel arranged herself by the 'spring', smiling myopically.

"A little sip," instructed Zach. "Triffic... and another one." He went on snapping until the glass was empty. "I need a few rolls, it's a big spread."

"Don' mind t'all... " said Christobel, her voice already a little slack.

"And of course, an in-depth interview with you. I don't think any of the papers have carried that?"

"No." Christobel's face turned sulky. "They've all been with Grace Fry. As if she knows anything about it."

"I'm sure she's completely ignorant of what really goes on here," agreed Zach. "But we can put that right. My editor himself wants to talk to you."

"Your editor?" Christobel's eyes veered further towards her nose. She was clearly impressed. Zach nodded emphatically. "He only does the big interviews. He'll call in a moment."

Right on cue, Christobel's vidi-fone began to ring. Excitedly, she reached for it and pressed the answer button. Paul Jacobs' face came on the screen, smiling seductively. "Miss Steel. Paul Jacobs, *Independent Satellite*. How are you?"

"Oh... fine, thank you." Patches of red appeared round Christobel's exposed neck.

"Young Zachariah not working you too hard?"

"Ha, ha. Not at all... he's been... " She cast a suggestive glance at Zach "...spiffing!"

"Good, good." Paul turned brisk. "Now Miss Steel, what I want is a chat with you about your first hand experience. A to Z at the Centre."

Zach moved closer and mouthed, "While you're talking, I'll pop back to the factory... get a few more shots."

Christobel waved, distractedly. Paul was asking her how she'd come by her charming name. Taking this for an answer, Zach headed for the exit.

"Won't be a mo'," he called. He looked back to see Christobel roll onto her back, and stretch like a bunny being stroked. He had to admit Paul had a talent, almost as good as his own, for schmoozing.

Zach cantered back to the factory, flashing his pass at anyone who looked curious, and with it his broadest smile. "*Indie Satellite*. Photos. Miss Steel's right behind me."

By now word had got round about the photo session and most of the security officials and minders had seen Zach and Christobel together. He was assisted through the encoded doors and floors without question. Once back in the clacking, humming factory, he hunted quickly for the workstation he'd noted on the earlier visit. Eliana Kodaly's name, with 'Team Leader' above it, was prominently placed at the station. Like the other workers, she smiled docilely as he raised his camera. He took a snap then leaned in, as if examining the work to which she was applying herself assiduously. Focussing for a close-up on a *Ransorange* condom, he muttered into her ear, "Eliana, listen to me carefully. I've come from Grace Fry."

Eliana couldn't help a startled glance, but Zach went on quickly.

"Just smile as I photograph you." Raising his voice, he said, "... And another, that's topping." Then in a whisper, "I'm looking for your sister-in-law and nephew. Can you help me?"

Eliana, nodded, still smiling.

"Good. So... just get up and follow me."

Eliana did as she was bid. The workers were all locked in a trance of Digi-tranquillity and no one paid attention as Zach took photos on their passage to the door. When they arrived at it, he announced loudly,

"Topping... and how about one with this gentleman here?"

The security guard, duped by the compliment, brushed the crumbs off his uniform – he'd been eating a brancake – and gave an obsequious snigger. Zach snapped him with the giant condom over his head. He and Eliana slid out of the door and along the corridor, while the guard was still re-composing himself.

At the corner, Eliana took the lead and after many twists and turns and clanging doors, they arrived at the hospital wing. Zach repeated the flattery routine with the guard there and then with the nurses and orderlies inside the wing. Everyone stopped and smiled, taken in by the friendly photographer. It was amazing, he thought, snapping away, what people would do for a picture in the paper.

In a small scullery at the end of the main ward, Eliana located her orderly friend. She spoke to her softly in their own language, while Zach took a picture of her bucket and mop. The orderly, Chrystyna, nodded and pointed the way to a door marked, 'Rehabilitation Unit.' She took a swipe card out of her overall pocket and handed it hurriedly to Eliana.

None of the zombie-like staff noticed Zach and Eliana silently pass through the door Crystyna had indicated, finding themselves in a much smaller ward, with a number of curtained cubicles. A swift glance showed that inside the cubicles lay people wired up to bleeping machinery, in what appeared to be various stages of coma. When they came to the fourth cubicle, Eliana darted to the bed and shook the recumbent figure.

"Anna, Anna!" she hissed, then murmured something in the same foreign language.

While Eliana urged Anna round, Zach kept a watchful eye through the curtains. There was no one on duty, except a nurse, who was snoozing in the corner. Eventually, Anna's eyes fluttered open and she stared at Eliana without understanding. Eliana snatched a bottle of pills off the bedside table and thrust them at Zach.

"This, what we made to take," she whispered, fiercely. "Medication. Say no, no see husbands, wives, children. Still say no, taken to psychiatric wing. They say danger to ourselves and others. But I clever. No take. Destroy. Act like all others. If they find out..." She paused, then raised a stubborn chin. "They kill me."

Zach quickly pocketed the pills and with Eliana's help, pulled Anna upright and swung her legs out of the bed. Eliana spoke to the bewildered woman softly, explaining in their native language.

"Come, Anna. You are going to Imre. This man will take you. He is a friend. First you must walk. Go to fetch Janos."

Anna nodded dimly, seeming to take in a little. At least she was conscious now and Eliana quickly swapped clothes with her. She placed her Team Leader armband high on Anna's sleeve, then wearing the hospital gown climbed into bed, waving them away.

"Go. I stay here 'til you have time to find Janos and get out. Go, quickly!"

Zach didn't need telling twice. The place was spooky. With
Anna leaning heavily against him, he negotiated the short walk
back to the door and out into the main ward.

"Left foot. Right foot," he instructed in a whisper. "And just
keep smiling."

Anna did as she was bid, but her uniform was enough to ensure
anonymity. All faces looked alike above it.

At the Youth Protection unit, the guard made a perfunctory
check of her Team Leader badge and Zach's ID, but after posing
for a smirking photo, let them through without further question.
Inside the self-contained wing was a large, airy common room
with dormitories, showers and kitchens leading off it. It may
have been a prison but it was a comfortable one. The main room
had luxurious sofas, state of the art sound and game facilities
and a huge telescreen playing the usual *StoneTV* docu-soap.
Several youths lounged in front of it. One sat a little apart by the
window, playing a game on a palm-pilot.

Anna gazed round dazedly. After a moment, her eyes fell on
the boy at the window and she took a faltering step towards him.

"Janos..." she called.

The boy looked up, casually. His eyes widened in disbelief as he
recognised his mother.

"Mamma?" he said uncertainly. He stood and ran forward,
catching Anna as she fell towards him.

Zach left them and raced back to the leisure centre. In the
steamy water gardens, he found Christobel, now stripped to a
sausage-pink corset, twirling on a lilo in the jacuzzi. She was still
in vidi-fone connection with Paul Jacobs and as Zach entered,
was shrieking with laughter, her legs flopping, her bosom
exploding from its catgut constrictions. Zach took a couple of
quick shots without her noticing.

"Ooh, you naughty boy!" Christobel snickered into the fone.
"What a suggestion!" She waved the fone at Zach and yelled,
"Your editor!"

"What's he like!" agreed Zach, beginning to strip off his own
clothes. In seconds, he was down to his jockey shorts and sliding

into the water. He held the camera above his head and snapped as he waded towards Christobel. She tossed the vidi-fone onto the bank of the pool and began to pose, shamelessly, on the lilo.

"Wanted to know all about my private life," she continued archly. "I told him, I haven't got one."
She puckered her lips towards Zach as if inviting him to change that. He gave a sexy, answering pucker, still keeping his distance. Christobel threw her legs in the air, almost tumbling off the lilo.

"But I know plenty about other peoples'. Oh yes... " she winked broadly at Zach. "My own little pension fund... just in case."

"Just in case?" Zach gave an encouraging leer.

"In case they don't give me what they promised. I have to have it!" Christobel lunged at him, her arms flapping.

"Have what?" Zach paddled closer.

"Seashoram of course! When Grace Fry gets de-selected."
She whooped with laughter. "Oh Gideon! Let the cat out of the bag!" Her lips pursed. "Miaow, miaow!"

"So that's the plan, is it?" Zach spoke softly, as if to himself. He allowed Christobel to fling her arms round his neck.

"And who's promised you that?" He pressed against her bosom, encountering stiff resistance from the corset.

"Well," Christobel sighed. "Seth's hinted... " She withdrew slightly and frowned. "Not that you can trust a word he says... but I've got good friends in the constituency."

"I bet you have." Zach gave her another squeeze.

"About these private lives... " he murmured, nuzzling her nose. "Who are we talking about?"

"Wouldn't you like to know?" Christobel tempted, rubbing back vigorously. Zach nibbled her earlobe. "Yes, I would."
Christobel began to breathe heavily. Her arms tightened their grip on his neck. "You can see for yourself, 'wicked'. You can even join in if you want to."

"That sounds fun." Zach stuck his tongue in her ear. Christobel shuddered with pleasure.

"There's a party tonight. At Lord Ransome's."

"It's a date," murmured Zach. "Let's have a little warm-up, shall we?"

He plunged one hand into her cleavage while with the other, he held the camera high. Christobel heaved and moaned and as her breasts oozed clear of their corseted moorings, clutched at Zach with such ferocity she fell off the lilo. There was a mighty splash as she sank into the whirlpool, almost dragging Zach with her. He struggled to hold the camera above the waves as Christobel surfaced, blowing bubbles like a great pink whale. She gave gasping giggles and Zach joined in. He felt like laughing. He had not imagined the Club Gothique pill would work so spectacularly. The pictures would be killers.

He was distantly aware his fone had begun to ring in his jacket by the poolside. But Christobel now had her legs round his waist and, as he grappled with her boa constrictor crunch, this was not the moment to answer it.

Half an hour later, Zach, his hair still very wet, exited the building. With him were Anna and Janos Kodaly. They looked quite normal, though someone observing closely would have seen that Anna was wearing a selection of boy's clothes and needed a lot of support from the young man at her side. Fortunately, the guard at the gate was not an observant person.

"I'm taking a couple of your residents, Anna and Janos Kodaly, out for a photo-shoot," Zach told him. "Miss Steel has given permission."

The guard turned automatically to his screen and tapped in the name Kodaly. His search revealed the residents' log, with the data Zach had adjusted. There, clearly on the screen, was the authorisation for them to leave the premises. It was unusual, but the guard could think of no reason to challenge it. "Miss Steel's coming with you?" he asked, to be on the safe side.

"Er... no," said Zach. He grinned, conjuring the vision of Christobel as he'd left her, comatose and bound to the spinning lilo by her corset. "She's a bit... tied up," he said, cheerily.

CHAPTER TWENTY-FIVE

Grace made several more attempts to call Zach, all unsuccessful. The first time there was still no answer; the second, his fone gave the engaged signal. Had Grace but known it, Zach was on the line to Paul Jacobs sharing the news that he'd barely escaped from Christobel's clutches with his life, let alone his manhood.

"She nearly had me balls off! Christ, the stuff you expect me to do for a story!"

"Your idea, boy," chuckled Paul. "Never mind your balls, did you get the pictures?"

"Think so," said Zach. "There may be a few splashes."

"They'll certainly make one," assured Paul and they both roared with laughter.

Though the call waiting light was flashing, Zach switched off the fone out of deference to Anna. The rickshaw in which they travelled bumped and jolted up the steep path to Luke's villa and Anna, propped on Janos' shoulder was looking extremely poorly.

At the other end of the line, Grace sighed with exasperation. She checked herself in the Drome Dames' mirror, brushed a speck off the widow's weeds to which she had returned, freshened the respectful pale lipstick and modest bluebell-scented perfume and steeled herself to return to her gaoler. She'd had to beg to get five minutes alone in the lavatory. Any moment now, Jimmy would be tagging her.

The market in the Drome foyer was in full promotional bustle, all the companies making the most of the last few days of Conference. Potential buyers crowded round the stalls, examining and sampling the products. On the cyclorama were shots of a school playground, with lines of children in knee-length shorts springing through 'physical phitness' routines. The boys did hefty push-ups while the girls twirled hoops and batons. Isiah's monotonous drone expounded the benefits of:

"Children brought up in the righteous ways of Albion."

At the 'Brit-Grip' stall to which Grace returned, Jimmy Wang, as the company's chief euro-executive, was demonstrating various instruments known in the trade as 'Stability Equipment'. He offered Jonathan Temple a brand new People Prodder that looked, to Grace's jaundiced eye, like a giant dildo. Jonathan handled it lovingly, displaying it for the benefit of the *Stone TV* camera crew, which was still shadowing him.

"Super," he murmured, stroking the baton's leather length. He pressed a button and the end of it sprang into life, ejaculating a foam which Jimmy assured the camera was "palarysing."

Jimmy grabbed the jerking baton and with a grin, poked it towards Grace. "Good for wife... eh, Glace? If not obedient." He went into a braying laugh, showing his cavern of golden treasure.

Jonathan Temple, now examining a pair of spiked testicle-cuffs, turned to her with a teasing glance.

"You're not going to let him get away with that, Grace? Be careful Jimmy, our Grace is a feisty lady. She's more than likely to use it on you!"

Grace smiled tightly, aware she was in shot.

"Ah..." said Jimmy. "You know each other?"

"Indeed," said Jonathan, suavely. "I've always felt a strong bond with Grace. I think she joined the wrong party." He gave an admiring laugh. "She could have been the 666's new Leaderene!"

"Kind of you, Jonathan," said Grace, as graciously as she could manage. "But I'm perfectly happy with my own party. I don't think you and I would find ourselves in agreement."

"Ooh, I don't know..." Jonathan raised his eyebrows provocatively. "You and I found ourselves very much in agreement when we were on that select committee. I recall happy trips to Amsterdam."

"To report on the pornography," said Grace, shortly. The camera crew tittered.

Jonathan gave her a smouldering look. "It was, as I remember it, fascinating." His hand slipped along a Brit-grip collar and chain. "We joined forces to get it outlawed."

"Mmm." Grace forced herself to laugh. "A marriage of untrue minds, Jon!"

"Touché," acknowledged Jonathan, returning the laugh. The camera crew chipped in sycophantically.

"Excuse me," said Grace, spotting Miriam across the foyer.

" Where you go?" growled Jimmy.

"Just to see my friend... over there," Grace pointed to Miriam who had taken up her place behind the *ET* stall. "I won't be a moment."

She whisked away before Jimmy could say any more. She'd had as much of the loathsome Temple as she could stomach. She well remembered their 'happy trips'. Jonathan had always positioned himself next to her on the flights and despite the wife and two kids left at home, propositioned her relentlessly. Though she'd coldly rebuffed him, he insisted on believing she was as obsessed by sex as he was and only her fear of discovery prevented their having a fabulous affair. She'd never discussed his behaviour, except with Martha and, of course, Mim, knowing that she would be seen in a bad light — if anyone believed her.

Miriam was not at all welcoming. She pretended to be busy with *ET* demo appointments and was brusque to the point of rudeness. "Grace, I really don't have a second. I've got people arriving from Pakistan and – "

Grace cut her off, determined that this time Miriam was not going to evade her questions.

"Mim. I know you've got something to do with these *Sunday Prophet* 'revelations'."

Miriam shuffled graph papers, avoiding Grace's eyes.

"I don't know what you're talking about."

"I'm not a fool," said Grace, her voice low and angry. "I've worked it out. Only you and Luke knew about the pregnancy. Only you knew for sure what I did about it. Whatever Luke thought, I always told him I miscarried."

Miriam's eyes flickered over Grace and back to her paperwork. She patted a few stray wig-hairs into her chignon, fighting for time. "Maybe Dan told people... his wife."

"Oh, please." Grace shot out a hand and caught Miriam's arm, at the same time pinning her with a damning stare. "You were the person I turned to when my marriage broke up. You and Jim were my second home. My first home. There's nothing I haven't confided to you over the years. Miriam... how could you?"

Miriam's face trembled. She looked down, close to tears.

"I was threatened," she said, after a pause.

"Your life?" Grace was appalled.

"No. Much more important. My job."

"Ah." Now Grace understood everything.

"My Chairman," Mim went on, as though once started, she could not stop. "He called me and said it would be in my interests to co-operate with *The Sunday Prophet's* investigation."

"Your Chairman. Right. He's on the Drome Unit Thoughts-tank, of course."

Miriam nodded miserably. "He implied if I didn't, I'd lose my job." She looked up at Grace, her eyes desperate. "At my age I'd never get another, you know that."

Grace did know. Miriam, like herself, was over forty.

"So you decided to... sacrifice me," she said slowly. Miriam's hand flew to her throat, as if to strangle her voice. "I only confirmed what they already knew," she choked. "They'd got the nursing home records somehow. I never trusted that doctor."

Her voice faded away and they both stood a moment in silence. As though they were at a bereavement, thought Grace. For the past. For the baby. For their relationship.

"What else did you tell them?" Grace said at length.

Miriam shook her head. "Only that you were very unhappy in your marriage."

"Oh? Did you mention that my husband, the celebrated human rights lawyer, regularly beat me up, blacked my eyes, accused me of being an alcoholic, a nympho-maniac and worse?"

Grace's face twisted into a wry smile. Miriam had been the one to whom she'd always run during trouble. Who'd nursed her, helped her cover up the bruises. Put her back on her feet.

"No. Honestly." Miriam's voice was barely audible.

"That'll stay our little secret, then," said Grace. "Along with the bother you've had with Jim."

Miriam looked up, her face registering sick horror.

"You wouldn't?"

"We'll have to see whether I lose my job." Grace gave her a nasty look. "But I don't think your Chairman would be very impressed by an executive married to a secret transvestite."

Leaving Miriam to deal, as best she could, with the boulder she'd dropped on her, Grace sauntered away. Her heart was beating fast, tears of rage and disappointment pricked behind her eyes, but the performer in her took over and her outward demeanour was calm and measured. She waved blindly towards acquaintances who did not, on the whole, return her salute and stopped to talk to others, forcing them to offer condolences, which she graciously accepted. She would not be seen to buckle under pressure. Indeed, there was a certain bitter satisfaction in knowing you were completely alone and surrounded by enemies. This was, she realised as never before, where Dan had been. And what he had schooled her for.

She caught sight of Jimmy, searching the crowd for a sight of her and set her face in a welcome. After the encounter with Miriam, she needed blood and at least with him, she might get it. She would command him to take her out. Somewhere with steak on the menu.

The gun emplacement was lit with candles and oil lamps. They glowed as warmly as the re-union between Imre and his family demanded. There was laughter, there were hugs and tears and much explanation in their own language.

Luke and Zach watched sympathetically. Luke had brought food — bread and vegetables, even a little cheese from his daughter. Anna tried to eat, though she was very weak. Janos shook his head disdainfully and took chocolate from his backpack. Zach gave Eliana's bottle of pills to Luke.

"I'll take a couple with me," he said. "Get them analysed. You put the rest somewhere... you know."

Luke nodded. Secret. Safe. That was what Zach meant. If such a place still existed.

"Does Anna remember anything?" Zach asked Imre.

The refugee dragged his attention away from his wife and answered. "A little... she given large doses of those." He pointed to the pills. "Then many tests... then more pills."

"Human guinea pigs," muttered Luke.

"Many people disappear... she sure they die."

"Working out how far they can go?" Luke raised his eyebrows questioningly.

"Bound to be a few 'mistakes'," Zach agreed. "I'll run it by my friend, the chemist."

"Came for asylum," Imre began in a low impassioned voice. "Look! Look what we get!" He pointed to Anna, now slumped, her eyes closed, on the makeshift bed. "No dignity. No freedom. No love." He hung his head as though the revelations were shaming to himself. "We leave this bad country. Go home."

"I don' wanna go," Said Janos.

It was the first time he had spoken and his voice was quite different from his father's. He had no trace of the native accent. The whiny tone, no doubt picked up from other lads in the Care facility, was totally streetwise and southern Albion. He was unpacking his bag, a rather handsome leather rucksack, and was surrounded by designer tee-shirts and techno toys; not at all the sort of possessions one would expect a refugee to have, nor indeed any one who wasn't part of the Elite circle. Imre's eyes grew large looking at them.

"Where you get these things?" he demanded.

Janos ignored the question, continuing instead, "I ain' goin'. I like it 'ere."

"I can see why," Zach said, his eyes lingering on a matchbox-sized, digi-camcorder amongst the toys. "I'd kill for one of those."

Imre, however, appeared incensed at his son's cavalier attitude. He spun Janos in his chair and took hold of his shoulders. "You bad boy. Bad son. You tell me now... where you get these!"

Janos stared at him insolently. Anna stirred on the bed and opened her eyes.

"Please... Janos," she said weakly. "Do not... disobey your father."

"He learn bad western ways." Imre was beside himself. He shook Janos' shoulders. "Lie. Cheat. You steal these things! You steal! This is why they say I bad father!"

He was almost weeping, but Janos was unmoved by his distress and sat dumbly, a slight sneer on his face.

Zach picked up the tiny digi-cam and looked through the lens, zooming it in and out, testing its tricks and powers.

"Neat," he said, grinning at Janos. "Mind if I borrow it?"

CHAPTER TWENTY-SIX

The walled, kitchen garden to one side of Lord Ransome's mansion was in silent darkness. Zach, bent low, scurried between the raspberry and blackcurrant bushes. As he got close to the black, pseudo-gothic pile, faint lights and sounds became evident. He crept round the building until he came to a large bay window, overlooking rolling lawns at the front of the mansion. The sill of the massive window was quite close to the ground and might provide a foothold. Zach scrabbled in the granite crevices for a grip then, grunting slightly from the unusual exertion, hoisted himself up until he could see over the sill. Heavy, swagged curtains were half-drawn, but through the red-lit gap came music and the sounds of revelry. The sill was broad and after testing it for weight, Zach crawled cautiously along it.

When he reached the gap, he almost fell off the sill. The sultry red light coming, he now saw, from rose-shaded chandeliers, lit figures engaged in what appeared to be an orgy. After a moment frozen in shock, Zach quickly extracted the toy digi-cam from his pocket and pressed the red button. A faint whirr came from it as it recorded the grand table loaded with meats and wines, and a huge venison carcass turning on a spit. A belly dancer gyrated by, her dimpled bottom in close-up. Beyond her, a male stripper was doing strange things with a python and two female ones were simulating the act of love.

Others – celebrities Zach recognised from sports, law, the arts, the media – were genuinely engaged in it. In twos and threes, they rolled and thrashed while others watched and indulged themselves singly.

Lord Ransome sat on a throne, naked except for a laurel wreath round his head, being fondled by playful nymphets. Jethro Stone, in a red robe, held Father Christmas court close-by. He was taking presents from a large sack – current must-have techno toys – and distributing them amongst the naked boys who lay around him. Peter Priest, dressed in a baby's nappy, was being fed from a teeted bottle by a Teflon-clad dominatrix. Last, but most stunning of all, Isiah King, naked except for a loin thong, lay strapped, face down, to an oak refectory table.

Zach held the camera up, twisting it about for the best angle, silently cursing the crazily swaying dancers who got between him and his prey. The new millennial pipe music – Zach recognised it as a piece Piggy Creede had composed for the royal wedding – came to an end and in the lull, the dancers subsided. Zach and the camera had a clear picture of two tall, strapping women approaching Isiah's table with whips. Judging by their wigs and the size of their hands and feet, they were men in drag and they certainly wielded the whips with manly ferocity. Each lash fell on Isiah's buttocks with a resounding crack. Isiah writhed in agony, or perhaps ecstasy. Now the music had died, his cries could be heard ripping the air, though few paid any attention. As the lashes reached their zenith, Isiah's familiar Old Testament boom was wrenched from him.

"Punish me!" he bellowed. "Harder! I'm wicked! Harder!"
The drag queens didn't need telling twice. They scourged him in a frenzy, which they themselves seemed to be relishing. Isiah's buttocks were striped and bloody but with a smile on his face, he continued to scream.

"Beat me! Bugger me! Screw me!"
The drag queens gave each other a glance, then as one, dragged off the shreds of Isiah's cloth and set about obliging him.

Zach filmed until the tape ran out, then slid down the wall and dropped the last couple of feet to the ground. He clutched himself in silent glee. Some party! Just let *The Sunday Prophet* try and ruin Grace Fry. He'd got enough to hang them all! He giggled out loud at the thought of his part – and the attendant promotion it would bring – in the public lynching. A sound in the bushes stopped him and he fell quickly to his knees. A shower of water rained down close to his head and above it, a voice addressed him. "Hello, pretty boy. Lost your way?"

The transvestite shook his member and tucked it away, tugging at his tight skirt. He peered down at Zach through curly false lashes.

"Ah. Who's a shy boy then? Don't worry, I won't bite."

He extended a hand with long lilac nails and wrist bangles, but before it could reach its target, Zach was up and crashing through the bushes as though the devil himself was after him. The trannie's voice pursued him.

"Spoilsport! Don't run away. The party's just beginning!"

But Zach had reached the garden wall and begun to shin up the grapevine trellis. By the time he reached the tartan car rug chucked over the broken glass at the top, the voice had diminished to a faint wail.

Luke, his cold pipe clenched between his teeth, was waiting anxiously in the car. As soon as Zach flung himself in, he started the engine and cranked down the lane.

"Phwoar!" exclaimed Zach, wiping his face with the rug. He was panting and sweating.

Luke chuckled. "It's easier when you're a lad. Jake Ransome and I used to scale that wall regularly to go scrumping. Even then he swore he'd own it all one day."

Zach leaned back and breathed deeply. "I'm out of practice."

"Get what you wanted?"

Zach nodded. "Stolen fruit." He held up the digi-cam. "Certainly confirms Janos' story!"

Zach had taken the boy for a walk and got more sense out of him than his father had managed. There'd been, said Janos, many orgies to which boys – and girls – from the Protection Unit had been taken. It wasn't wise to say no. Children who did, 'disappeared'. Jethro, he claimed, had favourites and he was one of them. He even produced some crumpled love notes from him – "My darling, you looked like an angel, asleep... I could hardly bear to leave you." They were all signed simply, 'J'.

In the glove compartment, Zach's vidi-fone began to ring. He took it out and touched the 'view' button. Grace Fry's face flashed onto the screen. "Zach! I've been calling you all day! Where the hell have you been?"

Zach picked a twig out of his hair. Grinning, he said, "I've been to a naughty party."

Grace's expression turned furious. "Terrific!" she spat. "I've been worried sick about you!"

"Ah," Zach's voice became caressing, "nice to know you care... pusscat."

Pacing her hotel room in regency-stripe silk pyjamas, Grace did not forbid herself a smile at the word. Something more than relief had seized her, at the sound of Zach's voice. A kind of exultation. A certainty that, no matter what, he was on her side. As he poured out the story of his day – and night – she let out a squeal of delight. This was better than her wildest dreams. "Gold star!" she cried. "Great White!"

Her own evening had been wretched. At her insistence, Jimmy had taken her to an exclusive, private dining club, where there was indeed, steak on the menu. Grace was fascinated, never before having glimpsed this Elite world. It was as subterranean as the one to which Zach had access – in this case, literally – as the restaurant was in a disused underground car park. After covertly checking the clientele, mostly corporate types with much younger women, Grace ordered a plate-sized sirloin. But forced to tolerate the increasingly lewd remarks Jimmy made, his leg pressed insistently against hers, she ate it without enjoyment. Perhaps, she worried as she chewed on the bloody hunks, she was losing her carnivorous instincts.

Afterwards, she accompanied Jimmy to an illegal gaming club where he lost many euros. Only the effect this had on his libido, prevented his goodnight attentions from turning into hand-to-hand combat. There was every indication he would prove an exhausting husband.

Grace didn't mention any of this to Zach. It could wait, along with her other revelations, until they were together.

"Are you going to stay with Luke?" she asked instead, and when Zach confirmed that he was, she cautioned.

"Be wary. Both of you. They know we're onto them."

Zach promised he would. They'd take it in turns to sleep and keep lookout.

Grace nodded. "OK. I'll see you tomorrow. Goodnight and sweet dreams." She paused, then added with tender provocation, "Pusscat."

CHAPTER TWENTY-SEVEN

The next day, a Government limo carried Grace to the funeral of Josie Andrews. It also carried a bloodshot-eyed Seth Thomas, who was silent for most of the journey. He stared out of the smoked glass windows at the farmland rolling by, occasionally swearing, as the car drew up in the dusty lanes behind a herd of cows, or slowed to let a cart, trundling *Osso* barrels, cross. He didn't address Grace at all, though she caught him observing her slyly when he thought she wasn't looking. She wondered what he was really feeling. Were the red eyes a sign of grief – or over-indulgence? She longed to ask him about his relationship with Josie, but that way lay disaster. It was essential to keep up the facade of ignorance. She'd pretended to be honoured when he'd called her early that morning and given her instructions on the travel arrangements. Behind them travelled another limo carrying a posse of Adam Solomon's boot-boys, a sick-looking Christian among them. At least Jimmy Wang had not insisted on coming to the funeral. No doubt, the presence of the Drome Unit bullies was considered vigilant enough.

The sleek car glided past flowering *Ossophate* and *Ransome* billboards, into the outskirts of Seashoram. Grace straightened her suit; a flattering black, with pencil skirt, vest and waist-nipping jacket. Seth cast a sideways glance, a hint of appreciation in it, at her legs, well displayed in sheer black stockings and patent leather stilettos.

They were deposited, a little late, at the lychgate of Saint George's church, where a crowd of local press and bystanders had already gathered. For the first time, the glorious Indian Summer had broken and the day was overcast, suitably mirroring the doleful watchers. Some of the press boys took photographs as Grace emerged from the limo. Seth, as usual, hung back and shielded his face from the cameras.

Grace, at the head of the Drome posse, entered the ivy-clad churchyard as the coffin, borne on the shoulders of the frock-coated undertaker's men, was making dignified progress from the great door of the Gothic church to the open grave in the cemetery. It was followed by the officiating clergyman, who dispensed drops of water from a large urn labelled 'Ransome's ', and a choir of young men and women in flowing white, who were swaying and clapping. Grace was reminded of the religious cults of her youth. Before Oxford Street had its travelator, bizarre groups had wandered it, banging tambourines and chanting. The waiting pit was in the shade of a magnificent chestnut tree, still in its autumn splendour and surrounded by other well-kept plots, with marble headstones and flowering zucchini patches. It sent the dark smell of freshly dug, damp earth into the air.

Grace scanned the mourners for Zach, noticing that few amongst them seemed of Josie's age. She'd been curious about the girl's friends. Perhaps she had none. As for family, if what she'd said was true, there was only Sam.

She spotted Zach in a dark suit and gave a relieved nod to him. He looked unusually smart in the well cut Beatle-suit, his hair slicked into tidy waves. She thought again, almost dispassionately, how good-looking he was.

The bearers reached the graveside and the vicar and choir took up their places. As the plain box, with its covering of the red-crossed Saint George's flag, was lowered, they embarked upon a joyful committal.

"Our Dear Sister, mistakenly took pills to make her sleep," commenced the vicar in a sing-song falsetto.

Rather longer than she intended, thought Grace, exchanging a tiny flicker with Zach.

"And sadly died," continued the vicar. "But she is not lost to us."

"Lost to us... lost to us..." carolled the choir.

"Her body will go to feed the soil."

"Feed the soil... feed the soil..." The choir drove home the message.

"Sooner or later to this we all come."

"All come... All come... "

"All become vegetables."

"Vegetables... Vegetables..." At this point, the choir lobbed cauliflowers and cabbages onto the coffin. One or two of the mourners joined in, Christian chucked a leek and Seth, a carrot. Grace threw a single red rose, almost defiantly. The bearers stood back from the grave in a neat line, their stovepipe hats clutched before them, their heads bowed. Grace noticed that one of them, a slight blond man, was wracked with sobs. He obviously took his job very seriously.

"Earth to earth." The vicar intoned the age-old words. "Ashes to ashes, dust to dust... "

"Earth to earth..." the choir chirruped, illustrating the sentiment by scattering handfuls of soil. The vicar finished by giving the coffin a generous sprinkling of *Osso* from a tub held by the churchwarden. This was the completion of the ceremony and was accompanied by applause all around the grave and a soaring chorus. A patch of pale blue sky appeared and the sun broke through the pall of cloud, as though to add its blessing.

As the small crowd drifted from the graveside, Grace managed to signal Zach to follow her. She assumed she'd be marshalled into the limo with Seth and whisked back to Conference. She was determined to get a few words with Zach before that happened. She crossed the daisy-spotted grass between the graves, deliberately choosing the narrowest path, tricky in her high heels, and stopping to examine the other graves. Zach caught up with her at the tiny grave of a baby. Grace was reading the headstone.

'Zebediah. Gone to the Earth aged two months. Good Gideon protect him.'

"Anyone would think Gideon was the Pied Piper," Zach muttered.

"Where he leads, we all follow," rejoined Grace, *sotto voce.* "Speaking of which..."

Before she could say more, she felt a slight tap on her shoulder and turned to see the blonde coffin bearer behind her. Close to, she could see his face was blotchy and his eyes swollen with weeping.

"Miss Fry?" he queried, urgently. "Grace Fry?"

"Yes?" confirmed Grace, wondering what he could want. A donation perhaps. Some pallbearer's charity.

The young man dropped his voice so low Grace had to bend to hear him. "I'm Sam. Josie's brother. Sam Andrews."

Grace stood back, startled, for a better look. The young man before her bore no resemblance to the one she had seen in Sam Andrew's flat.

"Sam?" she said, doubtfully.

The young man nodded vigorously. "I know I look different. I did it to hide. But... it's me. I must talk to you!"

Grace looked swiftly around. Though Seth was standing at the lych-gate with the Drome posse, he was looking in their direction.

"Not here," she said. "Far too dangerous."

Thinking quickly, she fumbled in her pocket and brought out a tissue. She raised it to her nose as if to give a tearful blow and behind it hissed.

"Go to Luke Counsel. Seaview Villa. The Cliffs. Seashoram. Can you remember that?"

Sam mumblingly repeated the address, breaking down into sobs again.

"You can trust Luke with your story," Grace impressed him. Out of the corner of her eye, she saw Seth approaching.

"I'll come there as soon as I can," she finished hurriedly, then changing her tone, said loudly, "Thank you so much for your condolences. Kind of you." She blew her nose, tearfully. "Yes... yes... in one so young, very tragic."

Seth caught the last phrase as he came up and took hold of her elbow. Sam walked swiftly away, rubbing his face with the sleeve of his frockcoat. Seth gave him a hard look but said only,

"You're wanted in your constituency office, Grace. We'll give you a lift."

Zach started after Sam, but before he'd taken more than a step, Seth's hand descended on his shoulder.

"You, too," he said with an unpleasant smile. "Your editor wouldn't want you to miss this."

Without further explanation, he propelled Grace towards the purring limo.

CHAPTER TWENTY-EIGHT

Neither Grace nor Zach, bundled unceremoniously into the back of the limo by Seth and a boot-boy minder, dared say anything on the short ride from the church to Grace's office. Grace could not imagine what was coming next in the mercurial routine to which she was being subjected, but she knew it wasn't going to be pretty. She tried to communicate as much to Zach with eye-rolling glances.

Her offices were in a Victorian building once the main bank, near the centre of Seashoram. A large crowd, which included journalists and photographers, seethed about outside. Grace hastily took out her cosmetic bag and applied a slash of lipstick. In her powder-compact mirror, she saw Zach start at so many familiar faces, obviously as mystified as she was. The car drew to a standstill by the building and the paparazzi rushed towards it, thrusting their cameras up to the windows. Seth leaned forward and opened Grace's door. Now she could hear their shouts.

"Is this the end, Grace?"

"Are you being de-selected?"

"What's in the Chief Whippy's report?"

"Any comment on you and Dan Jefferson?"

She shrank back against the upholstery, as if the comforting leather could save her from the horrifying gauntlet she was, apparently, expected to run. Seth, with the same humourless smile he'd had during the ride, said.

"Now, now Gracie, it's the press. You love the press. Off you go."

He gave her a shove, so she half-fell into the jumble of people and cameras. Zach leapt out of the other door and tried to force his way round to save her, but the crowd pushed against him, thick and bellicose. The shouts had become random now.

"Allegations!"

"No confidence!"

"Nervous breakdown!"

"Sex, sex, sex!"

Grace scrambled upright and cast an agonised glance back to the car. Seth slammed the door and poked his face out of the window.

"You're on your own." He raised his eyebrows, his glance saying – this is what you get when you don't play onside. "Bye-bye, Gracie."

The smoked glass slid over his grinning face and the limo sped away from the chaos.

Mustering as much dignity as possible in the circumstances – she was furiously aware of her ruffled hair and the ladder running down one stocking – Grace, head held high, stalked through the swarming paparazzi to the entrance. She was just able to catch sight of Zach being stopped by the Security Wardens on the door, as she herself was shoved through it.

The constituency office was upstairs, in what had been the bank's main accounting room. The Security Wardens hustled her along the corridor so fast her feet didn't touch the ground. They allowed her barely a moment to adjust her clothing and smooth her hair, before throwing open the polished oak door to her office.

The scene that greeted her was that of a quasi-court. The room had been re-arranged with rows of benches, a dock and a magistrate's table, behind which sat Noah Petty. He stood as Grace entered and she saw he was wearing a spanking new, brown uniform with epaulettes and a lot of toggles. He looked extremely pleased with himself and, checking swiftly round the room, Grace could see why. The benches were filled with his support group, a caucus of female delegates famous for their moral fervour and commitment to duty. This they expressed by hand-sewing Noah's uniforms and knitting pastel bootees for Baby throughout constituency meetings. In their biscuit-brown clothes and mousy wigs, they sat whispering, nudging and pointing at Grace. The clacking of their needles, pearl and plain, pearl and plain, never ceased for a moment.

Grace was marched to the 'dock' and up its steps to confront this audience. None of them liked her, she well knew. To them, she represented all that was unacceptable in a woman. The whole coterie had long wanted to unseat her and now, it looked as if they had their chance. Though she had many supporters in the community – ordinary people, whose burdens she'd helped to lighten – none of them were present. Attack, she decided, was the best means of defence and before Noah could speak, she braced herself and demanded angrily,

"What on earth is the meaning of this insanity?"

The delegates took a communal breath, which expelled itself in a disgusted hiss. They sounded like so many geese, thought Grace. Noah was more like a turkey with his round, unblinking eyes and absurd coxcomb wig. Taking his time, he wagged his head and said in a smug tone,

"You're the one who appears to be 'insane', Grace."

He gave a moment for jeers and sneers from the floor to assert themselves over the needle-clicking.

"We've had... " Noah plucked a sheet of paper off the desk, "... a very nasty report from the Chief Whippy on you."

The noises from the floor became more pronounced, transforming themselves into phrases.

"Disgrace to womanhood."

"Immodest behaviour."

"Unholy adultery."

Each phrase was punctuated by the jab of several needles. Yet the clacking went on uninterrupted.

"It alleges... " Noah left a more impressive pause. "Behaviour likely to bring the Government into disrepute."

Grace looked round wildly, for means of escape. The only other exit, a window, was two floors above ground level and she could hear the crowd outside, still baying.

"I have no idea what you're talking about," she said, with as much disdain as she could muster.

"You will if *The Sunday Prophet* run this muck!" Noah waved the sheet of paper at her. It was the cue for an outbreak of honking from the floor. The delegates half-rose in their seats, pointing and crying in unison.

"Harlot!"

"Filth!"

"Baby-killer!"

Grace went cold. It appeared they knew everything.

"We won't tolerate that kind of publicity for Seashoram!" Noah was shouting now. "We'll have to de-select."

Fear gripped Grace. It was her worst nightmare realised. But in a second, all the sacrifices she'd made – home, love, children, privacy – flashed through her head and fear was replaced by total rage.

"I've given my life for this constituency," she cried.

Noah gave a complacent smile. "We could all say that, Grace." Having hit his target, he subsided, patting his orange toupée. With icy clarity, Grace saw his plan. He, as witch-finder general, would accumulate the glory. Inherit her mantle. Take her seat.

"You sanctimonious sod!" she screamed. "What have you done for this town? Dressing up and strutting about! You're just a potty little Hitler!"

There was a moment's horrified silence from the floor. Even the needles were stilled. Noah seemed shaken by her attack. White-faced, he got to his feet and said tremblingly,

"You can insult me all you like, Grace. It won't make any difference." His voice gathered strength. He shook a finger at her. "It's the Drome Unit you've got to appease. Otherwise you're finished."

A low rumble had started in the room, now it built into a howl. The delegates stood, thrusting their knitting needles at Grace.

"Fin-ished! Fin-ished!" they chanted manicly.

One or two left their seats and moved towards the dock; others quickly followed. In a moment, Grace was surrounded. The mob chanted and poked as if possessed.

"Fin-ished! Fin-ished!" The needles pecked her flesh as if intending to execute the sentence. Terrified, Grace backed from the podium; the needles followed, forcing her to the door. Once there, she turned and bolted down the stairs. Even the hounds of hell outside were preferable to the jury of crazed knitters.

At the bottom of the stairs, Grace stopped, fumbled in her bag and clamped on a pair of sunglasses she'd brought for the funeral. Then with a set jaw she pushed open the front door and thrust her way through the pack, which immediately recommenced shouting and jostling. The hacks barred her passage, tweaking her clothes and thrusting cameras under her nose. She said nothing, for once turning her head away from the lenses.

Zach struggled through the throng towards her. Catching sight of his face, she knew she'd never in her life been so glad to see anyone. He grabbed her arm and jerked his head at a waiting rickshaw. They hustled through the bodies, Zach lashing out to right and left, and tumbled, at last, into the hard seats. Zach waved a fistful of euros at the driver, who set off at a startled gallop.

The rickshaw was pursued for a while along the main street, but the rickshaw boy was young and healthy and the journalists were not. The little carriage gathered speed and soon left the straggling hacks behind. When the only sounds were of street vendors and the slapping of the boy's shoes on the cobbles, Grace snatched off her dark glasses. For the first time, Zach could see how she felt. Her eyes were hurt and scared, but not without humour. Her lips twisted into a sardonic smile.

"As I always tell people. Get the media on your side," she said dryly.

CHAPTER TWENTY-NINE

The front door to Luke Counsel's villa was hanging wide open when the rickshaw drew up on the clifftop. Grace left Zach to negotiate with the rickshaw boy, whose appetite for euros had risen with every sweating, panting yard, and approached the house cautiously. There was no sound from the interior, but she was perturbed to see the signs of a scuffle in the hall. The hatstand had been overturned, the clothes and walking sticks scattered. On the mat lay Luke's precious Briar, broken.

Grace picked it up and stepped inside, calling Luke's name softly. There was no answer. She edged forward until she could see into the living room. Everything was upended, thrown about, smashed. It was obvious it had been completely ransacked. A sound behind her made her jump, but it was only Zach in the hallway. He looked over her shoulder into the room.

"Hmm. Drome Unit boys got here before us," he said shortly.

Grace leaned against the doorjamb and put her head in her hands.

"They must have followed Sam," she said, dully. Then, as the full implication of that dawned on her, "Oh no... No! The Kodalys!"

Zach crossed quickly to the open french windows. "I'll check on them," he said. "You have a look round in here."

Oblivious to danger, Grace ran from room to room calling Luke's name. The house was eerily silent, but every room had been raided. In Luke's bedroom, drawers and cupboard doors had been wrenched open and his meagre possessions strewn across the floor. Pictures were cracked, photographs torn, ornaments smashed. The bully boys had done a thorough job of degradation.

Grace came sadly downstairs, sure now her friend had been arrested on some pretext. Sam too perhaps, if he had made it this far. She sat heavily on the arm of the dear, familiar sofa and looked round the destroyed living room. All the furniture had been slashed, the few books were ripped, even the lovingly tended pots outside had been broken, their soil and plants dumped over the patio. It was as if the intruders had been looking for something. Tears began to run down Grace's cheeks. They were hot but silent. A great piece of her life too, had been demolished.

Zach re-entered to find her bent double with pain of stitch-like intensity. He put an arm round her shoulder and held her for a moment. "The good news is, the Kodalys are alright. They heard noise... shouts and crashes, but they kept very still and nobody came near the bunker."

Grace nodded. With their history, the Kodalys would be skilled in silent hiding.

"Luke isn't here," she said, wiping her tears. "Nor is Sam. They've been taken away, I'm certain." Her voice broke again and she said though sobs, "It's all my fault."

"Don't be silly." Zach's tone was brisk, but he gave her a comforting squeeze. "How can it be?"

"I led them into it. Luke tried to tell me. I wasn't... I didn't... pay attention."

"You're straight," Zach said, without irony. "They play a dirty game." His tone was full of contempt. "No rules."

"How can we prove it?" said Grace wearily. A terrible thought struck her. "You didn't leave that video here?"

Zach patted his inside pocket. "No worries. Hasn't left my body."

Grace stared down at the debris scattered at her feet. In amongst it, she spied the toy Tyrannosaurus Rex and Luke's words about it came back to her. She picked it up and cradled it to her cheek, hearing Luke's voice say,

"Sometimes I feel like this. Extinct."

To her surprise the little toy rattled. She held it out and shook it again. This time Zach heard it too. They looked at each other with a glimmer of hope then, feverishly, Grace scrabbled to take it apart. The plastiflex seams fell into halves and revealed a tiny postage stamp CD, a bottle of pills and a scrap of paper. Grace snatched up the paper and read aloud.

"Grace. Sam Andrews came. This disc is the bespoke programme he created at *Ossophate*. Sam and Abbie destroyed everything in the lab before she died, so this is the only evidence."

Grace gasped. She could hear Luke giving a slight chuckle as he wrote his last sentence.

"If you're still a carnivore, you'll find it."

"Oh, Luke," she whispered. "I am. I am!"

She clutched the locket round her neck and pressed a tiny button. The locket sprang open, displaying a smiling photo of Dan Jefferson. At another touch, the photo slid away and revealed a minute computer. Grace slotted in the CD. On the heart-shaped screen in the other half of the locket lid, lists of data appeared.

Zach let out a low whistle as the chemical symbols flashed by.

"It's the components of the drug."

He rattled the bottle. Text now replaced symbols on the screen and peering closely, they both read:

"The drug *Doze* is guaranteed to make people happy, hard-working, docile consumers. Multi-purpose, for use in the workplace, home, centres of learning, sports and detention, it is intended for ultimate People control. Currently undergoing tests at *Ossophate* and Seashoram Re-location Centre."

They were both struck dumb by this information. After a moment, Grace returned to Luke's note, in which there was a further paragraph.

"Sam thinks only King and Ransome are involved, but I believe the Drome Unit is the cancer at the heart of it."
There was a gap and then a hurriedly scrawled post-script,
"I can hear a car outside... must hide this now... Get to the fertiliser."
The note tailed away and Grace imagined Luke scrambling it into the hiding place, as the front door was battered.
"Get to the fertiliser?" murmured Zach.
They stared at each other in silence, as each tried to fathom how they would do that.

The neat streets of the suburb, in which Margie and Tony lived, were empty except for the occasional cat washing itself in a sunny patch. The trees shook their autumn russet gently. The sky was the hyacinth blue of late afternoon, the air with a touch of frost in it.

Zach drove Luke's car, while Grace pointed out the route. He swung into Margie's street, notable only for the large *Ossophate* Security van parked outside their bungalow. As they pulled up, Grace and Zach saw there was a rickshaw piled with furniture and household belongings, on the road behind it.

"What's going on?" wondered Grace, getting out of the car.
Margie came down the path loaded with boxes of pans. She deposited them in the rickshaw and when she straightened up, Grace saw tears were running down her face, under her glasses.

"Margie," she called. "What is it? What's wrong?"
Margie swung her head blindly towards her. She pushed up her glasses and wiped her streaming eyes with her pinny.

"Oh, Grace..." she said and burst into sobs again.
Tony stomped down the path with a garden hose and buckets.

"We're being exiled, " he shouted furiously at Grace. "That's what's wrong. Sent to a bloody Home Zone!"

"What? No!" Grace couldn't believe what he was saying. "But... why?"

"When the Neighbourhood Committee released me from the stocks," Tony said sourly, "I spat in their bloody faces!"

"And then I swore at the Happiness Warden," added Margie. Her voice was so choked with sobs, Grace could hardly make out the next words, "I said 'damn and blast happiness'."

The couple's three sons had now crowded into the doorway. They made rude hand gestures.

"Useless old gits!" they jeered.

"Serves you right!"

"Bad Citizens!"

"Bad Parents!"

Curtains twitched along the road and windows opened.

"Hurry up, Tony," pleaded Margie. "Let's go. I can't stand the shame of it."

"Stop!" exploded Grace, dragging a case from the rickshaw. "I won't let you... I won't let this happen!"

"You should have thought of that a long time ago." With a hostile stare, Tony grabbed the case from her. He took Margie's arm.

"Come on, m'duck."

He helped her aboard the rickshaw, then positioned himself between the shafts and grunting, heaved away from the pavement. Grace followed, saying hopelessly, "No. Tony! Stop it!"

Margie looked back at her. "It's too late... too late, Grace."

Her words cut across the sound of the trundling rickshaw like some terrible prophecy.

Grace stood in the middle of the road and watched until they disappeared round the corner. The other watchers at windows and doors melted away as the rickshaw passed its pots and pans clanking in leper-bell warning. Grace's heart was like a stone and she set her face to match it. It was only too late over her dead body.

CHAPTER THIRTY

Margie and Tony's three boys seemed at a loss, once their parents had actually gone. They fell back to let Grace and Zach into the house, then followed Grace past the many posters of Gideon to the kitchen, whining that they were hungry.

"We need our greens," demanded Steve.

"Yeh. We're starving," chipped in Darren, though he was gnawing on a sausage. Presumably, black market.

"She's a bad mother!" growled Kevin.

"OK, boys," said Grace, with a nannying smile. "I'll cook you something. Why don't you go and watch TV?"
She could hear strains of the *Stone TV* docu-soap coming from the living room. Clearly the youths had not allowed their parents to take the telescreen. They sloped off, still moaning about their mother's deficiencies.

Grace dropped the smile instantly, full of outrage for her friends. Through the window she could see Zach in the garden, hovering over a drum of *Osso*. He scooped a little into a flowerpot from Tony's shed. Grace looked round the bare kitchen. Margie had removed all her samplers and family certificates and in their place were more large posters of Gideon giving his sympathetic, global beam. For the first time, Grace looked at them with something approaching hatred.

There was no sign of any food but Grace recalled Margie had a larder and hurried across to it. There was half a loaf of Margie's home-made bread, a few hoarded tins and a plate of bubble and squeak left ready for the boys' tea. Grace gave a small grunt of satisfaction. She picked up the plate and took the bottle of *Doze* pills out of her pocket.

"Right," she muttered, with a dark glint of pleasure.

"Greens are good, you little bastards."

Half an hour later, the three youths were sprawled, snoring in front of the telescreen, empty plates by their sides, and Grace and Zach were rifling through Steve's bedroom. Zach was already dressed in one of Steve's *Osso* Security uniforms. Grace spotted another – thanks to Margie's 'bad mothering', ready washed and pressed – hanging on the back of the cupboard door. The sleeves and trouser legs were a little long, but in Margie's bedroom she found a box of pins and with Zach's help adjusted them. Her short hair disappeared completely under the cap and she swapped her stilettos for a pair of Margie's abandoned boots. With a faint grin, Zach pointed out she was still wearing lipstick. Grace looked in the mirror to scrub it off, then stood back to survey the whole effect.

"Bloody Gideon," she commented, confronted with a small, but credible, security guard. "Even Naomi would approve of me in this outfit!"

Steve's security pass and the *Osso* van keys were conveniently resting on top of his chest of drawers. Zach pocketed them and, leaving the slumbering boys to the mercy of *StoneTV*, they tiptoed out of the house.

Grace bundled their clothes into the boot of Luke's car, while Zach climbed into the *Osso* van. It started without any trouble, unlike Luke's car. Grace eventually managed to engage the big old-fashioned clutch and a few moments later, they were heading out of Seashoram. On their way, they passed through the peripheral Home-Zones and caught the desolate sight of Margie and Tony unloading the rickshaw, watched by a line of glum women with pushchairs.

Ossophate's chimneys towered in the near distance and Grace pointed a hand out of the window to warn Zach they should turn off into the narrow country lane skirting the complex. The light had faded into cloudy, moonless, evening. The woods, the lane soon dipped into, added to the darkness. And the sense of danger.

Grace parked behind bushes in a secluded spot and waited for Zach to draw up. They got out of their vehicles and faced each other. Each knew the other's heart was beating fast, from fear, but also something more. They clasped hands, then, irresistibly, drew together and kissed. It was a quick trembling kiss, but it said everything necessary. A moment later, Grace was off, bent low, diving through the trees. Zach watched her, willing her to be lucky. He knew now, that for him, this was far more than just a job. When Grace had completely merged with the shadows, he got back into the van and drove round to the main entrance.

At the massive security gates, it was already almost night. Any moment now the huge arc lights would click on. Zach pulled his cap well down and keeping his face averted, handed the guard Steve's security pass.

"Hiya, Steve," said the guard, grinning. "How're you doin'?"

"Er... good," Zach muttered, trying to emulate Steve's callow gruffness.

"Changed yer shift?"

"Yeh... yeh." Zach thought fast. "Mate gettin' married tomorrow... "

The guard put his head in the window and lowered his voice. "If he needs anythin'... You know, booze, burgers, whatever..." He rubbed his nose meaningfully. Zach gave a sideways glance at his badge.

"Right... er... Deen."

"Jus' let me know." The guard gave another smirk and withdrew his head. The gates opened and Zach released the clutch and drove shakily through, thankful all was still lightless.

Bobbing and weaving, Grace made her way through the woods, ever alert for cameras. She had done the same trip so recently, she could remember roughly where they were positioned. Nothing had prepared her for the dread she felt, however. The trees loomed blackly, threatening spectres in the dark, each tiny sound sent panic through her. A couple of times she stopped and pressed her hands on her hard-beating heart, trying to instil it with courage.

She edged out into the clearing before the high fence by the gate through which she'd seen the lorry enter. It was closest to the phallic factory and against the still black sky, she could make out the spirals of pale smoke from its chimneys. A camera whirred and she ducked behind a tall rhododendron, then threw herself full-length beneath it, as the first arc light raked over the clearing. She counted the seconds between beams, and after the next flood of white, crawled forwards on her stomach. At the other side of the gate, she could just see a dim figure approaching. The black uniform was hard to distinguish from the surrounding dark, but Zach gave their agreed signal – a rather diffident owl hoot – and opened the gate with Steve's smart card. Counting the seconds, four, five, one to go, Grace scuttled through and fell into Zach's arms and down to the ground. The lights scanned back, only a centimetre above their heads. They lay perfectly still for another second, waiting for any sound, but when nothing happened, Zach scrambled to his feet and grabbing Grace's hand, dragged her along behind him.

They headed for the factory, speeding over the open space, dodging behind stationary vehicles and vast dumpbins whenever the lights threatened. Close to the entrance they crouched, breathing fast, behind a cluster of metal bins and watched as a large covered lorry drew up. Workers in security guard uniforms began to unload it, carrying black plastic bags into the factory. It took two workers to lift each bag; they were obviously heavy.

Eyes dilated, Grace and Zach looked at each other, then by unspoken consent, strode out and in a busy moment, mingled with the workers. No one paid them any attention or indeed, even seemed to notice, as they took each end of the next bag off the trailer. Grace staggered slightly under the weight, but after an extra hoist from Zach, quickly righted herself. Carrying the sagging sack, they shuffled to the entrance.

Inside the factory, despite the bright light from a central, buzzing generator, there was a foreboding dankness. The workers, all wearing white coats and dome-shaped hats, moved about in an unsmiling and seemingly automatic pattern. There were boilers, vats, urns, grinders and at the end of a conveyor belt on which the bags were dumped, a huge glowing oven. The oven's gates were open like a red mouth and the material it devoured burned fiercely. Ash from the backside of the burner shot, smoking, down a funnel into a steel cooler. This joined barrel-thick pipes, which ground and clanked, transporting what appeared to be chemicals to vast vat-like mixers. Grace watched as custard coloured powder poured in on top of shell pink and cobalt blue. One powder she saw was a particularly bright white. She glanced quickly at Zach and saw, by his slight nod, that he too had noticed. Out of chutes the other end, poured the now grey mix: the magic *Osso* fertiliser.

It took only a nanosecond for Grace and Zach in their heightened state, to absorb all this. Meanwhile they heaved their bag onto the conveyor belt and watched as its plastic coating was ripped away at the oven gates, revealing a mess of decomposing fruit and vegetables. As they followed the other workers out for more bags, Zach whispered. "Must be rubbish from the Re-location Centre. I saw on the computer *Ossophate*'s got the disposal contract."

Made sense, thought Grace. Compost was exactly what good fertiliser needed and the Centre would have plenty of it. Another little deal for King and Ransome's mutual benefit.

They humped another bag onto the belt, but this time instead of going straight back, Grace made her way through the white-coated workers to the Ransome's watercooler near the great, labelled vats. Workers with small containers were removing samples of the fertiliser for testing. Grace filled a water beaker, and checking no one was watching, chucked the water away and swiftly scooped some of the grey powder into the beaker. She stuffed it into her boilersuit pocket, then wiping her mouth, turned to rejoin the line of security guards. In her haste, however, she caught her belt buckle on one of the plastic bags and as it moved onwards, a wide hole was torn in it. Something flopped out of the hole that did not look vegetable.

Grace peered closer and in a moment of frozen horror, saw it was a human hand. Hypnotised, she followed the bag's progress to the oven where, as usual, the plastic was stripped away. No one else seemed to have noticed that inside this bag was a body. Before it slid into the oven, Grace saw the face quite clearly. It was that of Eliana Kodaly.

Grace's hands flew to her mouth to stifle a scream. She looked wildly round for Zach, but he had his back to her as he exited for a bag. She positioned herself as near as bearable to the oven's heat and scrutinised the other bags as they approached it. The plastic on the next was ripped away, revealing peelings, tealeaves and garden waste. The one after contained grass cuttings. The third, rotten fruit and eggshells.

The bags went on normally for some time – Grace almost began to think she'd been hallucinating. But then came one with an unusually round bulge in it. Without waiting for the stripping machinery to engage, Grace slit it with her buckle. Compost oozed out, but in the middle of it, face decorated with *Nut-Noggin* grounds, eyes gazing sightlessly upwards, nestled the blond head of Sam Andrews. This time Grace could not help an exclamation. One or two workers looked round as she yelped his name, but the bag was now consigned to the flames and, seeing nothing more than a security guard apparently stifling a cough, they immediately resumed their mechanical activity.

Grace moved along the conveyor belt, losing count, tearing at the bags ever more wildly. "Quality control!" she barked at the workers who showed any curiosity.

On the fourth or fifth bag, quite close to the entrance, her gash revealed what she had most feared – the sad, benign face of Luke Counsel. This time, Grace let out a howl so loud it was impossible to ignore. Several workers stopped and stared. Guards glanced towards her. Zach, entering with another bag, saw Grace nailed to the spot, hands clasped over her mouth, as the contents of the split bag burst out around her. The rotting vegetables fell away swiftly, creating a large pile at Grace's feet. In moments, Luke's body, still in his old pinstriped suit, was clearly on show, jolting towards the furnace. Workers began to point and mutter. Not at the body, which they seemed to take for granted, but at Grace. Security guards at the entrance conferred and a couple moved towards her.

Zach looked round desperately. Grace was lost, unaware even of her peril. Somehow he must create a diversion. His eyes fell on the monstrous power generator with its arm-like lever. It wasn't too far above the floor – if he stood on a nearby pile of *Osso* sacks, he could just about reach it. He hurtled across the floor, between the whispering, nudging workers. All eyes were on Grace and the body of Luke Counsel. Zach climbed onto the sacks as if for a better view and keeping his back towards the genny, felt for the lever and yanked it down.

The factory was plunged into darkness. The machinery and grumbling conveyor stopped dead. There were exclamations, cries and shouts. Only the red glow from the oven lit the stumbling confusion. In this, Zach managed to locate Grace. She was completely inert. He had to half-drag, half-carry her from the stinking compost mountain. He looked back once to ensure they weren't followed, and saw a vision from hell; the dark shapes of panicking people silhouetted against the licking flames of the furnace.

Outside all was soot black. The generator governed the arc lights and, Zach hoped, the entire security system. People were shouting commands. Boilersuited guards ran about, colliding with each other. Zach skidded to a halt, took Grace by the shoulders and shook her hard. "Wake up, pusscat. We've got to run!"

Grace stared at him without comprehension, as lifeless as the bagged bodies.

"Sharks!" shouted Zach. "Run. Damn it, run!"

He knew it could only be a matter of seconds before someone restored the power. When Grace still didn't respond, he put an arm round her waist and, lifting her, staggered towards the gate where they'd entered.

The barrier was stuck at 45 degrees, arrested by the power failure. A lorry about to enter was jammed beneath it and the driver was out of the cab, examining the damage and swearing at the guards. In the darkness and shouting chaos, none of them saw the two figures stumbling by. Zach, tugging a catatonic Grace, ran through the barrier and into the woods. They crashed through the undergrowth towards Luke's car, as the lights and sirens blasted out behind them.

That night, Grace and Zach stayed with the Kodaly family in the gun emplacement. They rolled, exhausted, into the makeshift bed on the floor, covered themselves with coats and, in Zach's case, fell instantly asleep.

He awoke some time later, alone in the bed. Confused by the strange surroundings, he felt automatically for the hidden evidence. It was still where they'd carefully stashed it the previous day, in the lining of Luke's ancient overcoat. Relieved, Zach raised himself on one elbow and peered towards a faint glow. Grace, a coat wrapped round her, was sitting at the rickety bamboo table reading by candlelight. Luke's files and papers lay spread on the tabletop. The book in her hands was leather bound and looked, from the embossed date on the front, like a diary. She turned the pages feverishly, skipping chunks, muttering the words out loud, occasionally exclaiming.

"Grace?" said Zach, uncertainly.

She was so absorbed she didn't hear him, but continued with her fraught, broken monologue.

"And Dan said... no, no... but Adam Solomon and Gideon..." She fell silent, though her lips still moved and little whistles of breath came through them.

Zach scrambled off the mattress, picked up his tee-shirt and went across to her. She paid no attention until she felt his arm on her shoulder, then she looked up and said with great excitement. "It's all in here, Zach. Luke's diary. He's kept it since Dan died."

"Grace..." said Zach again, this time more firmly. "We'll read it in the morning. You've got to sleep."

"No, no! You don't understand." Grace shook off his arm, impatiently. "This *Doze* thing. It goes back to the Flame Quenchers strike and the ideas they experimented with then."

"This way madness lies..." Zach looked longingly at the bed. He was, in fact, beginning to be seriously worried for Grace's sanity. Grace gripped his wrist. "Abel Gauntlet – does that name mean anything to you?"

Zach puzzled sleepily, then said, "I think so, wasn't he a flame–quencher? The leader of the illegal strike?"

"He was the Wat Tyler *de nos jours*!" said Grace, then seeing Zach's confusion, "Well, of mine anyway. I guess you don't know who Wat was either?" She shook her head. "Jesus, I don't know why your generation bothered to go to school. Listen." She pinned Zach with Ancient Mariner urgency. "Dan had a lot of sympathy with the Flame-Quenchers but he was out-manoeuvred by a cabal in his cabinet – Gideon and Adam Solomon amongst others. What Luke says in here... " She caught up the diary and held it to her breast, "...is that unbeknown to Dan, this faction co-opted Isiah King to make a quelling drug, Lord Ransome to foot the bill and Jethro Stone's news empire to spread 'reports' on the strikers. No need to tell you how they were represented!" Her look was corrosive, she'd been there herself so recently. Zach thought better of interrupting.

"So...?" Zach stared at her bemused.

"The drug– ! It was *Doze!* "

"But–?"

"Obviously after they'd succeeded in doping the strikers, they saw the benefits of extending the experiment!" Grace overrode any objection. "Luke says..." She flicked a few pages, "Yes... here we are. Their long-term project is to have a dumb population who present no challenge, no dissent and have no voting rights."

"No voting rights..." repeated Zach, fighting waves of exhaustion. "They've never suggested that."

"Not yet," Grace agreed. "But think about it... First it was political apathy and disaffection among the people, then voting started to be actively discouraged. It's only a few short steps to taking rights away. You wait..."

She gave Zach a searching look. "Luke thinks Dan died because he wouldn't go along with it. Listen..."

She rifled through the diary until she found the relevant lines.

"The idea was put to Dan in a late-night session, when he was very drunk. Even so, he immediately vetoed it. Three days later he was dead."

Grace put the diary down and stared into the blackness outside the pool of light. "Luke tried to tell people what was happening. Me amongst them. No one would listen. He was called irrelevant. A dinosaur." Her face crumpled and she was wracked with silent sobs.

"Why?" she gasped. "Why didn't I listen?"

Zach tightened his hold on her shoulders. Her head fell heavily against him and he murmured soothing words, aware as much as anything, of the Kodalys asleep in the inner room. This was not for their ears.

"I've been blind." Grace went on. "Blind with ambition. Always wanting the glittering prizes."

"Stop it, Grace. Hush now, stop."

But Grace would not hush. It was as though, for the first time in years, she was truly speaking from the heart.

"...And you know the worst? I feel cheated, finding out all of this now. Cheated! Because I still want the prize, no matter what! Can you believe that?" She butted her head into his chest. "I still want it!"

She subsided, her words spent, and Zach stroked her shoulders.

"Come to bed," he suggested.

Grace pulled back and looked up at him. It was a straight, raw, questioning look. Zach returned it as frankly.

"Don't you think we've earned it?"

He bent forward and kissed her; at first lightly, but then with increasing passion until she responded. Their tongues inter-locked and she strained into him, all her pent-up anger and grief flooding into the kiss. He picked her up and carried her to the bed. When he laid her down, she clung to his arms and pulled him into her with a desperate, primitive ferocity.

CHAPTER THIRTY-ONE

They left Seashoram, Zach driving Luke's car, early the next morning. The Kodalys sat in the back of the car. Anna seemed a little better and even spoke occasionally in their own language. But, apart from the odd blast of heavy techno from Janos' headphones, and a call from Zach on the vidi-fone to Paul, the journey was tense and silent.

They went their allotted ways at Conference Town, where for most people, the day was just beginning. Grace's wrist-bleep, now firmly back in place, bleeped her to an unscheduled breakfast meeting with Rachel, the Chief Whippy. She showed it to Zach, shrugging silently. In low voices, they made contingency arrangements.

Zach's first port of call, after his hotel, was the illicit laboratory of Charlie, his chemist acquaintance. Charlie fed him black market coffee and heavenly bacon sandwiches. There was more than one benefit, Zach was reminded, to having contacts in the underworld. When they'd wiped up the last dribble of grease, Charlie poured the grey fertiliser Grace had collected in the factory, onto a sheet of paper and pushed it under the microscope. After a few mutterings and jottings, he let out a little whistle.

"What?" said Zach. "What's in it?"

"Well, definitely traces of that same drug... what did you call it, *Doze*? And..." He returned to the 'scope as though he couldn't quite believe his findings. "Human bones and tissue."

Zach nodded, slowly. "That's what we thought. No wonder it's so bloody effective."

Charlie was still staring, mesmerised, into the 'scope. "Very ingenious," he murmured, almost admiringly. "Put the drug into the food chain, through the fertiliser."

Zach took out the envelope with the *Osso* he'd scooped from Tony Griffiths' tub. He offered it to Charlie.

"This was taken from an ordinary garden."

Charlie examined the sample and nodded.

"Yep. That's the same."

"So it's already out there?"

The question was rhetorical. They both stared at the ashy powder trying to take in what this meant.

"May be very recent. Not fully assimilated?" suggested Charlie.

"Perhaps," agreed Zach. It was the best they could hope for.

"Incidentally, I heard rumours about that recreational version you brought in. The guy selling them... a Goth, I think you said... is a relation of Lord Ransome's. Nephew or something. 'Course, Club Gothique's owned by Ransome."

"Is it?" Zach whistled. "Is it, indeed?"

"Unofficially," Charlie went on. "The Russian mafia run it for him." He gave an ironic grin. "Makes you wonder what's left, doesn't it? They've even got the underworld sewn up."

"Corporates leave nothing to chance," said Zach, wryly. "Ransome's not funding you is he?"

Charlie grinned. "I wish."

They punched each other playfully, back on their schoolboy rugger pitch.

"So..." Charlie said, "You reckon the aim is to flood the market with various versions of this?" He poked gingerly at the grey granules.

"Cover every eventuality. Think about it. 'Illegal' drugs for those who want to be cool."

"I wouldn't mind trying it," smirked Charlie. "In fact, I wouldn't mind a piece of his action. We haven't come up with anything nearly as interesting."

"It's in the Earth... In everything you eat. And last but not least. Water."

"What, the old reservoir trick?" Charlie grimaced.

"Nah, tap water's only for washing." Zach's eye fell on an open bottle by the microscope.

"But, everybody drinks *Ransome's*."

Grace spun the half-empty bottle of *Ransome's* on the table in front of her. She'd ordered it to be correct, even had a sip or two to show willing, but there was something about the taste of it she'd never been able to get used to.

She and Rachel were in the breakfast room of Rachel's five star hotel, where the menu consisted of the usual fruits and breads. As a concession to the five stars, they were highly priced and came with paper doilies. Rachel's plate was piled with healthy, 'organic' prunes. Grace didn't even pretend to eat. The events of the last few days had left her totally without appetite. To Rachel, she pleaded a tummy upset by sour yoghurt. She had no intention of admitting how devastated she really felt; indeed, she was making every effort to appear 'normal'. She'd made a quick visit to her hotel, surprisingly untouched, and donned a smart but subdued midnight blue suit and rather a lot of makeup. Next to Rachel in her beige wig and matching frock, she looked like a film star.

Rachel popped the last, dutiful prune into her mouth and pushed the dish aside. "So Grace..." she said, chewing vigorously. "A rather unpleasant experience yesterday, I imagine."

"Mmm," said Grace, cautiously. The constituency 'court' had already been mentioned. "Not one you'd want to repeat."

It was hardly a question and Rachel took Grace's answer for granted. Picking a shred of prune out of her teeth, she continued. "There's no need. We can deal with Noah Petty. Seth Thomas could spike *The Sunday Prophet* story..." She left these enticements dangling.

"Yes?" Grace simulated grateful hope. Safe in the knowledge that she had the upper hand, she was fascinated to hear what was on offer.

"Yes." Rachel wiped her lips on a napkin. "I've been authorised to offer you a deal. Damage limitation."

"Damage limitation? What, you'll hold pages one, two, three and the photos?" Grace couldn't keep irony from her tone.

"We can't work miracles, Grace. You have had rather an... unfortunate, shall we say... Conference." Rachel gave a smug little smile. "After it started so promisingly."

"So, what's the deal?"

"Gideon values you, Grace. Loves you even."

Grace dipped her head modestly. "So he always tells me."

"But he values loyalty more. We want assurances you'll play onside. A member of the team. No more going your own way, regardless."

"Oh, Rachel..."

Grace sighed, thinking of the many times in the past, in Dan Jefferson's day, she and Rachel had stood shoulder to shoulder. She wondered what Rachel was really feeling.

"I know it's hard for you, Grace. You're such... such... an original." The word sounded unaccustomed, distasteful even, on Rachel's lips. "Your combative spirit is all very well in the right place..." She paused and sipped her *Nut-Noggin*, then added firmly, "But it's out of step, now. You're speaking the wrong language."

"So am I to understand all will be well, as long as I keep my gob shut?"

"Really Grace!"

Rachel gave a cough and replaced her cup. "You see, that's typical of your 'style'. Loud. Rude. Confrontational. No wonder Naomi's had such problems."

"Been complaining, has she?"

"Not about your work. We all know you're tireless. Too tireless on occasion. Take Seashoram."

"What about it?" Grace's nose quivered.

"The feeling is... you should stay away."

"You've made that pretty clear."

"We had no choice. You weren't listening."

"But why, Rachel?"

Grace was dying to see how much Rachel would admit. "It's my constituency."

Rachel paused for a moment, then answered carefully.

"You're too close to it. Too involved. You'll see the benefits with hindsight."

"Yeh. Really."

Rachel frowned at Grace's satirical tone.

"If you agree, the PM will announce a ministry for you. In his closing speech this afternoon."

"Mode." Grace did not attempt to keep the disgust out of her voice. "A harmless backwater."

"An influential one," Rachel reproved. "Really Grace, you should be grateful."

"Rachel, Rachel."

Grace looked directly into her one-time compatriot's eyes. "A few years ago we were on the same side. When I think of the campaigns we fought together. benefits, trial by jury, freedom of information..."

"We lost," said Rachel, bluntly.

"So... we stop fighting? What if they brought in ethnic cleansing for blue-eyed blondes, or women over forty? Would you vote for it?"

There was a silence. Rachel dropped her complacent expression and returned Grace's straight look.

"Take what's on offer, Grace. Anything else would be suicide." She glanced around, automatically, but there were no cameras in the Elite hotel.

"Frightened we're bugged?" Grace waved her wrist-bleep. "Easy enough to put in these."

Rachel gave a small, awed laugh. " Grace, you're incorrigible."

"Finish your breakfast."

Grace pushed Rachel's plate of multigrain bread and groundnut-spread towards her. Rachel shook her head.

"I've had enough."

"Feeling sick, pusscat?" Grace put on a caring face. "It's all the lies you've had to swallow."

Thanksgiving for Conference was being held in the same church, Saints George and Gideon, as the opening service. Grace hurried up the steps to the 'modernised' Gothic doors, a little late from her meetings. Inside, the church was crammed with Drome officials, PRs, delegates and guests. Lord Ransome and Jethro Stone, with various other VIPs sat under the carved pulpit, which took the form of a vicious-looking Gryphon. Gideon and his gang were not there – they'd be busy with the preparations for the closing ceremony – but Grace spied Hettie straight away, on her knees beneath a particularly lurid depiction of the Beast from Revelations.

Grace dipped her fingers in the 'holy' *Ransome's* water, taking care to wipe them swiftly on her skirt, and made the obligatory Saint George's cross. The choir was just finishing the joyous anthem, "Praise, Oh praise Saint Gideon's garter," as she slipped into a pew full of journalists. Paul Jacobs, who'd squeezed in a little further along, gave her a nod. He had placed himself next to *The Sunday Prophet's* Peter Priest, who looked bloated and weary. He'd obviously had a good Conference.

The choir's last, echoing note died away and after some shuffling of feet as people re-arranged themselves, Isiah King mounted the pulpit. He towered over the Gryphon, his flowing hair and beard making him, too, seem mythical. "Brothers and sisters," he began in his cathedral boom. "We are gathered together to give thanks for a successful Conference and to pray for Albion to vanquish her enemies and long continue in stability and peace."

"Stability and peace in our time." The congregation gave the ritual response.

"Let us pray."

There was a pause for people to sink to their knees on the uncomfortable, hand-embroidered hassocks. Paul Jacobs took the opportunity to whisper to Peter Priest.

"Peter... a quick word. We're running a piece by Grace Fry... allegations of a Drome conspiracy... stitch-up of democracy..."

Peter shot him an evil look.

"Up to your old tricks, Jacobs?" he muttered. "It won't work. We've got the pictures."

"Yes..." Paul smiled. "We'd like *The Prophet* to drop them. Along with the rest of your 'colourful' story. In fact, we'd like your support on this. She's going to challenge Gideon."

Peter gave an audible hoot. "You're joking boyo! What've you trousered?"

Paul Jacobs smiled grimly.

"This."

He extracted the tiny digi-cam from his pocket, pressed the 'play' button and poked it under Peter's nose. Zach's recording of Ransome's country house orgy flashed onto the screen. Peter's pouchy eyes snapped open, wide as the Drome itself. He almost fell off his hassock when he saw his boss Jethro Stone featured. He clutched at his collar, breathing heavily.

"Thought you'd be impressed," grinned Paul.

"God bless our great nation and its families..." Isiah intoned, from the pulpit.

"Families," responded the congregation.

"Mmm," said Paul, offering the swaying Peter a supportive arm. "Nice to know Jethro, as a family man, can let his hair down, eh?"

"Devout, clean and English." Isiah's voice was rising

"English," parroted the obedient congregation.

"We pray for release from all bodily lusts and temptations." Isiah's voice burned with passion. Flecks of spittle appeared at the corners of his mouth.

"Lusts and temptations," crooned the congregation.

Paul pressed another button and the sound came up on the digi-cam. Isiah King's voice blared out of it.

"Harder!" he screamed. "Beat me! Bugger me! Screw me!"

In the pulpit, King stopped abruptly, his eyes starting from their sockets. Everyone in the church recognised his distinctive voice and all eyes turned to the source of it. Paul stood and held

the little camera above his head so the faithful could take a good
look at the man they'd chosen to follow. The whip-wielding
transvestites were at their busiest.

"Front page blow-ups tomorrow," promised Paul, his voice
echoing round the church. There was a scandalised silence.

King hung over the pulpit clinging to the Gryphon's head as
if he were drowning. With a great roar, he lunged himself
towards the camera. He crashed to the floor at the Gryphon's
feet and writhed about, horse-like snorts and gargles coming
from his mouth. After a moment's teetering on the pulpit's edge,
the great bible fell on top of him.

Outside the church, stretcher-bearers carried Isiah King to an
ambulance. He wrestled with his bonds, frothing and whinnying,
as though fighting the devils of Hell. He seemed to be strangely
enjoying the battle. The congregation piled outside and watched,
mostly mute; there were one or two hysterical giggles.

On the pavement near the ambulance, Zach was conducting
a photoshoot for *The Independent Satellite*. There were light stands
and assistants. Zach looked through the lens at Anna Kodaly,
who sat on a bench, Imre and Janos close by her. Paul Jacobs
gave them a wave as he followed Peter Priest out of the church.
In front of them, Jake Ransome and Jethro Stone were
descending the steps. Jethro stopped in his tracks at the sight of
the Kodalys. Paul gave Peter a nudge.

"Keep an eye on your boss," he murmured.

Blood fled from Jethro's face, leaving it livid lemon. He clutched
Jake Ransome's arm and raised a trembling finger.

Janos beckoned to him, gaily. "Hi, Uncle Jethro."

"Ah," said Paul, "I see he's been recognised." He patted his
pocket.

"It's all on the video. I take it we can rely now, on support
from *The Sunday Prophet*? I'm sure Mr Stone wouldn't want his
little... peccadilloes... exposed by us. Nor indeed..." he chuckled,
"would Lord Ransome. There's even a charming bit featuring
you, Pete." He thumped Priest, jovially. "And a baby's bottle."
Peter Priest stared at him, gagging slightly.

"I know what you're thinking," Paul said, with a conspiratorial wink. "You're wondering how to fill all those blank pages left by the Grace Fry piece? Worry no more!"

With a flourish, he produced from another pocket a clutch of photographs. Peter's stunned gaze fell on Christobel Steel, gurning into the camera. She was on a lilo, merrily twirling, naked as the day she was born.

"Plenty more where they came from," promised Paul. "And a big splashy story. All about your boss's efforts to take over the world and make it totally secure for global capitalists. Comedy, eh? "

But Peter Priest wasn't laughing.

CHAPTER THIRTY-TWO

Grace stayed in the church, hugging herself. The outcome of Paul's plan, finalised in a hasty meeting at his office before the service, was better than she could ever have imagined. Alerted by Zach's fonecall, Paul had opened the infamous safe and searched back in *The Indie's* files for any hint of sexual misadventure by Ransome, Stone or King. He had much on their business dealings, but on sex he'd found only vague hints, all mention of which had soon been suppressed by Stone's newspapers.

"What a surprise," Zach grinned ironically.

Once Paul heard the full story and saw the evidence, he didn't need any further convincing.

"What a scoop!" he chortled, rattling the pill bottle. "Stone, King and Ransome, the unholy trinity bang to rights!"

"It's rather more than a 'scoop', Paul," Grace remonstrated. Really, sometimes she despaired of journalists. "It's no less than a conspiracy to totally stitch-up democracy!"

"Right. Right." Paul gave her a humouring pat. "That's our Gracie!"

Grace's hand strayed up to her locket, back in place round her neck. At least, now, she had the support she needed. Of the many terrifying things she had felt in the last few days, worst of all had been the loneliness. Her eyes filled with tears for Luke.

And for herself. Her father, mentor, friend, gone forever. If it wasn't for Zach...

Grace broke off her thoughts, remembering her quarry. Hettie was still kneeling under the picture of the Beast. Her head was bowed and she put up a hand with a tissue in it, to wipe her eyes. Now was the moment to pounce, as a skilled carnivore knew, but Grace hesitated. There was something pathetically vulnerable about the deflated shoulders and skew-whiff hairdo. Grace clicked her teeth – she really must give Hettie the name of a good wig-master.

She silently crossed the aisle and slid into the pew beside her former friend. Hettie raised a swollen, tearful face and drew back sharply at the sight of Grace. Her lips parted, but before she could say anything, Grace gently took her hand and embarked on her now-rehearsed story. She told Hettie everything she had discovered. Oddly, though Hettie's white face showed her deep shock, she did not seem surprised. Nor did she attempt to contradict Grace. As the story unfolded, she adopted a curiously resigned expression, as though the account had a terrible inevitability. By the time Grace finished, however, Hettie was weeping slow, inconsolable tears.

"I'm sorry, Hettie." Grace pressed the hand she still held.

"Oh... I knew." Hettie choked. "Really, I knew." She lifted an arm and wiped her face, uncaringly, on her powder blue jacket sleeve.

"All those 'missing' workers at *Ossophate*. And you... what they did to you! They were determined to silence you. They made Miriam..."

Grace held up a hand, "I know," she said, tightly.

"And Abbie and poor, poor David." Hettie's voice tailed away. She fumbled in her pocket and took out a pill-box which she opened, shaking two tiny white pills into her hand. They were halfway to her mouth, when Grace caught her wrist.

"Don't take those, Hettie."

Hettie stopped, her hand still suspended. She stared at the pills, a slow horror dawning.

"You think–?"

Grace nodded. But she could see Hettie already realised what she'd been taking.

"No. The bastard!" Hettie whispered.

"Who?"

Hettie trembled with suppressed emotion. "Adam, of course. He's the puppet master. He sent me to see the Drome therapist."

"And she prescribed... those?" Grace pointed to the pills. Hettie dipped her head.

"Very smart," murmured Grace.

"I was so depressed, I didn't think..."

"Why should you?"

"I should have realised." There was more than a trace of anger now, in Hettie's voice. "It all started when I discovered Gideon – " she broke off, as though the memory was too terrible to recount.

"Discovered Gideon... what?" urged Grace.

Hettie looked down. In a very small voice she said,

"I'd gone down to Chequers. There was a dog show I was judging. I came back a day a day early."

Her voice faltered then she swallowed hard and said with renewed strength.

"When I got to number ten, Adam was there. It seemed – alone. I went to the bedroom, I was going to drop my case, but he tried to delay me. He was in a panic. He grabbed my arm and started shouting. Weird things like... 'Don't go in! Offside Hettie! It really wouldn't be playing the game!' The more he tried to stop me, the more determined I became. We wrestled."

Hettie gave a snorting laugh.

"It was funny really. Adam's such a wimp. I could floor him with one hand." The jagged laugh stopped. "In fact I did. I shoved him so hard he fell on the floor. I opened the door and stepped over him. I saw... I saw..."

"Yes?" Grace could hardly believe there were further revelations.

"I saw Gideon in bed with Jonathan Temple."

"What?" Grace breathed.

Hettie's face was as hard as the granite church walls surrounding them.

"They were... fucking!"

Grace gasped. It was partly Hettie's use of the word – and the ferocity with which she pronounced it – and partly because it was the last thing Grace could have imagined. There was what seemed like a long silence. Then Hettie turned haunted eyes on Grace. "I could have forgiven him.. I would have accepted it, you know what my feelings always were on equality... if only I'd believed for a moment it was..."

"Love?" finished Grace for her.

Hettie nodded, then continued, bitterly. "But Gideon doesn't know the meaning of the word. It was opportunism. Pure and simple. He wanted Jonathan on his side. He was prepared to go to any lengths to get him."

"In bed with the enemy," murmured Grace.

"The hypocrisy!" Hettie spat the words. "With all the job losses and deaths... David and the others... Isiah King and aversion therapy!"

No wonder, thought Grace, Hettie had been so awkward in their conversation about *Ossophate.*

The sound of the church door opening alerted them both. A booted Drome Unit boy had entered and stood, lolling against it. Hettie's eyes grew fearful.

"My minder," she whispered. Then frantically, "Be careful, Grace. No matter what evidence you've got. Adam will stop you if he can. He'll say you're mad, bad, a liar. You can't trust a soul. Your friends will desert you... "

She looked up at the apocalyptic vision which hovered over them. The Beast arising from the sea.

"He'll have power at any cost. What's that old poem?" She hesitated, then quoted, "'I kill where I can... because it's all mine. I'm going to keep things like this.' "

Above them, the face of the Beast expanded and glowed crimson. It smiled. The sharp-eyed, hawk-like smile of Adam Solomon.

In the room of perpetual night Adam watched the screens, without smiling. On the contrary, there was a look of intense malevolence on his face as he saw Grace Fry exit from the church with Hettie – the boot-boy minder a step behind them.

In the dressing room attached, he could hear Gideon having a temper tantrum. Gideon was halfway through his beauty preparations but on hearing of the events at church, leapt from the chair, his face covered in cucumber slices. He stormed up and down the room, blobs of cucumber flying off him.

"Ninnies!" he shouted. "Dolts! Loonies!"

His ire was directed at Seth Thomas who was slumped in a chair, his head in his hands. In a corner, Christian was sobbing.

Adam's eyes narrowed. It was he who had fielded the enraged fone calls, Stone, Ransome – thank Gideon, King was too gaga to make one. He glanced with contempt at the unravelling trio. None of them was up to dealing with the situation. As usual, he would have to take charge.

Not for nothing was he the puppet master.

CHAPTER THIRTY-THREE

Grace put the finishing touch, Dan's locket, to her costume and took a step back to look at herself in the mirror. She had deliberately chosen the suit she'd worn for her pinnacle of success at the opening, award ceremony. She gave the mirror a bitter smile. How long ago that seemed. Despite the ravages of the past few days, however, she looked good. The white sharkskin shimmered, moulded to her body like a second skin, her hair was newly washed and shiny, her face carefully made up. She gave herself an approving nod. She felt ten years older, but miraculously it didn't show. No one would guess the painful rite of passage through which she'd travelled.

She opened the briefcase containing trophies from the dangerous ride and took out Luke's little T-Rex. She held it tightly for a moment, closing her eyes and hearing Luke's voice,

"Are you sure you're still a carnivore, Grace?" then slipped it into her pocket. She was going to need all the luck she could get. Even without Hettie's fearsome warning, she knew very well that exposing Gideon's cabal in public was a high risk strategy.

She tried out a different smile in the mirror, coral lips wide, teeth bared. Better, but something was missing. She snatched up her perfume bottle and drenched herself head to toe. The scent of the carnivore.

In the foyer of her hotel, Zach was waiting with Paul Jacobs and Imre, Anna and Janos. They'd decided they should all walk to the Drome together. There was safety in numbers. Paul Jacobs was grinning and rubbing his hands. He couldn't wait to get started. His grin widened to a triumphant laugh when Peter Priest joined them, outside the hotel.

"Peter!" he cried, giving him a jovial slap. "Thought old Jethro would see it our way."

Peter looked as sick as a pig. There was a sticking plaster above one eye. He had obviously been three rounds with Jethro.

The day was cheery with sunbeams. A playful breeze accompanied them along the promenade, ruffling hair and waves; the National bunting fluttered madly. Shouts from paddlers and the barks of a dog came from the beach. All was well in Albion. As they entered the Drome aura, its white light breathed over Grace's suit. She glittered like the star she was. Shortly, it would again be recognised.

The foyer was packed with people heading for the Great Navel. For once, however, the cyclorama was blank and there was no prophetic warning from Isiah King. If people were puzzled by this, they did not comment. There was a palpable tension in the air as they shuffled in a long queue, into the hall. This, the culmination of Conference, was both expectant and alarming. Who knew what Gideon would spring in his closing speech? Always rallying – indeed comparisons with Henry V at Agincourt were frequently made – he could also delight or distress with sudden, surprising announcements.

No one seemed aware of any other surprises. Grace was greeted cordially enough. Naomi gave her a forced smile. Rachel, the Chief Whippy, even patted her. Grace nodded to left and right, keeping a bland smile on her face. In the scrum, Zach pressed her fingers. He, and he alone, knew she was terrified.

The intimidating Navel was swagged with purple and shining silver, the grand platform brilliantly lit, the flag of Saint George outstretched above it. The 'BarleySugar Bunnies' in Saint George and the Dragon armoured suits were finishing a jolly jousting number. Grace's posse drew close around her. Paul Jacobs put an arm round her back and led the tight group off to a table close to the rostra. It was decorated with flowers, in the red and white of Saint George and a carafe of Ransome's water. Grace placed her Titanium briefcase firmly in the centre.

Heads nearby turned at the sight of a minister, flanked by newspapermen and what appeared, by their scruffy dress, to be a refugee family. The Kodalys shrank together, overawed, but Paul Jacobs waved merrily at the watchers.

The lights dimmed and over the rousing Piggy Creede overture, 'Glorious Albion', a female voice announced:

"And now... the man for whom we have all been waiting, whose great example inspires us all... the Prime Minister, Gideon Price!"

There was an intense hush and then howls of adoration as Gideon, looking fresh as a daisy, his bouffant hair immaculate, bounded on stage. Behind him, the rest of the Drome Unit, more subdued, filed into a semi circle. There was Adam and Seth and Matt and Gabriel and the other members of the inner circle. Everyone was smiling except Hettie, who came on last, propelled by a push from a bootboy.

Gideon embraced the microphone and held up his arms for the howling to subside. It was a heroic pose, especially as his shiny, pewter-coloured Teflon suit had the suggestion of medieval armour. The music died to a still patriotic but background level, and Gideon began to speak.

"When I first came to power, I promised you a new dawn. A caring, sharing Millennium of Stability, Security and Belief!"
Cheers and clapping burst from the assembly. Grace and Zach exchanged an ironic flicker.

"Our fair Albion was facing Hard Choices. Wracked with panic. Tortured by terror. Scourged by smut. Our homeland fractured. Threatened. Torn." He paused to allow in a memory of the bad times. Everyone bowed their heads.

"But...We rode the challenge. Expunge all Evil! Stabilise or die!"
Gideon let these words ring round the domed ceiling. On stage, there were supportive nods from the circle.

"The spirit of the people was with us. Together we have forged the New Utopia. Radical. Historic. Modern."

Gideon's face shone with self-belief.

"We boldly went where none had dared before. Created an ideal. Cherish Heritage, but merge it with brave future. Strong. Confident. Just. Prosperous. Rock, not shifting sand. Poised to take back Albion's rightful place..."

Here, Gideon paused for dramatic tension. The audience was breathlessly still, longing for the release of the next crescendo.

"Global Centre!" Cried Gideon, raising an arm.

The audience blasted the roof with its clamour. One or two among it were weeping.

"Now," Gideon quelled them with another theatrical suspension. "New concept. Proud to tell you. Great step for mankind. We have secured the support of the 666 Opposition party."

A confused hush fell. People exchanged glances, uncertain they had heard properly. Grace sat bolt upright in her seat. Under the table, Zach's knee nudged hers urgently. Gideon seized the moment.

"Yes, brothers and sisters, that's what I said. The finger of destiny points." He pointed it. "Today, the 666 Party join us in Historic Partnership. Together, we give birth to a new, all-inclusive vision. The One Nation Party!"

A red and black banner with the logos of the Government and the 666, entwined, unfurled above Gideon's head. In the crowd, there were astonished gasps and murmurs. Several people stood. Paul Jacobs gave a raucous laugh. Jonathan Temple walked on stage and joined Gideon at the central podium. He smiled broadly and waved at the crowd. Gideon put a brotherly arm of welcome around him. Everyone behind them applauded, – everyone with the exception of Hettie, who stood up, dropping her handbag, and ran from the platform.

The Whippies began clapping and moved swiftly around the Navel, orchestrating the audience to join in. At first, the applause was fitful, but as the Whippies cracked in, it became more confident. At last, it reached a sufficient level for Gideon to take the microphone again. He kept one hand on Jonathan, as he entered the final, fervent charge.

"The One Nation Party will be a beacon for the World. A World to restore the old moral order. A World to unite all those who share our values. A World for the Great and Good of our Magnificent Country. Albion's very own Brave New World!"

By now, the clapping and cheers were at full strength. Whistles pierced the air. Delegates stood on chairs, stamping. The assembly espoused the message, as though never a doubt had crossed its mind.

A nod went round Grace's table and she stood, grasping her briefcase. With a smile from Zach and a slight push from Paul Jacobs, she took a step towards the platform. Her heart was thumping so hard she thought it would burst, but she must be brave. This, she knew, was the moment to grasp her own destiny.

She was three paces from the platform when Gideon saw her. He beamed at her like the sun king. Taken aback, Grace stopped mid-stride. Gideon calmed the applause and still watching her, said:

"For this Historic Bequest, I announce the creation of a new all-powerful ministry. The Ministry of Drome."

More surprised mutterings broke out in the hall, and indeed on the stage, but Gideon over-rode them.

"Drome will span all others. Have free reign to command and control. Keep always in mind, the Cosmic Vision."

His voice rose, as it usually did when he invoked the cosmos.

"Secretary of State for Drome will carry a tremendous burden. Only one with total conviction, courage, loyalty and yes, style, charisma... and grace, can do the job. I have chosen a person whom, I know, has those qualities in abundance."

Gideon left a slight pause. There was a shifting in the Drome semi-circle. All those who considered themselves potential candidates looked self-consciously at the floor. Naomi crossed and uncrossed her legs. Rachel plucked at her wig nervously.

Gideon held up the mike stand as though it was a lance. Jonathan Temple ducked out of the way, as he brandished it.

Pointing at the shining white figure of Grace, Gideon let rip in full battle cry.

"Friends, Albionites, Countryfolk, I give you our own, our very own, dear, Gracie!"

Grace thought she was about to faint. The room spun like a mirror ball, Gideon's hand, luring her onto the stage, at the centre of it. Behind him, Adam and Seth rose to their feet, followed more reluctantly by the rest of the Drome Unit. Their faces, set in chilling rictus, went in and out of Grace's blurred focus. She was vaguely aware of the Whippies as they wove between the Navel tables, stirring up a chant:

"Grace Fry! Grace Fry!"

At first it was low, but soon it filled the air, victoriously.

"Grace Fry! Grace Fry!"

This time there were no knitting needles.

Clutching her briefcase as if for life-support, Grace looked back at her table. Zach and Paul were on their feet, their faces expressing dismay. The Kodalys clung together, not under-standing, but knowing something was wrong. Peter Priest was laughing.

Other faces – Margie's tear-streaked, Tony's angry, Miriam's ashamed – reeled past her. She heard snatches of their voices, imploring her.

"It's too late... too late."

"You should have thought of that a long time ago!"

"They threatened me I'd lose my job."

Dead faces floated in, Dan, Sam, Abby, Luke, their eyes mournful. They held out ghostly arms and called to her.

"Grace – be staunch. Don't abandon us."

Through all the faces, Zach's eyes were burning into her. She saw the love, the possible future in them.

In this second, her whole life, with its hard choices, sped before her and all the while the vast Navel reverberated with her name. Grace wavered, giddy and sick, unable to take a step in either direction. She scrabbled for her locket, willing herself to have strength.

"Dan," she whispered. "Help me."

Before she could touch the charm, Peter Priest rushed forward, as though to her rescue. In his hands, he held the carafe of *Ransome's* and a glass. He poured the water into the glass and handed it to her. Grace stared at his face – kindly, with twinkling eyes, the face of a friend – then at the glass. It foamed and bubbled. In the depths of the fizzing water, she saw another face. It too was smiling, the lips drawn back to show carnivore fangs. It invited her – no – seduced her, to drink. Come, be one of us, said the smile. Join the Elite, keep our secrets. Grace's body flooded with heat followed by ice, in the grip of the terrible temptation. The swirling water was hypnotic. Perhaps – she was just conscious enough to think – Adam really was the devil.

Zach made a move towards her, but was stayed by Paul's hand. It was Grace's soul. Only Grace could take this decision. She put out a hand and all in the Great Navel suspended breath, held in thrall to one question.

Would Grace Fry sip from the poisoned chalice?

EPILOGUE

0011: Grace Fry's Diary (Extract)

I've established a possible form of contact with GW. For the moment, he still has his job and if I can get information to him by one means or another, he promises he'll break it in the appropriate place.

So, here I am talking to myself - ha! nothing new there - in Luke's bolthole. Thank God he revealed it to me. Where else could I have hidden when I came under suspicion for Gideon's death!

It's lonely here - and dark - I daren't light more than a couple of candles. But at least there's food - a stash of tins - and a small stove to cook on. Living like this reminds me of the Great Panic all those years ago. I never thought I would come to it again. What was the prayer, well mantra, really, I'd mutter then to keep my spirits up?

> 'Be bold and mighty forces will come to your aid.'

I think it's Goethe. I used to chant it when I was climbing onto the roof to steal pigeon eggs. The answer, as far as I recall, was an eyeful of birdlime.

0011: Letter

My Dearest GW

If only I'd realised how brief my triumph would be, I'd have thrown over everything to be just with you. Heaven knows, you warned me enough at the time - but I really thought I could make it work. I should have realised they would never let me - or Gideon - get away with it. Have you any clue yet who was behind the 'heart attack'? I fear the hand of Adam Solomon. He and Matt Penny are thick as thieves again - and were even before Gideon's sudden death. Poor Hettie - it will be a long time before she comes out of that Mental Correction Facility, if ever.

I'm in a safe place - as safe as I can be anyway, and can hole up here til the sisters find me. They're not as bad as everyone believes - they're not terrorists, just women working in their own way to tell the truth about the Government, and this so-called 'Worldwide War on Terror'. God knows I got nowhere trying to go it alone. I'll get all the information I can to you, and you must be as good as your promise and get it out there.

I miss you Great White. You've been my best friend, as well as my lover and my sometime saviour. Take care of yourself, my darling. One of us has to bear witness.

Your Pusscat.

0012: Grace's Diary (Extract)

I hope they come soon, I'm down to the last tin.

Dear Luke, how like him to think ahead - canned vegetables and rice, chocolate, (goodness knows where he found that) and even some illegal frankfurters!

Today I made nettle soup. It wasn't so bad and staved off the hunger pangs quite tolerably. I shall write the recipe here for future reference.

Pick nettles (at night and preferably with gloves on).
Steep in water and vinegar.
Heat over teeny calor gas stove.
Add salt, pepper and any other spices to hand
(I put in a bit of Luke's nutmeg).
Cool off.
Drink broth, chewing rope-like nettle roots (slowly).

How GW will laugh if he ever finds this.

I never was much of a cook.

0012 Notice in personal column of *The Independent Satellite.*

```
GW - PC's health much better now she's at home
with her sisters.
```

0012: List in Grace's notebook

Sisters - C, P, A, H, M, with me, six at present

Targets

BIG
MP
JS
AS
PP
LR

0013: Grace's Digicam Diary (Commentary Extract)

'We crept through underground tunnels for miles until we saw a
dim yellow light ahead. C gestured me to get down and she and
I, with P close behind, dropped silently to our stomachs. I had
the camera – the tiny digicam GW gave me before we parted –
and I crawled forward, inch by inch with it.

The tunnels opened into a cave-like space and I could see,
while hidden behind a huge boulder. Kneeling on the floor was a
prisoner, a man in a camouflage jumpsuit, bound hand and foot.
His face, which I could just make out, was a white, terrified blur.
There was a group of men standing behind him, masked and
draped in black. They had weapons – Kalashnikovs, I think.
One, with a pointed hood over his head was shouting and
gesticulating, as if to rouse or frighten the others. While I
watched, he caught hold of the prisoner by his hair and forced
his head back. The prisoner's eyes rolled, as his captor produced
from his black drapes, a large hatchet-like knife.

With a sudden violent lunge, the guard sliced into the
prisoner's neck. There was a terrible scream and a great jet of

blood, but the man's head was not yet parted from his body. It took several more hacks with the knife before the captor held up the severed head, the eyes almost starting out of it.

Now I could see it was the head of the missing media man, whose face had been on Television and posters.

There was a shudder in the group and then wild shouting and laughing. Sick to my stomach, I crouched shivering, but somehow managed to keep the digicam going.

The guards kicked over the body and then jumped on it. One took out his member and urinated. Before they left, one or two of them snatched off their masks. To my shock, I saw that far from being 'terrorists' as I had imagined, they were men from Adam Solomon's old Drome Unit posse – one in particular, Christian, I recognised...'

0013: Newspaper cutting: *The Independent Satellite.*

The Independent Satellite board today decided unanimously to sack long time Editor in Chief, Paul Jacobs. Jacobs had come under increasing pressure to resign, after repeatedly publishing so-called 'evidence' of Government instigated torture and mistreatment of prisoners during the War on Terror. The reports, including several photographs of a supposed 'beheading', have all been completely discredited by other non-governmental agencies. The photographs were unattributed, but are thought to have been smuggled to the paper by a member of a terrorist group calling itself, The Sisterhood.

Mr Jacobs was given the news of his dismissal at 11.45am and escorted from the building at noon. His place is taken by Peter Priest, who is a new appointment to the IS. Mr Priest's first statement as Editor-in-Chief was a warning that other

'dissidents' at the IS would soon be following in
Mr Jacobs' footsteps.

0013: Notice in personal column of *The Independent Satellite*

PC – Moving on to GBC. Take care of your health,
all my love, GW.

0013: Newspaper cutting: *The Independent Satellite*

The giant agro-chemical company, *Ossophate,* has
just landed a massive Government defence contract.
The Prime Minister, Matt Penny, denied allegations
of cronyism, saying that Baron Isiah King's
company was the most skilled and ahead of its
rivals in the biochemical industry.
'People must grow up and learn to be less
squeamish about WMDs,' said PM Penny. 'In these
times of global terror, it is prudent to use every
weapon available to us, and *Ossophate* is first in
the field.'

0013: The beginning of a last letter from Grace.

GW

must leave asap, as we fear our security here has been compromised.
There's a chance we may be able to get out of the country. I'll try to
contact you through the usual sources, but I can't promise

"The letter breaks off there. That is the last anyone heard of
Grace Fry, she is presumed... "

Zach Green hit the shutdown button on the plasma screen and sat back, whistling softly through his teeth. He still could not bear to look at the last, blurred image of Grace, as her hand slipped from the digicam. What had happened at that moment? Capture? Hurried departure? Battery failure? He would probably never know.

The re-editing of his acclaimed '*Depeches*' documentary, '*Grace Fry's Hard Choices*', had been painful, but it was nearly over. The finished film was to be entered for the prestigious Euro-Federation Festival Golden Gryphon Award – and the word was that it would win.

Something was missing though; some final statement, something more – what? – more personal. He couldn't get it from Grace, that was for sure.

Zach glanced around the editing suite where he'd been viewing the final cut, and his eye fell on the rostrum camera. He sat down in front of it, ran his fingers through his unruly hair and straightened his collar. Then he switched on the camera and spoke directly to it.

"Let me end this story of fear and flight, courage and daring, on this note. Grace Fry was – is – a remarkable woman and an inspiration to many.

It's taken me years, and much difficult research, to uncover the history of what happened after she 'disappeared', but I know, however contentious it may be, it's important to share it with you.

I was privileged to be Grace Fry's ... friend, and if I knew anything about her... "

Zach stopped at this point. He brushed a hand across his eyes and, after a moment resumed, his voice a little shaky.
"If I knew her at all, I know that rumours of her death are much exaggerated. This is Zach Green saying goodbye from me... "

Zach reached into his pocket and held up to the camera his favourite vidisnap of Grace, blonde and smiling in the sunshine of their last day together.

"... And from Grace Fry, 'Au revoir'. "

aurora metro press

Founded in 1989 to publish and promote new writing, the press has specialised in new drama and fiction, winning recognition and awards from the industry.

new fiction
Sacred by Eliette Abecassis
ISBN 0-9536757-8-5 £9.95

How Maxine learned to love her legs *and other tales of growing up.* ed Sarah Lefanu ISBN 0-9515877-4-9 £8.95

new drama
Lysistrata – the sex strike, adapted by Germaine Greer
ISBN 0-9536757-0-X £7.99

Harvest by Manjula Padmanabhan
ISBN 0-9536757-7-7 £6.99

Warrior Square by Nick Wood
ISBN 0-9546912-0-2 £7.99

Jonathan Moore: Three Plays
ISBN 0-9536757-2-6 £10.95

Eastern Promise *plays from central and eastern europe,* eds. Sian Evans and Cheryl Robson. ISBN 0-9515877-9-X £11.99

The Arab-Israeli Cookbook by Robin Soans
ISBN 0-9542330-9-3 £7.99

and accompanying cookery book
The Arab-Israeli Cookbook by Robin Soans
with a foreword by Claudia Roden
ISBN 0-9515877-5-7 £9.99

www.aurorametro.com